Winter Wonderland

Jane Blythe

Bear Spots Publications
Melbourne Australia

bearspotspublications@gmail.com

ISBN: 0992418003
ISBN-13: 978-0-9924180-0-7

Cover designed by QDesigns

Also by Jane Blythe

Detective Parker Bell Series

A SECRET TO THE GRAVE

DECEMBER 1ˢᵀ

10:00 P.M.

First one for the year was always the sweetest.

It had a special almost magical feeling about it, kind of like a fairytale.

A whole year of planning, waiting, fantasizing, all culminating in this moment.

Pulling to a stop at the side of the road, flipping off the engine, and climbing from the truck. Breathing in the crisp night air, enjoying the feel of the freezing wind that whipped in-between the tall trees. It had been cloudy earlier with the promise of snow in the air but the wind had cleared the clouds away and now the sky was a huge black expanse dotted with stars that twinkled like Christmas lights.

Stretching deliciously, like a contented cat, in the cold then crossing to the back of the truck, unlocking it, and staring in at the cargo.

The precious cargo.

Snickering at the thought of the police desperately trying to guess where this package would be left. No one would ever figure out the plan. The world was full of idiots, which made the job that had to be done that much easier.

Setting to work, it was not an easy task to remove it from the back of the truck and set it up on the road, which, incidentally, was why this particular stretch of empty highway had been chosen.

A tremendous amount of time and energy went into choosing just the right location to leave it. Pick the wrong place and the whole effect could be wiped away in an instant like drops of rain on a windscreen, gone before they were even noticed.

It was beautiful out here. Even in the wintertime. *Especially* in the wintertime.

Winter had always been a favorite time of year, and it had nothing to do with Christmas. It was the cold, the barren empty landscape, trees stripped of their leaves, snow covering all with its thick blanket, making everything look the same, like one enormous rolling field of white. It was all so forbidding, so menacing, and yet so peaceful.

It was close to an hour before it was finished. Before everything was just perfect. Just as it should be.

Temptation licked and curled, trying to coerce into waiting for someone to stumble upon the body.

It was the most delicious time of any crime.

Better even than the kill.

The range of emotions that tumbled across the face of the person that was unfortunate enough to stumble upon the body was almost indescribable. The explosion of shock and fear and revulsion, always mingled with fascination, they did not want to look and yet they could not tear their gaze away.

It was thrilling knowing that you could have that much power over someone you had never even met. Making them do something against their will.

Power was what it was about after all.

Unable to resist the lure, after a last check of the body, locking up the back doors of the truck and climbing back inside, then driving the car into the woods. Deep enough to remain hidden from the road but close enough to be able to have a decent view of what was soon to happen.

Grabbing a bag of popcorn and a bottle of diet soda from a cooler on the floor of the passenger side and hoping that it wouldn't be too long a wait.

Patience was not a strong suit.

Thankfully, the wait was not long.

Mere minutes later a set of headlights sparkled along the horizon.

A scrumptious tingling starting in the toes and working it's way up to the brain, so that white spots danced. Controlling the pleasure with an effort so as not to miss a single second of what would happen next.

The car approached quickly, and then all of a sudden the body was illuminated in the bright glare of the headlights. The brakes applied so suddenly the screech of tyres was audible even from here, the car swerved, sliding on the slippery road and almost careening into a tree.

The occupant scrambled from the car and stared in shocked silence at the body placed strategically in the middle of the road. Then a scream sliced through the quiet night and the lucky customer dropped to their knees at the side of the road, shoulders hunched.

With a chuckle and a last look, the truck merged quietly into the inky night.

* * * * *

11:18 P.M.

She was in an empty room.

A familiar room.

One from a long time ago, but that she still remembered as perfectly as the first time she had laid eyes on it.

The room was empty, just as it had been that day.

She tried to move but couldn't.

Looking down she saw the rope that bound her wrists to the arms of the chair.

Something sharp stabbed at her fingertips and she looked back down to find her hands streaked with blood, the ropes now lay at her feet.

Her heart beat hard and fast, her breath catching, as her eyes stared at the blood.

She hated the sight of blood.

It terrified her.

Blinking, when she opened her eyes again she was at the window.

Outside it was snowing.

The ground covered in a thick mantle of white that made her think of the old Christmas song.

Snowflakes swirling in the air, flicking and spinning through the sky like children chasing one another. The moon, hidden behind a layer of clouds, cast a hazy glow, the only light in an otherwise dark night.

It hadn't been snowing the first time she was here.

Then it had been early fall, the weather still warm, a hint of red and yellow tinting the otherwise green leaves was the only acknowledgment that summer had ended.

However, it had been snowing the night she had last been here, exactly one year ago.

Turning she saw the face behind her just as she had known she would.

He sneered at her, his mocking hazel eyes staring accusingly.

Guilt flowed through her just as it always did.

She'd used him, taken advantage of his instability.

A bang like a firecracker going off above her head startled her.

She didn't have to look at her hands to know what had happened.

The gun had gone off.

He dropped to the ground. His eyes, now blank and empty, continued to bore into her in the relentless stare of death.

The pool of blood from the single gunshot wound that had ripped through his heart, killing him instantly, slowly but steadily grew.

Frozen in place, fear preventing her from gaining control of her limbs, she watched in horror as the ever-growing pool of blood inched its way across the floor towards her.

A shrill scream filled the room; she knew it was coming from herself even though her mouth was closed.

Then she was in a tunnel.

Images swirled around her.

Unwanted images.

Pictures from her past that she wanted to keep buried away.

Her scream reverberated in the tunnel until it pounded in her ears, deafening her.

The tunnel changed into a deep hole that was slowly filling with blood, it dripped down from some unseen source, more and more until she was drenched in it.

Pairs of eyes filled the dirt walls.

Accusing eyes.

They stared at her with unblinking hatred before crying tears of blood.

She screamed again.

One loud long howl a combination of pain and terror and guilt.

Hands grabbed at her.

So many hands.

Clutching and clawing at her.

Shaking her.

"Tessa."

With a start, her eyes snapped open.

Struggling to draw breath.

Pulse pounding loudly in her ears.

A fuzzy face slowly falling into focus above her.

"Shh, it's okay, it was only a dream."

* * * * *

11:25 P.M.

Practically dancing down the street thrilled about how perfectly things had gone this evening. Earlier while quietly leaving the scene several police cars had gone tearing past, sirens wailing, lights flashing.

Suppressing a smile, as pleasurable as today had been, when out hunting for prey one did not want to attract any unnecessary attention.

As thrilling as the killing had been it was time to focus on what lay ahead. True, things would be different without Stacey Wood around, having spent the last couple of months in her company, but soon there would be a new houseguest, the prospect of which was almost excruciatingly exciting.

Slipping into a late night coffee house and taking a seat a suitable distance from the object of tonight's hunt, close enough to keeps tabs on the girl but not so close as to seem suspicious.

The place had a warm and cozy feel to it, small and intimate. The walls were painted a deep scarlet and dotted with flickering candles, the fabric of the chairs and booths the same color as the walls, the floor and ceiling a bright cheery yellow. Although the colors ought to clash, they seemed instead to perfectly complement one another.

Ordering a coffee, weak and black, as coffee was not a favorite drink, and a muffin, then grabbing a copy of the paper from a nearby table and beginning to casually flip through it. Despite the late hour, the place was nicely full and it was several minutes before the waitress appeared with the order and a harried apologetic smile. Sipping the burning liquid and taking a bite of the stale muffin while subtly studying the young woman at the nearby table.

Elizabeth Rose Landry.

Known to most as Lizzie, eighteen years of age, a college freshman, smart, pretty, with big brown doe eyes and shiny auburn hair, the life of every party. Right now, she was surrounded by a group of young men and as the only female in the gathering she was the absolute centre of their adoring attention. Lapping it up, Lizzie was gesturing animatedly as she regaled the boys with some wild story about the night she and a friend flirted with a cop to get out of a speeding ticket.

Tuning out the girl's irritating and overly enthusiastic voice as she droned on and on, her young companions continuing to remain utterly captivated, while finishing off the coffee and blueberry muffin. Casting a glance at the clock on the wall and then back to Lizzie, hoping that the girl wouldn't be much longer otherwise more food would need to be ordered so as not to draw suspicion.

About to make a move and wait for the girl outside when Elizabeth suddenly glanced at her chirping cell phone and pushed away from the table, her chair scraping along the tiled floor. Making a big show of kissing each of her male friends, who continued to be enthralled by her every move, on the cheek as way of goodbye.

Clad in skin-tight jeans and a bright red turtleneck with a huge pink love heart on the front every eye in the place was on her as she pranced towards the door. Enjoying being in the spotlight, Elizabeth beamed at the men who ogled her and their girlfriends and wives who eyed her with open jealousy. Watching as Lizzie started down the sidewalk pulling a pink scarf tightly around her neck to fight off the cold night.

Waiting a minute or two and then sidling out of the coffeehouse and following in the direction the girl had gone. Walking briskly in the icy night air, catching up to Elizabeth in minutes but remaining an unobtrusive distance behind.

After months of meticulous stalking, every aspect of Elizabeth Landry's life had been observed and recorded. A creature of habit despite the flighty attitude she gave off Lizzie was in fact a very mature young woman. At the age of ten Elizabeth, younger brother Devon, and mother Una, had been involved in a serious car accident. The drunk driver who had rammed into the family's car had walked away virtually uninjured; the Landry family on the other hand had not been so lucky.

Elisabeth's mother had broken her back and was paralyzed from the waist down, her little brother had suffered a severe head injury and was brain damaged as a result, Lizzie had suffered internal injuries but had fully recovered. Her father, not present at the time of the accident, had left his family just months later, overwhelmed by the prospect of living with a physically disabled wife and mentally disabled child. Little Lizzie had stepped up to the plate and taken on the responsibility of caring for her family.

Making order from chaos the girl had become as predictable as clockwork. Every morning she got up early and hurried to her classes, unlike most of the girls her age she lived at home and not on campus. After college she went straight to the café where she worked, the small coffee shop they had just left, and then before heading home she spent an hour or so with her friends. It was in this time that she really blossomed, eyes shining brightly like brown stars, face coming alive, she was vibrant and energetic and absolutely amazing.

These were the qualities that endeared her to every man she came into contact with and they were also the qualities that were going to lead to her death.

Following quietly but barely bothering to stick to the shadows as Elizabeth was lost in texting a friend. Waiting until they were deep in the back roads, far away from any traffic that might still be out on the streets at this time of night, before making a move. Lizzie took the same root home from the café every night so there was no need to keep her in sight.

Circling around behind a small block of apartments and settling in the spot chosen for the abduction. This particular location provided good cover and a relatively clear view of Elizabeth as well as the street in case any unexpected visitors showed up.

Thrilling electrical currents of excitement were tingling pleasantly and it was a struggle to stay focused on what needed to be done. Determinedly boxing away the pleasure to enjoy at a later date once everything was taken care of.

Slipping from the corner of the building as Lizzie came into view, approaching silently until she was just inches away. Reaching an arm to wrap around her throat and managing to remain unnoticed until the split second before it crushed against her windpipe. The effect was instant, the girl started thrashing wildly, legs swinging, hands clawing, like an animal caught in a trap, fighting for it's life.

Squeezing tighter and slowly, slowly, Elizabeth started to weaken, her body going limp; it was almost finished when . . .

"Hey!"

Head snapping around to see two figures in the distance, illuminated by the thin beam of a flashlight. Letting out a growl, from anger more than panic, reluctantly dropping Elizabeth Landry's now floppy body to the ground and taking off at a fast run.

"Hey, stop!"

Footsteps pounded along the ground but the interlopers were too far away to catch up. Reaching the van and swinging up inside, revving the engine and pulling out into the night before the intruders had a chance to get close enough to see anything that might hinder the plan.

Squealing off around a corner annoyed that the scheme had been disrupted but not thrown. Any clever logical thinking person always had a back up, a reserve, a fallback, a substitute.

This plan was no exception.

If you were not going to do something right then there was no point in doing it at all. If you wanted something to succeed then you had to go the extra yard. And that, was one of the many problems with the world today. Everyone wanted everything instantly, no wait, no hassle. Nobody wanted to put in the time and energy it took to do something properly. Luckily, that was not the case here.

If plan A had been disrupted, then it was on to plan B.

* * * * *

11:31 P.M.

"Here you go."

Parker handed a glass of ice water to his girlfriend Tessa Micah then tipped a couple of pills into her hand.

Taking the glass with a trembling outstretched hand, she took a shaky sip then set it down on the nightstand. Eyeing the painkillers that lay in her palm before tipping them out on the table beside the water. Shivering, with a weary sigh, she snuggled the blankets tighter around herself.

Studying Tessa as she sat in his bed, knees tucked up against her chest, arms wrapped around her legs protectively. A few white-blonde curls had escaped her ponytail and hung like springs around her face, which was paler than usual making the freckles scattered across her nose and cheeks stand out. Her aqua eyes were hidden behind blue-veined lids, and from her heavy breathing Parker knew that a headache was pounding at her temples.

"You okay?"

"I'm fine," Tessa replied with her stock standard answer.

This of course wasn't true nor was it the first night in the year they had been together that Tessa had awoken, screaming, from a nightmare. No stranger to nightmares himself, the dream that had plagued him since childhood had virtually ceased since he and Tessa had gotten together.

Things between himself and Tessa were moving slowly but definitely in the right direction. Tessa had clammed up about her past making it clear that Eleanor and Dylan Riley were both topics that were completely off limits. After that one night at her cottage she had replaced her emotional armor piece by piece. She had not shed one more tear or uttered one more word over anything that had happened to her. Parker knew that she was uncomfortable that he had seen her when she was not in complete control of herself.

While Tessa sometimes shared what she was thinking with him, she had not allowed herself to be exposed or vulnerable around him. Any time he brought up anything even remotely personal her eyes shuttered and she refused to answer. Tessa was like a closed book, no he thought, more like a teenage girl's locked diary, it took a lot of work and time and energy to get inside but once you did it was an enlightening fact-finding mission.

Tessa had not had the support of a loving family growing up and had spent all twenty-six of her years building a wall, one that reached high into the skies, to protect herself. She had been burned several times in the past, had lost every person that she had ever cared about, and was still reluctant to put her full trust in him now. But as stubborn as Tessa could be, he was more so and no matter what she said or did, he was not going to give up on her.

"Come here," he murmured sliding onto the bed beside her, he wrapped an arm around her shoulders and pulled her towards him. Tessa stiffened at first but then relented and nestled her head against his shoulder in the sweet way she did only when she was too exhausted to keep her barriers erect.

Running one hand up and down her arm, Tessa took his other hand and entwined their fingers together, her breath coming in warm little puffs against his chest.

While Tessa maintained her silence in regards to her family, her friends, and her feelings, Parker was starting to slowly draw out of her some of the things that she was passionate about. Tessa adored painting and drawing and was a children's book author who did her own illustrations. Her collection of works had recently been destroyed; so last Christmas he had bought her new supplies and the two of them had spent several days since out in the country with Tessa painting their beautiful surroundings.

Tessa also loved horses and was a very accomplished rider having entered and won numerous competitions, and had even undertaken the monumental task of teaching him to ride. Usually Tessa preferred to ride bareback, and watching her fly across the paddocks with the wind sending her white blonde curls whipping wildly, her eyes dancing, so completely in control of such a magnificent animal made his heart ache with love for her. This was where she was most at peace, where she was at her happiest, where she almost let her guard down. Sitting atop her huge chestnut colored horse Tessa looked both small and vulnerable, and strong and invincible, at the same time.

They sat together in silence for several minutes. "You wanna talk?" Parker asked eventually, knowing the answer before he even asked the question.

Tessa's head wiggled back and forth against his shoulder.

"Honey, it's one year today since it happened of course you're having nightmares, it would be weird if you weren't."

She said nothing but he felt her stiffen and shrink away, emotionally as well as physically. Face a blank slate as she rubbed her head tiredly and moved to the edge of the bed to be as far away from him as possible. Tessa was an expert at covering her emotions, at revealing nothing about what was going on inside her head, but they had been together for a year now and Parker was getting good at knowing what she was thinking.

"You still feel guilty," he told her flatly.

Tessa didn't confirm it but he knew he was right.

"Tessa, he was insane, you are not responsible for his death," he'd already told her these words countless times.

Raising a disbelieving eyebrow at him, Tessa pushed away the cream blankets and thick feather quilt and climbed out of the bed. Crossing to the window, she pulled back the blue curtains, the same color as the walls, to stare out at the night. It didn't matter how many times he told her that it was not her fault that Dylan Riley had died she wouldn't, couldn't, believe it.

Rising to follow her to the window Parker stood behind her, close but not too close, allowing her the space she needed to deal with her feelings. Tessa was too lost in a past she wanted desperately to forget to acknowledge his presence, so he stood gazing out at the clear night, the millions of tiny diamonds shining in the black sky. Thoughts straying briefly to the diamond ring he had hidden away in a corner of the spare bedroom wardrobe, tucked away behind a stack of unused jackets, waiting for when the time was right to bring it out.

Deciding he had given her enough space Parker crossed his arms around her waist and settled her against his chest. Tessa didn't relax into him but neither did she pull away, he took this as a sign to continue. "I don't care how many times I need to say it, you are not responsible for Dylan Riley's death. I am going to keep telling you that until it finally sinks in."

Opening her mouth to protest then snapping it shut, wiggling around so that she was facing him and burying her face in his chest. "I'm too tired to argue with you, Parker," voice muffled against him.

Holding her tighter, he rested his chin against the top of her head, her five-foot frame fitting perfectly into his own six foot one. Breathing in the sweet smell of the citrus shampoo she used, they both started as the phone chirped. Reluctantly Parker released Tessa to answer it, hoping that it wasn't who he thought it was going to be.

Snatching up the receiver before the person on the other end could hang up. "Hello?"

"It's Wyatt." Skylar Wyatt was his partner and friend of over twenty years. "We got a case."

Keeping one eye on Tessa as she resumed her sightless stare out the window. "What is it?" he asked trying to focus.

"Attempted kidnapping. Eighteen-year-old Elizabeth Landry. Someone tried to grab her while she was walking home from work, perp tried to strangle her but took off when a couple of guys showed up," Wyatt summarized. "I'll be there in fifteen minutes. And, Parker . . ." his voice trailed off.

"What?"

"It looks like it could be related to the Iceman case."

Parker felt his blood turn to ice at the mention of the serial killer who had stalked the city the previous winter. "Why?"

"Well for one thing it's December first, plus he left a sprig of holly at the scene," Wyatt filled him in, holly was one of the Iceman's signatures.

"Did they find a body?"

"Yeah they did."

Catching the sadness in his partner's voice. "Was it . . .?"

"Yeah it was her."

Closing his eyes and letting out a measured breath, even though they'd been expecting this it didn't make the news any easier to hear. Casting another glance in Tessa's direction then turning his back and lowering his voice, "Wyatt, I'll come to you. Today, it's one year since . . . I don't want to leave Tessa alone . . ."

Interrupting, "I'll bring Casey," Wyatt told him referring to his wife. "She can stay with Tessa at your place."

"No, no, I don't want to impose, you've got the kids and . . ."

"It's no imposition," Wyatt reassured him. "The kids are with Casey's parents, and we weren't sleeping anyway."

"Thanks." Wyatt was one of the reasons that Parker had become the person he was today. After being abandoned by his mother as an infant Parker and his twin sister Matilda had grown up in foster care, the last place they had been sent to live the worst by far. Not long after their tenth birthday, Luka and Laura Bell, a couple that had lost their only son, Taylor, to cancer, had adopted them. Wyatt's family had lived next door to the Bell's and Parker and Wyatt had quickly become firm friends despite the five-year age gap. Because of the steadfast love and support of his adoptive parents and Wyatt, Parker had changed from a withdrawn and angry little boy into an open, loving and empathetic child.

"We'll be there in fifteen minutes," Wyatt reminded him before hanging up.

Listening for a moment to the dial tone, then replacing the phone in its cradle and crossing the room back to Tessa.

"I don't need a babysitter, Parker," she snapped irritably as he came up beside her.

Surprise flickered through him; he had thought he'd been discrete. He shouldn't be surprised, he knew that Tessa was always on guard and aware of her surroundings, even when she didn't appear to be. "I know," he nodded emphatically, although he wasn't entirely convinced, instead of dealing with the events of the past year Tessa just acted as if they hadn't happened. "Wyatt's gonna be here soon," he told her.

Relenting she softened her gaze. "I'm fine, really, Parker, go do your job, save some people," reaching up on tiptoes she pressed a quick kiss to his lips.

Kissing her back, he wrapped an arm around her waist and lifted her so that they were eye to eye. "I know you don't like it but I worry about you."

Studying him for a long moment with eyes that seemed to see all and yet reveal nothing. "I know that you do, and I love you for it," she finally said, "But I'm okay, I really am."

* * * * *

11:44 P.M.

"Here you go."

Someone pushed a steaming paper cup of tea into her shaking hands.

Blinking, she looked up into the kindly face of one of the many police officers swarming the area.

"Thanks," she murmured softly. Her voice was croaky, partly from the shock of everything she had been through tonight, and partly from the man's hands that had wrapped so tightly around her throat. Lizzie chocked back a terrified sob as she remembered her life flashing before her eyes as his hands had squeezed tighter and tighter and each intake of air became harder and harder. Her lungs felt like they were going to explode, her eyes like they were about to pop, blood pounded in her ears so loudly she couldn't hear anything else . . .

"Miss Landry!"

Hands gripped her shoulders and shook her firmly sending hot tea splashing over the sides of the cup she still clutched tightly.

"Miss Landry," the voice spoke again, a commanding voice, calm and sure. "It's okay, you're safe now, it's all over."

Forcing her vision to clear she saw the watchful face of a paramedic peering down at her with bright blue eyes.

"Miss Landry?"

Giving him a shaky nod as he gently removed the cup from her hands and took hold of her shoulders again, this time to ease her down to the ground.

"There we go," he smiled reassuringly. "I'm just gonna check you out," he explained as he knelt beside her. Ensuring she didn't have any other injuries before examining the necklace of black and purple bruises encircling her neck, checking her vital signs, taking her pulse and her blood pressure. His partner joined them shortly and wrapped a scratchy grey blanket around her shoulders.

Elizabeth was barely aware of the medics as they poked and prodded, her thoughts were too busy swinging from her family to a shadow of a memory that remained tantalizingly out of reach. After those two men had shown up and her attacker had run off, she had been out of it, struggling to draw a breath, struggling to control the panic that continued to pulse through her and she hadn't been able to properly process everything.

Then once she had been able to pull herself together her first concern had been her family. Controlling her tears and forcing her voice to remain steady, she'd called home to tell her mom that she was okay but had been held up. Resisting the urge to blurt out everything that had happened right there and then, she didn't want her mother to worry and decided it would be better to explain things to her in person.

Looking up once again as someone patted her on the shoulder.

"All done," the medic smiled at her.

"Thank you," she whispered hoarsely.

"You don't need to go to the hospital," the other EMT told her. "But if you still have a lot of pain in your throat in a couple of days then see your doctor."

Lizzie nodded but she barely felt the dull ache in her neck, it was fear and shock that kept rippling through her like relentless waves on the seashore. She watched absently as the two paramedics packed up their things and returned to the ambulance, following it with her eyes as it weaved off down the alley.

Scanning the crowd, police officers, CSU techs, reporters down the end held at bay by a couple of officers who looked not much older than herself, searching for the two men who had without a doubt saved her life. Sighting them off in a corner Lizzie felt a shiver of relief flood through her; she didn't know how she could ever thank them enough for what they had done for her.

Trying unsuccessfully to grab once again for the thread that kept flitting into the edges of her mind only to dart away whenever she reached for it. Frustrated because she knew that whatever it was it was very important, perhaps it was even the key to catching her would be murderer.

"Miss Landry?"

Starting once again this time she glanced up to see a police officer hovering beside her. "Can I go home now?"

The officer shook his head. "We need you to talk to some detectives who'll be working the case."

"I already told you everything I remember," she protested weakly, recalling the numerous questions she had been asked when the first officers had shown up at the scene.

Shooting her a sympathetic smile as he offered her his hand and pulled her to her feet, guiding her with an arm around her shoulder to the back of a police car. "I'm sorry but we really need you to talk to them, anything that you can tell them might help them to save someone else's life."

"What?" she asked him, confused.

As he opened the car door and helped her inside he looked her straight in the eye, his deadly serious brown eyes boring into her own sending shivers up and down her spine. Then he uttered words that chilled her to the bone and made everything else that had happened tonight seem like nothing more than the harmless ups and downs of a rollercoaster. "We think the man who attacked you was the

Iceman."

* * * * *

11:48 P.M.

Shaking.

She couldn't stop shaking.

Neither could she shake the picture of what she had seen from her mind.

Squeezing her black eyes closed she shook her head from side to side as fast as she could as though, like in one of those old Etch A Sketch's, that would somehow dislodge the image from her brain.

She wanted to leave, get out of her clothes, take a shower, try to rid her body of the scene she had stumbled upon, a scene that felt like it had permeated her very soul.

She wanted to go home . . .

No, Winter Hamilton corrected herself, twisting her black hair around her fingers, something she had done since childhood whenever she was stressed or scared, home was the last place she wanted to be right now.

Remembering with a violent shudder that made her feel as though an earthquake was exploding in her stomach, the tremors reverberating all the way out to the tips of her fingers and toes, exactly what she had seen that had ruined her night.

Driving aimlessly through the streets, fifteen years old and an only child with few friends, it was something she did regularly especially late at night. Winter's mother was more self-involved than any one of the vain cheerleaders who tormented her daily at her school, she had never met her biological father and her stepfather could be . . . no she wouldn't think of that now.

She had come to a screeching halt when the moonlight had reflected off something placed in the middle of the road. From a distance she had been unable to tell what the thing was but as she had gotten closer, the image in front of her growing steadily larger with each advancing yard, a sinking feeling had started to develop. And then she was close enough that her headlights lit the horrible scene, as though it were a stage set for a play and Winter wished with all her heart that was all it had been.

When she slammed on the breaks the tyres had slid on the wet roads sending the car heading straight for a tree. Managing to regain control over the vehicle before a collision had occurred, she had jumped out, standing on legs as weak and wobbly as a newborn foal's.

Taking a step towards the enormous block of ice, at least seven-foot square, she had stared in numb shock at the emaciated, naked body encased inside it. The young woman who looked only a few years older than herself, the black eyes that seemed to be looking out at her from beyond the grave as though the woman's soul was trapped within her icy grave. Black hair hung, frozen in place, around the shoulders, the legs crossed at the ankles, the hands clasped, encased in elbow length gloves, against her breast, a sprig of holly clutched by the thin white hands.

The girl looked so real and yet so fake. For a second Winter had allowed herself to believe that it was just a mannequin, that the whole thing was just someone's idea of a sick joke.

Another glance at the body told her that this was no game.

Before she knew it, she was screaming wildly. Gut protesting over her late night snack she'd lurched to the side of the road, thrown up and then promptly called 911 with fingers that shook so badly she'd dropped the phone several times before managing to place the call.

Alone in the eerily quiet woods, the towering trees closely bordering the small road, some dressed in their ever-present green attire, others reaching twisted grey fingers to the sky. The only sound the soft scratching of leafless branches as they tangled together in the breeze. While Winter sat in her car waiting for the police to arrive, shivering despite the blast of warm air the heater spouted directly onto her face, her swirling mind had recalled every gruesome detail about the Iceman case.

Now the harsh florescent lights the police had set up around the huge ice block had replaced the milky moonlight. The cacophony of voices, whirring of cameras and general bustle of police and CSU techs drowning out the soft sounds of the woods.

When the police had arrived they had peppered her relentlessly with questions; had she seen anyone? No. Had she heard anyone? No. Had she seen a car hanging around? No. Had she noticed anything unusual? No. Did she come this way often? Yes. Had she seen anything suspicious any other time she had come this way, maybe a car hanging around at the side of the road? No. Had she touched anything? No.

By the end of it Winter felt like the most useless person on the planet.

Now, however, they had finally left her alone. Asked for her number in case they had any follow-up questions, left her a card in case she thought of anything important, then dismissed her and told her she could go home.

But Winter wasn't ready to go home yet, and so she sat in her car, the engine off, the car as cold as . . . ice, she thought dismally the connection made her feel ill as the image of the girl in the ice block came rushing back into her head.

As sick as she felt picturing the horrible scene just outside her car, she felt even sicker when she thought about . . .

No, she told herself, forcing the notion from her mind.

"It's just a coincidence," she mumbled aloud. "It has to be."

Forcing herself into action she reached out a hand and switched on the engine, startled when cold air blasted out at her. Switching off the heater and whirring down the window, Winter enjoyed the freezing air that whipped inside. The cold numbed her delightfully, dulling the images that seemed burned onto her eyelids and deadening the trepidation that filled her at the thought of what might be awaiting her at home.

* * * * *

11:52 P.M.

The Iceman always referred to itself in the third person. Shrinks might say it was a way of assuaging guilt over the killings, to remove responsibility as though someone else committed the murders. But shrinks thought about things way too much. In truth, the Iceman did it because it was amusing.

The Iceman loved the name the press had come up with, thought it was hilarious, albeit not very clever. It failed to encapsulate each carefully chosen aspect of the crimes making them seem more simplistic than in reality they were, still as monikers went it wasn't so bad.

Already the failure of the evening forgotten.

Iceman had moved on.

On to poor Hayley Geoffries.

A perfectly meticulous planner the Iceman always had not one but at least four or five backups and this time that replacement was a twenty-two year old named Hayley Geoffries.

Just as pretty as Elizabeth Landry although not nearly as sure about her looks, Hayley was half Japanese, with beautiful almond shaped brown eyes, smooth, straight black hair that she had highlighted with streaks of red. Hayley was as different in personality from Lizzie as it was possible to be. While Elizabeth liked to go out with her friends and party, Hayley preferred to stay home alone and read a book or watch a movie. Where Lizzie loved to be the centre of attention and was outgoing and talkative definitely an extrovert, Hayley was quiet and withdrawn ever the introvert. There was one characteristic common to both young ladies; they were both very responsible for their age, especially in regards to their families.

Iceman had to admit it was a little disappointing not being able to spend the next month with Elizabeth. She would surely have been the most challenging girl so far. It was a toss up as to whether it was more fun breaking their spirits or actually killing them and it was always a little sad when the time came to do the deed.

Still, ever the optimist, perhaps Hayley would be a surprise and turn out to be just as entertaining as Elizabeth surely would have been.

Standing in the deliciously icy night, huge piles of grey clouds were slowly starting to fill up the sky and the promise of snow was in the air. Standing in the backyard of a simple brick two-storey house, the yard contained nothing but a small rectangle of grass and a single apple tree, now bare and grey in the wintry night. Hayley Geoffries still lived with her parents in the home in which she had grown up.

Slipping from a pocket some lock-picking tools, the Iceman skillfully got the backdoor unlocked in a matter of seconds and once inside made a beeline straight for Hayley's bedroom. During many mandatory recognizance visits to her house a mental map of the floor plan had been formed.

Careful not to make a single sound, not wanting to wake Hayley or her parents, heading cautiously up the stairs remembering perfectly which ones creaked and which were safe to step on. Down the hall, coming to a stop in front of the last door on the right, Hayley's room.

Hand on the knob; trembling with anticipation; pushing gently on the door, it swung slowly open. Inside the room, in the midst of piles and piles of books, was a bed upon which lay a snoring Hayley. Snuggled under a rainbow-striped comforter Hayley lay flat on her back, making the job all the more easier. Crossing the room and pulling a gun from another pocket, Iceman placed a hand over the sleeping girl's mouth and nose, completely cutting off her air supply.

It took a moment before she sprung awake, arms flailing, legs kicking, eyes bulging open, the first thing they saw was a gun pointing at her head.

Lowering the hand a little so that Hayley could breath through her nose, Iceman continued to cover her mouth so that she couldn't scream and lent over, close to her face. "Hello, Hayley."

She went completely still as though her body had turned to stone, terrified eyes darting around the room trying desperately to seek out some form of salvation. Unfortunately for her there would be none.

Cocking the gun and whispering in her ear, "If you make a sound I will kill your parents."

Giving her a moment to let the words sink through the terror that was clogging her brain and register in her consciousness, noting with glee the exact second where understanding dawned on her face.

Leaning close once again, "I'm going to remove my hand, if you scream I will shoot your parents and make you watch. Understand?"

Watching the internal struggle in her eyes. The ultimate choice, herself or her loved ones. Really, there was no choice. If she screamed her parents would die, but the result for her would be the same.

Hayley gave a shaky jerk of her head.

Tentatively the Iceman removed the hand that still covered Hayley's mouth, the girl opened her mouth to take in a huge gulp of air but didn't make a sound.

Smiling at her and nodding appreciatively, the Iceman loved it when people made the sensible choice, demonstrating that they were a logical thinker. It was much harder to deal with an emotional person than a rational one.

"Let's go."

Standing and walking to the door without bothering to look back and see whether Hayley was following since not a doubt lingered that she would be. Opening the bedroom door and waiting while Hayley went out first, keeping the gun pointed at her in the unlikely instance that she tried something stupid. Hayley's steps were slow and shaky, like she might collapse at any second, but to the girl's credit she managed to keep herself upright.

Waiting until they were outside then bending and placing a single sprig of holly on the back stoop, one of the Iceman's favorite signatures. Then wrapping a hand around Hayley's arm and yanking her around the side of the house and out to the street heading toward the van.

Plunging the syringe into her shoulder, as she wobbled and started to pass out the Iceman whispered in her ear, "Stay strong and I'll let you live." This wasn't true of course but hope played an important role in the game. Without hope you had no reason to live and a despondent prey was no fun at all. For a second Hayley's eyes twitched furiously as the prospect of a way out flooded through her and then she was out.

Slamming the van's doors closed and climbing into the driver's seat the Iceman headed towards home with a deep sense of satisfaction of a night well spent.

DECEMBER 2ND

12:03 A.M.

"I don't want to talk about it."

Tessa felt herself closing off, slotting away her feelings into the appropriate boxes and locking them safely away. While Parker had taken a shower she had come downstairs, made a pot of steaming tea, set some cookies on to bake and curled up in one of the armchairs in Parker's living room. Although she had been practically living here in Parker's house for the past year she still thought of it as his home.

When he had first asked her to come and stay with him she had been reluctant, but her cottage was destroyed and she hated the main house, a huge stone mansion, on the estate she had inherited from her grandparents. In the end she had given in, partly because she had nowhere else to stay, and partly, although it scared her to admit it, because she wanted to be close to him.

"Talk to me, Tess," Parker pushed gently as he knelt in front of her and placed his hands on her knees. Sometimes he could be relentless.

A twinge of guilt mixed with apprehension, she knew that Parker wanted her to be an open book but it just was not who she was. About to give him her usual answer and tell him it was nothing but when she looked at him, at his face full of genuine concern, she reluctantly relented. To be fair Parker had shared a lot more about his own troubled past than she had and she knew that if they were going to move forward in their relationship then she was going to have to learn how to trust him.

Sighing, she began unenthusiastically, "I was thinking about the fire."

Fear flashed across Parker's face and she knew he was

remembering the night, just over one year ago, when he had rushed inside her burning cottage and saved her life. At first he had assumed that the attempt on her life was related to the serial killer who was stalking her. Eventually she had admitted that it was in fact related to an earlier event from her past and so Parker now lived in constant fear that this person would come back and finish the job he started.

"If he comes back . . ." Parker began fiercely, his amber eyes flashing with panic and anger. "I won't let anyone hurt you."

Offering a weak smile, Tessa reached out and smoothed his wild black hair. "I know, but I'm not afraid of him."

They sat together for a few moments each lost in their own thoughts. Tessa happy to put off sleep for as long as possible, although she tried to hide the terrifying dreams, flashbacks really, that plagued her almost every night it seemed that she wasn't as good at covering her feelings as she had been twelve months ago. Around Parker she was starting, inch by inch, to slowly let her guard down. She no longer bothered to hide her emotions behind carefully blank and expressionless eyes but neither did she shout her feelings from the rooftops. It still made her feel uncomfortable to allow him to glimpse her vulnerable.

"Tessa?"

She blinked as Parker shook her gently. "What?" obviously she had missed whatever he had been saying to her.

"You okay?" he was watching her closely now, brow creased with concern. After everything that had happened Parker had a tendency to treat her like a china doll, as though she might break into a million pieces at any second.

"I'm fine," she told him as he swung her up into his strong arms, plopped down in the chair and then settled her on his lap. She snuggled herself against his hard chest. "What did you say?" she offered as bright a smile as she could muster, and rested her head against his shoulder.

Wrapped safely in Parker's arms was like being wrapped in the world's softest, warmest blanket, and she felt a tingle of nervousness bubbling in her stomach, this was all so new to her. Before Parker she had actively avoided any kind of relationships, not just romantic but friendships as well. Life experience had taught her that people, even those who were close to you, couldn't be trusted, that they invariably let you down. She had tried her hardest to push Parker away, but like a bad smell, he had been impossible to banish.

"I said," he began patiently, "Maybe we could go out to dinner this weekend."

Parker's voice sounded nervous almost scared and she wondered what he was up to. "Sure, that sounds nice," about to add more but the doorbell chimed.

"That'll be Wyatt," Parker announced, stating the obvious since they were expecting his partner, not to mention that it was the middle of the night so visitors would be highly unlikely. Parker set her on the ground then hurried off to answer the door, grabbing a scarf from the coffee table as he went and wrapping it around his neck.

"Hey, goldilocks," Wyatt said enthusiastically a moment later as he entered the living room.

Tessa's face brightened into a real smile at the sight of him. "Hey, Skylar," she threw her arms around his neck and laughed as he lifted her feet off the floor and kissed her cheek. She loved Parker's partner like a brother, a wonderful big brother who looked out for you, teased you and whom you could count on. Things were always so easy with Wyatt; there was no pressure, no expectations. With Parker she was always so aware of trying to be what he wanted, to live up to his expectations, something she wasn't sure she could ever do.

"Casey's on her way," Wyatt told her. "She took her car cos she has work in the morning."

"Thanks, Skylar," she smiled as he set her back down on the ground. Tessa was the only person, other than his mother, that Skylar Wyatt allowed to use his given name and get away with it. The last of five boys his mother had been sure during her pregnancy that she would be having a girl, when Wyatt was born, another boy, she had decided to stick with the name she had chosen. As a small child Wyatt, occasionally dressed in pink and forced to take ballet, had grown to hate the name Skylar and all it embodied, and around puberty had started using his surname exclusively.

"Alright we better be going," Parker said gesturing at the door. "I don't know when I'll be back."

"Okay," she nodded, hating that she was a little apprehensive about spending the day alone, at least, she comforted herself, it was no longer December first.

"Love you," Parker tilted her head up and kissed her tenderly.

"Love you too," she murmured back. "See ya, Skylar."

"See ya, goldilocks." Giving her shoulder a squeeze, "Try to get some sleep."

She followed them to the door and watched forlornly as they climbed into Wyatt's car and drove away. Wandering back inside she found herself walking aimlessly from room to room ending up in Parker's bedroom. Retrieving the teddy bear Parker had given her for her birthday from the rocking chair. It was soft and fluffy, a beautiful light caramel color that matched Parker's eyes, a turquoise ribbon, the same color as her own eyes, tied in a bow around it's neck.

As a child Tessa had loved teddies, had a huge collection, but one lonely night after she had been abandoned by everyone who was supposed to have loved her she had snuck downstairs and taken a pair of scissors from her grandmother's sewing basket. Returning to her room she had taken the scissors to the bears and by the first light of dawn not a single whole bear remained. They were still in pieces in a bag in the back of the closet in her old room at the main house on her estate.

Sweet smell of baking cookies wafting though the house, Tessa took the teddy with her back downstairs, and after a quick check of the oven went to the living room and settled into one of the comfortable armchairs to await Casey's arrival.

Tessa loved Parker's house. When she had first moved in, he had been worried that she would look down on his house because it was not as luxurious as she was accustomed too. She had grown up in a very wealthy, albeit highly dysfunctional, family. The house she had lived in as a child was an enormous mansion but she had hated that house and had not been inside it in almost eight years. After inheriting the estate from her grandparents she had moved into the small cottage nestled in the woods at the back of the property. Tessa had loved that cottage and Parker's place reminded her of the one place where she had ever felt safe.

Mind wandering back in time to twelve months ago as she thought about the first time she had met Parker. They had met under the most unusual of circumstances. Parker, or Detective Bell as he'd been to her back then, had been one of the detectives investigating the case of a serial killer who had abducted a woman and left a list of clues pointing to nine unidentified women he planned on killing. She was one of those women. At first, she had infuriated Parker by refusing to reveal the identities of the other women. Eventually he had discovered her secret, that she intended to sacrifice herself to save her friends and had gone after the killer, Parker had followed, arriving mere moments after the gun had gone off, killing her tormentor.

Ever since he had refused to leave her alone intent on proving to her that he was the one person that she could trust, that he would never leave her or let her down. Although she wanted to believe that more than anything, she was still unable to fully convince herself that things would work out between them. Parker had done nothing to make her doubt him but she had been let down too many times in the past to trust anyone one hundred percent.

"Tessa?" a faraway voice broke into her daydream.

Gentle pressure on her wrist made her blink and Casey Wyatt's worried face came slowly into view.

"Tess? Can you hear me?"

Pulling herself together. "Hey, Casey," Tessa chirped pushing away her friend's well-meaning hands.

"Hey yourself," Casey responded replacing her fingers on Tessa's wrist and continuing to check her pulse. "Is everything okay?"

"I'm fine," Tessa frowned; she hated it when people fussed over her.

"Your pulse is racing, you sure you're okay," Casey asked producing a small light from somewhere and shining it in her eyes. "Have you taken anything?"

Once again pushing Casey's hands away. "You know I don't take medication. Ever." As much as she had grown to love Casey over the year they'd known one another she tended to fuss as much as Parker.

Tall and slender, Casey had been born in Sudan, orphaned as an infant, and adopted by an American family when she was fifteen months old. Skin as black as night, and deep dark eyes so black you could not distinguish between the pupils and the iris, corkscrew curls, tighter and smaller than Tessa's own ringlets, which Casey wore short. Originally a history teacher after the death of her and Skylar's daughter Casey had changed careers and was now a doctor.

"When I got here," Casey was saying, "I knocked and knocked, and when you didn't answer I started to worry, then I smelled something burning . . ."

"The cookies," Tessa interrupted moving to stand.

Hands on her shoulders Casey pushed her back into the seat. "Just stay still a moment," she murmured in her most annoying doctor voice. "I let myself in with my key and took the cookies out of the oven, then I found you in here completely blanked out. Are you sure you're okay?"

"I told you I'm fine," Tessa repeated keeping her voice calm with an effort. In her hurry to prove her case she stood too quickly causing blood to rush, pounding, to her head.

Swaying she felt Casey's steadying hands tighten on her arms and lower her back into the chair. "Stay put. When did you last eat?"

Stubbornly Tessa attempted to stand again but Casey held her firmly in place. "Maybe lunch yesterday," she murmured clenching her eyes shut to try to stop the swirling in her head that made it feel like her brain was riding a rollercoaster.

"Tessa," Casey exclaimed, "You have to eat. You have to start looking after yourself."

"Everything okay?" asked a voice at the door.

They both looked up to see Maisy Wallace, a relatively new CSU tech who sometimes worked with Parker and Skylar, peering anxiously over at them. Tessa had met Maisy at a Christmas party, at twenty-seven Maisy was only a year older than Tessa, they had spent the evening chatting and had been firm friends ever since.

"Tess isn't feeling well," Casey answered.

"Actually Tess is feeling just fine," Tessa shot back.

Narrowing hazel eyes at her Maisy tossed her red ponytail over her shoulder and crossed to them, addressing Casey, "What's wrong with her?"

Throwing hands up in the air in annoyance. "Nothing!" Tessa snapped.

Paying no attention to her Casey answered as though she was not even in the room, "Her pulse is racing, pupils are a little dilated, and she's dizzy."

"Should we take her to the hospital?" Maisy asked nervously, she was not good in medical situations. Like herself, Maisy hated the sight of blood, which sometimes made it difficult for her to do her job since working CSU she regularly had to collect blood evidence.

"I think she'll be okay. She just needs to take better care of herself," Casey added pointedly.

"You know I really do hate it when people talk about me like I'm not here," Tessa interjected irritably. Amused they both smiled back at her undaunted. "I'll get us something to eat," she scowled and tried to stand.

Once again Casey pushed her back down. "Just take it easy for a minute, okay? For me," Casey added upon seeing an argumentative frown brewing in her eyes. Relenting Tessa sunk back down, tucking her feet up underneath her. "Can you get her some water?" Casey asked, directing her question at Maisy, who nodded and headed off down the hall towards the kitchen.

"What happened to the cookies?" she called through a moment later.

"They burned while she was zoned out," Casey yelled back.

Returning, glass of water in hand, "Good thing I bought doughnuts then," Maisy commented handing over the glass to Casey then reaching into her huge red and green striped bag to ferret out a bag of a dozen iced doughnuts.

"Here drink this," Casey held out the glass.

"I'm not thirsty," she pouted stubbornly.

"Tessa," Casey warned.

Sighing long-sufferingly, she took the glass and drank a couple of mouthfuls of the cold water while Casey nodded approvingly. "So did you get conscripted too?" Tessa asked Maisy.

Looking up, eyes wide in innocence. "I don't know what you mean," Maisy could barely hold back her grin.

"I know Parker sent you," Tessa said to Casey. "And I'm sure he sent you too," she said shooting Maisy a suspicious stare.

"Actually, it was Marty who sent me over," Maisy laughed as she held out the doughnut box, Casey chose a chocolate iced one scattered with rainbow colored sprinkles.

Taking a plain one for herself, "Marty Jenkins?" Tessa asked surprised. "Your boss?"

Nodding, "Uh huh, I was planning on coming anyway but Marty rang me up, wanted me to come and check up on you. He was worried, especially because it's . . ." she let the sentence trail off.

Rolling her eyes. "So you're all ganging up on me now. You know despite what Parker thinks I do not need a babysitter."

"What you need," Casey sobered studying her with steady inky eyes, "Is to start dealing with what happened. You want to pretend like none of it ever existed, like Dylan Riley never existed."

"I wish he didn't, and now he doesn't. He's dead, it's over," deliberately forcing unwanted memories out of her mind.

"But he did exist, honey," Maisy said gently, balancing on the edge of the chair and putting an arm around her shoulders. "And he hurt you. You can't just keep pushing your feelings away, sooner or later they're going to come out and the longer you put it off the harder it will be to deal with them when they finally do."

When Tessa said nothing Casey reached over and took her chin, forcing her to look up. "You have to stop blaming yourself for his death, Tessa."

Gulping back tears, she hated for anyone to see her cry. "What about Janice, Tiffany, Bianca, Dorothy and Gina? Should I stop blaming myself for their deaths too? The facts are that if I'd done what Dylan wanted in the first place then all of them would still be alive."

"And you," Casey reminded her gently, "Would be dead."

A headache started to form at the base of her skull. "I don't want to talk about it anymore," she whispered, suddenly bone tired.

Exchanging glances, Casey nodded, "Okay we'll leave it be for the moment, but you know we're here whenever you want to talk."

Giving her shoulders a squeeze, Maisy nudged her over and slid into the chair beside her. "You will never guess what Luke said when he called me last night." Maisy began relating the next installment of the on-going saga in her relationship with long-term, off and on boyfriend, Luke.

Resting her head back against the chair and listening to her friend's cheerful voices, Casey and Maisy had become her lifeline over the last few months. Distancing herself from her former friends because it was too painful to be around them right now, she had only seen them a couple of times since Dylan Riley's death.

Focusing on the bright and bubbly voices Tessa was able, once again, to successfully lock away her feelings in regards to Dylan Riley. Casey and Maisy were wrong she could keep those feelings buried safely forever.

* * * * *

12:28 A.M.

"Elizabeth Landry?"

The eighteen-year-old looked up at him from the back of the police car with dull eyes. "Lizzie," she murmured, an automatic response.

Parker gave her an encouraging smile. "I'm Detective Bell and this is my partner Detective Wyatt, mind if we sit with you?"

Lizzie gave a half-hearted shrug as Parker slid onto the seat beside her, closing the door to keep out the cold. Wyatt took the front passenger seat, positioning himself sideways so that he was facing them.

Beginning slowly, "Lizzie, I know this has been a traumatic night, and I know that you've already gone over this a few times, but we're going to need to ask you some questions about what happened tonight. I know you're scared, and I know that it's hard, but it is really important that we know every detail that you can think of. Did someone tell you that . . .?"

"It was the Iceman who attacked me," Elizabeth cut in, shivering violently as though someone had dumped a bucket of ice on her head.

Continuing before Lizzie had time to dwell, "Why don't you tell us what you did today?"

Taking a deep breath Lizzie pulled the blanket that draped her shoulders tighter around herself then clenched her hands together in her lap as she began to recount the day's events. "I had classes this morning," voice growing stronger and surer. "Then I had lunch at the café and started work at about two. I worked till late, but I stayed around a little after my shift to talk with some friends, I got caught up and when I realized the time I left right away."

Parker noticed the hint of color that rose in her cheeks as she mentioned getting caught up at the coffee shop. Remembering what they had been told about the girl's family life, a disabled mother and brother, Parker bet that she didn't have a lot of time to spend with her friends and the time that she did spend with them just caused her to feel guilty about not being at home taking care of her family.

"When you were leaving did you notice anyone hanging around the café? Maybe someone inside who'd been watching you, or who left right after you did, or someone hanging around outside?" Wyatt asked.

"No, there was no one I can think of."

"What about a customer today who really stood out, maybe someone that asked after you specifically, or who was watching you?"

"No," Elizabeth shook her head.

"Do you remembering anyone following you when you were walking home?"

"No," Lizzie now looked on the verge of tears. "I'm sorry. I wasn't really paying attention. I was caught up in talking with my friends, and then on the way home I was busy texting because of this Christmas party we're planning. I wasn't looking around; I wasn't paying any attention to anything else. I'm sorry," she said again.

"That's okay," Parker reassured her. "You had no reason to be thinking someone was following you."

"But I should have been paying attention. I mean a girl walking home alone at midnight," shaking her head as she realized her own stupidity. "I even walk the same way every night, talk about making myself an easy target."

Parker couldn't disagree, Elizabeth had made herself a ticking time bomb for any lowlife to take advantage of but that was not the issue at hand. Redirecting her attention back to the night's events, "What happened next?"

"I was walking past there," the blanket slipped from her shoulders as she pointed a trembling hand down the alley. "The next thing I knew he was grabbing me from behind, his arm was around my neck and he was squeezing," her hands absently tracing the black and blue stripe that marred her neck. "He was so strong . . ." tears started to drip down her cheeks. "He was squeezing tighter and tighter . . . I couldn't breathe . . . I was pulling and scratching at his arms . . . but he was so strong . . . and everything was going black . . ."

Elizabeth was sobbing now and dropped her face into her hands, her entire body shaking. Parker put his arms around her and her fingers curled into fists, grabbing handfuls of his sweater and twisting it as she cried. Letting her weep until at last her sobs quietened to sniffles, then gently pulling her back, keeping a firm grip on her shoulders. Looking her straight in the eye, "Lizzie, I know that you are terrified, but we need to know anything you can tell us that might help us find out who he is. Right now he might have another girl."

She held his gaze; her fingers released his sweater and began to twirl the auburn hair that had escaped her ponytail around her fingers. "You really think that he took someone else?"

"Yes," Parker told her honestly. "The Iceman is meticulous, if your abduction was foiled he had a back-up."

Considering this Elizabeth studied them carefully trying to decide whether they were telling her this to pressure her or because it was true. Finally she nodded, closed her eyes and focused herself. "When he . . ." faltering briefly but quickly resuming control, "He grabbed me from behind, I . . . I never saw his face, but he was strong, really strong. He was wearing a black windbreaker and black gloves, I'm sorry I never really saw him . . ."

Her voice trailed off, eyes glazing over, Parker frowned and shook her gently. "Lizzie?"

No answer.

"Elizabeth?" a firmer shake this time.

Eyes clearing a little, a small smile curling her lips. "I thought of something," excited, her face becoming animated. "When he was choking me, the cuff of his jacket moved up a little and I could see the skin between it and his gloves. There was a scar, a weird one," she lifted her hand and used a finger to draw on her wrist as she described it. "There was a line that crossed straight across the wrist, then there were lots of little lines crossing it, kind of like a railway line with only one track."

"What color was his skin?"

"White, he was white."

She beamed up at them, both he and Wyatt smiled back encouragingly, the information probably wouldn't help them catch the killer but it would definitely work against the killer once they had caught him. Parker almost smiled at his own optimism, *once* they caught him, not *if* they catch him.

"That's great, Elizabeth," Wyatt told her.

Lizzie relaxed a little, reassured with the knowledge that she had given the police something helpful to work with, but she tensed once again at Parker's next words.

"Elizabeth, there's one more thing we need to talk about. The Iceman may have been following you for some time, watching you, learning your movements, your routines, gathering information about your family and friends."

Face draining of all color Lizzie swayed and rested her head against the back of the seat, for a second Parker was sure she was about to pass out. "He's . . . he's been . . . you think he's been watching me for a while?" her voice rising an octave, "for how long?"

"We don't . . ."

Cutting him off, eyes darting from himself to Wyatt and back to him again. "Days? Weeks? Months?"

Deciding honesty was still the best policy. "It could be as long as a year."

If it was possible her face went even paler. "A year?" she echoed.

"Do you remember anyone following you, hanging around, turning up repeatedly at places where they shouldn't be?"

Elizabeth shook her head.

"Have you had any unusual phone calls, emails, messages?"

Another shake of her head.

"Anything suspicious at all that you can think of?"

"No, I'm sorry."

Her voice had dropped to a mere whisper, she was completely drained, her energy spent, she'd had enough.

Patting her on the shoulder. "Okay, Lizzie, you've been great, really helpful, we're gonna get an officer to drive you home and we'll call to check on you tomorrow. If you think of anything, anything at all, however insignificant you think it might be, call us," he handed her his card, she took it was a quivering hand.

"Try to get some rest," Wyatt told her as they climbed from the car.

As another officer climbed into the driver's seat Elizabeth Landry once again wrapped herself up in the blanket, her own little cocoon, and the car took off towards her home. As he watched her go Parker's thoughts drifted to Tessa. Silent, independent Tessa, who lived inside her own self-made fortress, protecting herself from others at all costs so that she wouldn't be hurt once again. Thinking of the dinner plans he had made with her for the weekend, of the question he would ask her, he would prove to her once and for all that he was not going anywhere.

"Parker."

Blinking, he looked at his partner. "What?"

Rolling his emerald green eyes. "Thinking about Tessa?"

"What?" Parker repeated ignoring Wyatt's smirk.

Laughing Wyatt gave one of his easygoing grins and continued, "We gotta talk to the two guys who interrupted the kidnapping. Hopefully they got a better look at our guy than Elizabeth did."

"Hopefully," Parker echoed, but neither of them really thought that was the case. The Iceman was good there was no way he would go out without ensuring he was unidentifiable.

Approaching Lizzie's two saviors, Matt Kendra and Tom James, the two men looked up as they neared.

"Hi," Wyatt said when they reached them. "I'm Detective Wyatt and this is my partner Detective Bell. We need to ask you a couple of questions about what happened tonight, we're probably going to go over things you've already answered, but try to bear with us."

The two young men nodded earnestly. They looked to be in their early twenties, Tom was a blonde with deep dimples on his cheeks, Matt was a brunette with too tanned skin, both were fit and dressed in sweats.

"Can you tell us what you were doing out here at midnight?" Parker asked.

"We were out jogging," Matt answered. "We run together almost every night, but today . . . uh yesterday," he amended with a glance at his watch. "Yesterday we got held up at work, got home late, we rent a house together with Tom's girlfriend, so we decided to go this way instead of by the river where we usually jog."

"If we had got home at the usual time, gone for our run near the river, then Elizabeth would have been . . . we wouldn't have been here to save her," Tom added as both the shell-shocked young men shook their heads in amazement.

They were spot on, the Iceman would have followed Elizabeth Landry home several times to get an exact picture of the route which she took. He would not have been expecting these two boys to show up at just the wrong moment and interrupt things.

"What did you see when you got here?"

Matt once again took the lead, "When we came around the corner," he gestured down to the end of the alley, "We saw them. At first we were kind of far away and they just looked like two silhouettes but when we got closer we realized what was going on.

He had his arm around her throat, she was just kind of hanging limply in his grip . . ."

"We yelled out," Tom took over the narrative. "He turned to look at us, then dropped Lizzie and took off. Matt went to Elizabeth, I took off after the guy, chased him down the alley, by the time I rounded the corner he was screeching off in a white van. I tried to follow, to get a license plate, I didn't by the way," he added seeing their faces light with hope. "I found the holly on the ground, realized who it was and went back to Tom and Lizzie."

"Did either of you get a look at the guy?"

Matt shook his head. "I was mostly with Lizzie, she was pretty out of it by the time I got to her."

"At first we were too far away, when we got a little closer all I could see was a tallish guy, maybe five ten, lean but strong, and really fast, he was dressed all in black, windbreaker, dark jeans, gloves, baseball cap," Tom told them.

"It was the Iceman who tried to take Lizzie, wasn't it?" Matt asked them.

Parker nodded.

"Do you think he gave up when we ruined his plans or do you think he took someone else, another girl?"

Exchanging a glance with his partner Parker was about to answer when Matt jumped in, "He did didn't he, he took someone else."

"That's very possible, yes," Parker told them.

"So we saved Lizzie, but he still got a girl," Tom stared dismally down at the ground.

"Hey you can't beat yourselves up about that," Wyatt told them. "You saved someone's life tonight. Whatever else happens you need to hold on to that."

Tom and Matt nodded appreciatively then Matt asked, "How is Lizzie?"

"Someone's driving her home, she's shaken up but hanging in there," Parker told them.

"Thanks, guys, you've been great, here's my card, call us if you think of anything else," Wyatt handed them a card.

Taking it, "You'll keep us informed? About the case?" Tom

asked.

Parker nodded uncommittedly, "Call us if you think of anything else."

"We will," Matt told them as both he and Tom shook their hands and headed off down the street, heads bowed talking earnestly to one another.

"Not much to go on," Wyatt said eventually. "A white, thin, tallish guy, dressed in black who drives a white van."

"It's more than we had before," Parker commented with more confidence than he felt.

"True," Wyatt murmured softly. "But all I can think about is that right now he has another girl."

"Me too," Parker murmured just as softly. "Me too."

* * * * *

5:43 A.M.

Mesmerized, gazing up at the ruffled grey clouds, layer piled upon layer, piled upon layer, creating an intricate myriad of swirls and twirls so beautiful it was almost indescribable.

For the Iceman it was the perfect start to a perfect day, a grey day was a great day.

After throwing Hayley's unconscious body into the back of the van the Iceman had driven around through the still, quiet night, before heading for home. Arriving there the Iceman had secured her with another shot of sedatives and some thin, durable ropes around her wrists and ankles. Then creeping inside had taken a quick shower and tumbled into bed to catch a couple of hours sleep before waking ready to face another thrilling day.

Rising after only a few hours spent in slumber as fully rested and refreshed as though following a full nights sleep, Iceman did not need sleep to function at one hundred percent. Not bothering to eat, relying on adrenalin to sustain, the Iceman had descended the stairs to the garage and checked on the prey.

Hands had trembled with excitement and apprehension, not at

the knowledge that a kidnapped girl laid in the locked van, nor at the prospect of the police learning the Iceman's true identity. It was the possibility that Hayley Geoffries would not turn out to be everything the Iceman was hoping for. That she would turn out to be a dud.

Opening the van's backdoor to reveal Hayley curled up in the fetal position in a corner. Bound wrists wrapped as best as she could manage around her stomach, her eyes had been open but when light splashed across the van she scrunched them closed. A pitiful whimpering emanated from her crumpled form and the Iceman had rolled eyes in distaste then let the door slam closed.

Now, standing behind the building that was the centre of the Iceman's life, surveying the empty alley. It was still early, the day for many had not yet begun, and so they were alone in the small, narrow laneway. This was Iceman's favorite time of day not to mention the most important; it was at this time when plans were finalized, actions laid out in logical format.

This, in the Iceman's opinion, was another one of the many problems with today's society. Nobody bothered to put the time and effort needed into anything that they did, if they couldn't have it right away then they didn't want it all. Iceman could not understand this philosophy, anything worthwhile involved blood, sweat and tears, why other people couldn't seem to grasp that was beyond comprehension.

Taking a deep breath and enjoying the tingling of the cold air that whipped fiercely down the narrow alley. The Iceman prayed that it might actually snow today. Winter was almost upon them and still not a single snowflake had fluttered down from the sky.

Slightly off balance while swinging open the door to the van a well-placed kick to the chest sent the Iceman sprawling to the ground. Hayley stumbled from the back of the van and took off down the street, the ropes that had been wrapped tightly around her wrists and ankles all night made her slow and clumsy.

Apparently, while the Iceman had been daydreaming Hayley had been putting the time to good use, managing to loosen the bonds restraining her and get herself free. Balancing herself against the brick wall Hayley's progress was snail paced, the drugs still coursing through her system made her as wobbly as a baby deer.

Lungs reinflated after the blow Hayley had delivered the Iceman stood, brushed dirt and gravel off hands and pants, then strode, unfazed, after the hobbling girl. Catching up to her in seconds, Iceman pulled the gun from a back pocket and slammed it into her temple. Hayley crumpled instantly to the ground like a sack of rocks, a trail of blood dribbling down her pale face, which was already streaked with tearstains, her eyes closed, she was stunned but not unconscious.

Tucking the gun away and taking hold of Hayley's red, raw wrists the Iceman began to drag her back towards the building. Pulling her across the bumpy ground, Hayley offered a muted moan of protest but did not have enough energy to struggle. The small stones and pieces of gravel that littered the ground ripped at the exposed flesh on her arms and shoulders but seemed to barely register to Hayley.

Reaching the backdoor and unlocking it Iceman took a step inside and stood enjoying the quiet and solitude of the one place where everything was just as it ought to be. Taking hold of one of Hayley's ankles and yanking her through the door, leaving her shuddering body in a pile on the floor by the door, then swinging it closed behind them. Going to pull on a rope dangling from the ceiling, revealing a small set of wooden steps that led up to the attic.

Once again pulling out the gun Iceman gestured it at Hayley who eyed it defiantly, trying to decide whether she should risk making a run for it or not. Finally making the smart move, the only move, Hayley pressed her hands against the wall and slowly levered herself up. Gesturing at the steps Hayley looked at them and once again weighed up her options knowing that once she allowed herself to be taken up into an attic her chances of finding a way out decreased even further.

Grinning when Hayley hung her head and took a tentative step towards the stairs, the Iceman was convinced that the next month would indeed be an interesting one. All of the worry and uncertainty that Hayley would be weak and pathetic, that she would have no spirit, no fight, evaporated away. Her actions this morning showing that she would be as much fun as Lizzie Landry would have been or maybe even more.

Following her up the wobbly steps and into the dark, warm attic. The room always reminded Iceman of a den. A lion's den, or maybe a wolf's or a bear's, something strong and intimidating, something that was feared. Nodding approvingly, the Iceman was pleased with this apt analogy.

Once they reached the top the Iceman gestured for Hayley to cross to the other side of the room so that the thick carpet that covered the floor could be rolled up. Stopping halfway to reveal a small trapdoor in the centre of the room, opening it then waving Hayley over to show her what lay beneath.

Crouching at the edge of the hole Hayley's almond eyes grew wide as she looked down. At the bottom of the space was a tiny room, with a diameter of only ten feet, the smooth concrete walls were ten-foot high, and the room contained nothing but a bed a table and a chair.

Leaving Hayley to comprehend what lay ahead for her the Iceman crossed the attic and retrieved a ladder. It was obscured by a tall antique wooden bookshelf so that no one peering into the room from the top of the steps would be able to see it. Taking it to the circular opening and lowering it down so that the bottom just reached the concrete floor of the little jail. Hayley looked up, eyes pleading, begging, knowing what was coming but unable to accept it.

With a single nod of the head the Iceman indicated that her fate was already sealed, it had been from the moment the two men interrupted Elizabeth Landry's abduction. For a split second Hayley weighed her options and then made a quick dart for freedom. The Iceman merely suppressed a chuckle, best not to let her know how much fun this was just yet, and took a step towards her, wrapping a hand around her throat and slamming her against the attic wall.

"Do you want to live, Hayley?" the Iceman queried coldly, of course this was a rhetorical question on both sides. Hayley wanted to live but wouldn't, the Iceman wanted to give her hope when really there wasn't any.

Hayley managed a jerk of her head as the Iceman squeezed and squeezed her neck until her eyes rolled back in her head and she drooped forwards. Letting go the Iceman let her fall to the floor, dropping down beside her the Iceman simply sat and waited for her to come to.

Uttering a small moan Hayley blinked her eyes, drew in several shaky gasps, and pushed herself into a sitting position. Her brown eyes flashed defiantly but then she hung her head, accepting defeat and the pointlessness of resistance, Hayley moved to the ladder and backed down it. When she reached the bottom the Iceman pulled the ladder up and returned it to its place in the far corner of the attic.

Hayley looked up at the Iceman, the Iceman looked back down at Hayley, and for the first time since she had been snatched from her bed in the middle of the night, Hayley spoke.

"Who are you? Why are you doing this?"

Thrilled by her sweet, melodic voice, the Iceman thought it sounded even better now that they were up close and personal. Hayley Geoffries was turning out to be a worthy foe. She was strong, plucky, brave and confident despite her fears, not to mention she was optimistic despite the odds. The Iceman had judged Hayley too quickly, and never one to shrink away from a mistake, unfairly. Iceman had been too wrapped up in Lizzie and how perfect a prey she would be that what should have been obvious had instead been hidden from view.

If there was one thing the Iceman held to above all else was a challenge. To win against a mismatched opponent was not really a win at all. The Iceman loved a challenge, loved the time spent with the victims before doing what had to be done. It was not in the killing itself that the Iceman felt most alive it was in everything that happened before; the murder was nothing more than the inevitable, and necessary, final act.

Owing Hayley nothing less than the truth. "I am the Iceman and I do this because I can."

For what seemed like an eternity but in reality was not more than a couple of seconds their eyes remained locked, two magnets drawn together. Then the spell was broken and Hayley lost control of the façade of calm she had been holding onto by a thread. Letting out an animal screech she began to wildly claw at the concrete walls, trying unsuccessfully to find a foothold to throw herself up out of the hole.

Giving Hayley time to let out her frustrations the Iceman spoke in a quietly authoritative voice, "What happens next is up to you."

Managing to reclaim some control over her emotions Hayley collapsed on the floor and went still.

"If you are good, if you do as I say and respect my authority then I will give you food, water, light, books, paper, pens. If however you do not respect me then you will have nothing."

Respect. Another lesson the people of today needed so badly to learn. Respect for themselves, respect for family, for friends, for others. Hayley would learn, as those who went before her had learnt, that she would respect the Iceman. It was inescapable. One day it would not just be the girls that came to stay in this cell that would respect the Iceman, it would be the entire world.

Hayley pushed back to her feet with a tenacity that sent waves of pleasure rippling through the Iceman's body. Looking up with steady eyes, even from the attic the Iceman could see that she was shaking. "If I do what you want will you let me go home?"

It was a question not worthy of an answer and the Iceman's pride in the girl dipped slightly. Now Hayley would have to wait until tomorrow for food and water. It would be her first lesson, never disrespect your master by underestimating them.

Closing the trapdoor with a thud the Iceman left Hayley alone in her small pitch-black room to contemplate her future and what she would make of it. Sliding the latch into place and locking it with a combination lock the Iceman could just make out Hayley's desperate pleas for mercy, to bad for her that her pleas would not be heard by anyone else. The next stage of the plan was well and truly underway.

Life for the Iceman was good.

* * * * *

7:58 A.M.

"Nice of you to join us, Zak," J.J. huffed irritably as the door to his office opened and a curly head peeped around it.

"Jacob," Zak was the only person who called J.J. by his given name. There was no love lost between Lieutenant Jacob Jacobson and medical examiner Zak Fenton. Parker had to admit that as good as he was at his job Zak was one of the most infuriating people on the planet. An ex-model Zak was good looking and he knew it, he was in his early thirties, had big black eyes, curly hair and smooth cocoa skin. Zak had almost every woman he came into contact with swooning.

"Maybe now we can begin," J.J. glanced around at the small group assembled in his even smaller office. "Marty, why don't you start," he said addressing the head of the crime scene unit who was working the high profile serial killer case.

Marty nodded and rifled unnecessarily through the folder of papers laid out on the table in front of him. A widower in his mid fifties other than work Marty Jenkins had no other interests that anyone knew about he was completely dedicated to his job. "I don't have a lot to say I'm afraid," his serious, beady grey eyes were shadowed with concern. "We didn't find anything at either the Stacey Wood or the Elizabeth Landry crime scenes."

"Nothing?" Wyatt echoed.

Shaking his head emphatically. "Not a thing," Marty reiterated.

"How is that possible?" J.J. roared, every inch of his six foot eleven, three hundred pound frame quivering with anger. Between the history and the press coverage this case had everyone on edge, J.J. was particularly feeling the heat from every direction to break the case and make an arrest.

Marty looked wounded at the apparent implication that he had somehow been negligent in his work. Parker always thought that Marty looked like a bird, with a narrow angular face, graying black hair, beaklike nose, and thick black-rimmed glasses, he reminded Parker of an owl. "There was nothing, he didn't leave a single thing. No fingerprints, no hairs, no trace, no footprints, no tyre treads, absolutely nothing."

Running a frustrated hand through his thick brown hair. "Parker, Wyatt, what did you find from the Landry girl and those knights in shining amour?" J.J. asked apparently not in the mood to sooth

Marty's hurt feelings.

"We have a vague description of the guy," Wyatt answered. "He's, tallish, five ten or eleven, lean, strong, dressed all in black, drives a white van . . ." J.J. opened his mouth to interject but Wyatt ploughed on, "We did learn one helpful thing though. Lizzie Landry saw a distinctive scar on his wrist; she described it as kind of like a railway track. If we can catch the guy that will definitely help us ID him."

"Did the two young men who interrupted the kidnapping have anything helpful to add?"

"They gave the same description," Parker told their boss. "And the one who saw the van didn't get a license plate or a make and model."

"So once again the Iceman outplays us all," J.J. thumped a hand against his desk sending the family photos of him, his wife of thirty-six years, their four kids and fourteen grandkids, teetering wildly. J.J. was well known for his unpredictable temper, as sweet and gentle as he was capable of being with victims when he was pushed to the limits he had an almost manic air about him.

"The Iceman will slip up eventually, they all do," Wyatt placated.

Parker hated the nickname the press had come up with for the killer, hated it especially because it was the press who had come up with it. "At least we have more than we did this time yesterday. Any reports on the girl he took instead of Elizabeth?"

J.J. shook his head. "Are we positive he has another girl? Maybe he got put off when the abduction was foiled, decided to lay low for awhile."

"He has one," Parker was one hundred percent certain that this was true.

"Beth?" J.J. asked the psychologist who often worked with them on difficult cases to help them get inside the head of the killer they were hunting.

"He has one," Beth agreed.

"How can you be so sure?" J.J. pushed.

"This type of serial killer is highly organized and focused, nothing will stop him from deviating from the course he's set." Elisabeth

Bennett spoke with more authority than most. In the course of an investigation three years ago a psychopath she had been interviewing had attacked her in a desperate bid to escape. Slashing her across the face before plunging a knife deep into her abdomen, the man hadn't even made it from the room before guards overpowered him. The attack had left Beth self conscious about her appearance despite the loving support of her long-term boyfriend who had recently proposed after going into remission from his cancer. No one but herself had any doubt about Beth's beauty, with long dark brown hair that reached to her waist and serious brown eyes she was gorgeous, but with her wedding only weeks ago she had become even more paranoid about her face.

"So death or capture, those are the only things that will end this," J.J. commented to no one in particular. Sighing deeply he rubbed tired eyes, "Okay, Tim," addressing the only other occupant in the room, a silent, weary looking man who Parker knew was only in his early fifties but who looked closer to eighty. "Since Parker and Wyatt are now the lead detectives on the Iceman case why don't you get everyone up to speed."

Surprised Parker glanced at his partner who looked equally shocked. "We're taking the case?" he asked.

Shooting them a completely unapologetic smile. "Sorry I thought I told you two that already," J.J. answered. "Tim?"

Standing, Tim Underman began to pace around the small office as he spoke. "I caught the Iceman case on December first last year."

The night of the Iceman's first murder, it was also the same night that Parker had been fighting for Tessa's life after a lunatic with warped plans of a life spent with her had abducted and come within a hair of killing her.

"The body of a young woman," Tim continued. "Sixteen year old Hannah Green, was found on a deserted country road, encased in a block of ice and holding a sprig of holly."

"How long had she been missing?" Parker along with everyone else in the precinct, not to mention the city, knew bits and pieces about the case but he didn't know all the specifics.

"Hannah was a runaway," Tim explained and Parker could see in the way Tim held himself that he shouldered the blame for the Iceman's actions. "Been running away since she was thirteen, her mother gave up reporting her missing, said sometimes Hannah was gone for months then suddenly she just turned up again. We tried going by some of Hannah's haunts trying to find anyone who knew her, best we could come up with was she was last seen somewhere around Halloween."

"When did you find out about the next victim?" Wyatt asked.

"The next day we got a report that twenty-two year old Greta Hamburg had gone missing from work the previous night. Apparently she had been working late at the boutique where she was a saleslady, her car was still parked out back, the door was left wide open, her purse, keys, phone were all still inside the store, sitting next to a sprig of holly. We worked the case as though it was connected to Hannah Green's but we had no leads and no forensics, then on January first we found her."

Parker remembered the day Greta Hamburg's body had been found, by this time the press was all over the case.

Resuming his narrative Tim continued, "The same day we got the report that another young woman had been abducted. This time it was twenty-six year old Kelly Lorris, taken from her apartment, apparently she put up a real fight, the place was a mess. She was found on February first, body in the ice same as the other two, and Stacey Woods was kidnapped, her body found yesterday."

Parker noted a tremble in the man's voice and knew how personally he had become involved in the case. Becoming emotionally involved in cases was something Parker was prone to do with disastrous results. When he had put his trust in an insane teenager it had almost cost him not only his own life but also the life of an innocent baby.

Each sat listening to their own thoughts then Tim spoke again, more to himself than to anyone else, his haunted eyes fixed on something only he could see. "On March first we had almost the entire force out looking for any sign of the Iceman, but there was nothing. No bodies in ice, no missing women, nothing, it was like he just disappeared off the face of the earth until yesterday. All that time he was holding Stacey captive."

"Serial killers don't usually just stop killing for ten months then start up again do they Beth?" J.J. asked.

Addressing Tim Beth asked, "Were there any other cases in neighboring jurisdictions?"

"Nothing anything like this, either before December first last year or during the last ten months. It was like the guy just appeared out of nowhere and then went straight back to whatever hole he crawled out of."

"Some serial killers may wait in between kills. If he's working to a specific plan, organizing the murders around the wintertime. Besides he had Stacey Woods the whole time," Beth noted.

"He torture her, Zak?" J.J. asked the question they'd all been thinking.

"No signs of rape or physical abuse," Zak responded and the group let out a collective sigh of relief.

"And there were no forensics at any of the scenes?" J.J. asked baffled.

"None," Marty answered. "I worked each of the scenes myself."

"No witnesses?"

Tim shook his head.

"How does this guy do it?" Wyatt asked. "I mean how does he actually do it. Get them in the ice, get them unseen to the locations where they were found?"

Tim shrugged and said nothing; the case had clearly taken a toll on him.

"But he *did* he keep them alive after he abducted them right?" J.J. asked.

"It looks like he did," Zak nodded. "They had all lost a lot of weight since the time they were taken, their bodies showed signs of malnutrition, their hands were pretty badly battered . . ."

"Is that why he put the gloves on them?" J.J. interrupted.

"Possibly," Beth answered. "It may have been an effort to keep the body in as pristine condition as he could, keep the image as it is in his head, in his dreams."

"Anyway," Zak continued with a glare at J.J., he did not

appreciate being interrupted when he was delivering his findings. "There were old rope marks on each of the girls' wrists but they were mostly healed. He probably tied them up when he kidnapped them and then kept them somewhere where he no longer needed to restrain them."

"So he has to be keeping them somewhere that he isn't worried about them escaping," J.J. pondered aloud, "or being found."

"What was cause of death?" Wyatt asked Zak.

"On the first victim . . ."

"Hannah," Tim spoke softly.

"Hannah, she was smothered by hand," Zak paused for dramatic effect. "There were faint bruises around her mouth. The other three girls, Greta, Kelly and Stacey," he added with a look at Tim Underwood, "were smothered with something, probably a red pillow, I found traces of red fibers in their mouths and noses."

"Was there any connections between the girls?" Parker asked.

"None that we could find," Tim told them. "They were all different ages, different backgrounds, difference in appearance. We thought he chose Hannah, a known runaway, first as kind of like a practice run, picking a girl who no one would miss for a while," he looked to Beth for confirmation that he got at least this right. Beth nodded and Tim continued, "Anyway Hannah was a blonde, real petite pretty little thing. Greta was older, it was a riskier abduction, she was missed right away, she was Hispanic, crossing racial barriers with his second victim."

"There was nothing linking them together?" J.J. persisted.

"Went through their lives with a fine tooth comb, nothing. Kelly was larger, a little overweight, and a redhead, again she was a risky victim; she was missed by friends and colleagues and reported missing the day after she was taken. So he doesn't seem to be choosing them by race, or by appearance, going for a blonde, a redhead and a brunette, Stacey was a brunette too."

"Isn't that unusual, Beth?" J.J. directed his question to the psychologist who was sitting taking in all the information so she could put it together and form a profile.

"Unusual but not unheard of," Beth told them.

J.J. was about to push the topic when a nervous young officer tentatively pushed the door open.

"Yes," J.J. snapped.

The young officer looked startled but forged ahead, "We just got a phone call, a report of a missing young woman, her parents woke up this morning and found her gone. Her name was . . ." he consulted the piece of paper he clutched in his hands, "Hayley Geoffries."

"And . . ." J.J. whirled a hand at him to hurry him up.

"And outside, set on the back stoop of her house was a sprig of holly."

The tension in the room seemed to take on a life of it's own. This was the news they had all been expecting but all hoping, with a hope they didn't dare express in case they jinxed it, would never come.

Hayley Geoffries was Elizabeth Landry's replacement.

Hayley Geoffries was the Iceman's next victim.

* * * * *

5:15 P.M.

Her eyes had adjusted to the pitch black of the room, not enough to see clearly but enough to make out shadows.

Hayley had beaten her hands red and raw trying to escape earlier, trying to convince the Iceman to let her go, her throat was sore and scratchy from screaming. Now she had given up hope of fighting her way out of this room, there was no way up and the walls appeared to be made of solid concrete.

A part of her kept expecting the police to come crashing in, quickly apprehending the Iceman then carrying her to safety. She had to keep reminding herself that this was not a book, or a crime show, or a movie, this was real life and there were no guarantees that she was going to survive this, those other girls hadn't.

Lying here in the dark she'd lost all track of time, it could have been hours or days since the Iceman had left her here all alone. Her stomach was grumbling loudly she was thirstier than she had ever been before and earlier she had wet herself. For a time the humiliation of urinating on herself, the feeling that she had become nothing but a caged animal had overwhelmed the hunger and thirst.

Pushing aside embarrassment if she was going to talk her way out of this then she was going to need her wits about her. Hayley didn't think her chances of getting out of here were good but as long as she had hope then she had a reason to keep fighting and Hayley Geoffries was nothing if not persistent.

Recalling everything she could about the Iceman. The three murders the previous winter, three young women similar in age to herself, each woman found naked and encased in a giant block of ice. Hayley felt herself shiver at the recollection despite the stuffy heat of the room.

Images flashing into her mind, the terrified young women, naked and alone, she wondered what had happened to them before they had been killed. Had they been sexually assaulted, had they been tortured, had their deaths been quick, had they been alive when their bodies were entombed in ice? Hayley was a virgin; uncomfortable around men she hardly ever went out and had only had a handful of boyfriends in her twenty-two years. She preferred to stay at home with her family, reading or writing, she dreamed of becoming an author.

With thoughts of her family and her home flooding her mind Hayley could feel herself getting worked up again. Tears welled up behind her closed lids, her breath started to hitch, she could almost feel those dead girl's presence here in the room with her. For the next several minutes Hayley did nothing but cry, sobs that hurt her chest, her stomach, her throat, as she thought about all the horrible things that might happen to her here.

When her energy was spent she just lay on the firm mattress and rested. When she'd regained some control over herself she opened her eyes, not because she could see a lot but because it made her feel more normal, and was surprised to notice a small screen mounted near the top of the hole had sprung to life. Displayed on the monitor was a picture of a gigantic aquarium. It was enormous, full of brightly colored tropical fish, it was circular and . . .

Gasping aloud Hayley cast a glance around the small circular room where the Iceman had imprisoned her then looked back to the screen and she knew. That was where the Iceman was keeping her, somewhere nobody would think to look. Inside the middle of a giant aquarium.

DECEMBER 3RD

8:08 A.M.

Pulling the covers up over her head Winter tried to shut her mind down and go back to sleep. Really *back* to sleep was a bit of an overstatement she thought to herself, what she really wanted was to *get* to sleep.

The house was still and quiet. Her stepfather, a truck driver, usually left around five in the morning, her mother usually around seven, sometimes earlier depending on how much work there was to be done at the restaurant before they opened for the lunchtime rush.

By the time she had arrived home last night everyone else had been asleep, her parents in their room, her cat curled up on her bed, waking to offer a sleepy purr before promptly dozing back off. This morning she had told her mother that she wasn't feeling well and obtained permission to stay home from school, but hadn't said anything about what she had seen. She and her mother weren't close and Winter wasn't sure whether her mom was unaware of the nighttime drives or knew but chose to say nothing.

Deciding that lying in bed was a waste of time Winter slipped from under the covers, slid her feet into fuzzy yellow slippers and wrapped her soft, orange robe around her shoulders. Shuffling down the stairs, her cat, Mousy, racing past and almost knocking her over, in the kitchen she got breakfast for both the cat and herself, in that order, and dropped into a chair at the table.

Staring out the window as she ate her eyes wandered to the huge holly bush that covered the yard's back fence. A picture of the young woman in the ice jumped to mind; in her hands she had clutched a sprig of holly. It was just a coincidence, Winter told herself, lots of people had holly, especially at this time of year.

Suddenly nauseous she pushed aside the bowl of cereal and

51

climbed back up the stairs, walking down the hall to her parent's bedroom. Pushing open the door Winter stood on the threshold, surveying the room then crossed to her stepfather's dresser. Tentatively pulling open the top drawer she carefully rifled through, making sure not to disturb things too much, unsure of what she was looking for but certain she would know it when she saw it.

Slamming the drawer shut when she realized what she was doing. Her stepfather may be creepy but there was no way he could be a killer, could there? It had been almost five years since he had married her mom and moved in with them making him by far the longest stayer of any of her mother's husbands. Grant Hamilton was the sixth stepfather she'd had, her mom had been married another three times before Winter was born, none of them lasting longer than a year or two.

Grant was her least favorite of her mother's husbands, not that any of the others had been much better, her mother definitely had a penchant for creepy men. It wasn't that Grant had ever done anything to hurt her but sometimes she caught him staring at her and a couple of times just after they'd moved in he had barged into the bathroom while she'd been taking a shower pretending that he had forgotten she was in there. A few times she'd woken up in the middle of the night, sure that a figure had been hovering above her. She couldn't prove that it was Grant but whenever she was around him she felt something off.

Resolutely shaking away her discomfort, she'd check the other drawers and if she found nothing then she'd lay the whole thing to rest. Moving on to the second and then the third and fourth draws, discouraged Winter was about to give up but decided that she had nothing to lose by trying the last one. Lifting a pile of summer t-shirts that had been stuffed down here while they awaited the warmer months she saw a paper bag.

Pulling it out Winter hesitated, she wasn't sure that she wanted to know what was inside, she wasn't sure how she could even be thinking the things she was thinking. It couldn't possibly be true, could it?

Opening the bag she looked inside and her heart stopped.

* * * * *

8:23 A.M.

Climbing into the attic the Iceman couldn't think of anything that could make the day any more perfect than it already was. With the knowledge that Hayley was safely tucked away in her home for the next month, the same place that had been inhabited by Hannah, Greta, Kelly and Stacey, the Iceman had had the most wonderful night's sleep. Waking to feel stronger and more focused than ever the Iceman was looking forwards to seeing how Hayley had fared after her first night.

So far the Iceman's favorite guest was the first, young Hannah Green. The tenacious teenager had not even needed to be abducted, simply sweet-talked into following the Iceman straight here. Hannah had been quick and smart and it had almost been a disappointment to have to end the fun and kill her. Almost.

Crossing the huge attic floor to the cupboards pushed against the far wall the Iceman checked supplies, noting on the list pinned to the door anything that needed to be replenished. Deciding it would be more fun to let Hayley choose what she wanted, if of course she was behaving as she ought to be. Dialing the combination and taking off the lock the Iceman opened the trapdoor and looked down.

Below him Hayley was curled up on the bed, her arms wrapped tightly around her stomach an obvious indication that she was starving. When she heard the clunking above her she opened her eyes and quickly stood, she swayed slightly and placed a hand against the wall to steady herself.

The Iceman could see even in one day she was starting to lose weight, already she looked haggard and drawn. "How was your night?" the Iceman asked pleasantly, waiting anxiously to see how she would respond.

"It was okay," she answered squinting up, her voice strong despite the hunger and dehydration that must be already wracking her body.

"Did you sleep?"

Nodding. "A little."

Sniffing the air. "You have soiled yourself."

Red flushing her cheeks she nodded once again.

"You are hungry? Thirsty?"

"Yes."

Beaming down at her. "I'm impressed, Hayley. You have been very polite and you will be rewarded. I will give you a choice, you may have water and light, or food and a toilet."

Indecision battling in her chocolate brown eyes, her desire to feel human by using a toilet battling with her knowledge that without water her body would soon start to shut down.

The Iceman waited patiently while she made her decision, hoping that she wasn't going to be greedy and ask if she could have them all. To be greedy was to be ungrateful, and to be ungrateful was to be disrespectful, and if there was one thing the Iceman could not stand it was a lack of respect.

Finally Hayley sighed, "Water."

Nodding approvingly. "A wise choice," the Iceman told her and placed a bottle of water in a bucket, lowering it down to her and waiting while she retrieved it then reeling the bucket back up again.

About to re-close the hatch when Hayley spoke, "Excuse me, may I ask you a question."

Pleased with her politeness and her correct phrasing of the question, the Iceman found it distasteful when people substituted 'can' when what they meant was 'may'. "Yes, you may ask me a question."

"What day is it? How long have I been here?"

Seeing no benefit in lying to the girl. "It is eight-thirty in the morning on December third."

Her sluggish mind calculating how long that was since she had been taken, then her gaze flitted to the small screen mounted on the wall. She looked from it back up to the Iceman, the look in her eyes indicating that she had figured out her location just as the Iceman had hoped that she would. The Iceman was particularly pleased with the idea of placing the chamber inside a huge aquarium, making it completely invisible to anyone who might stumble upon it.

Once again about to close the trapdoor when Hayley called out, this time her voice was not controlled but filled with desperation. "Please let me go, I'll give you anything you want," she paused and swallowed audibly. "I'll do anything you want."

"I will return tomorrow."

"Please, don't go. Are you going to kill me?"

Disappointment washed over the Iceman, that was a stupid question and they both knew it, the Iceman started to close the hatch.

"Wait, what about the light?"

Half a mind to leave the lights off as a punishment for asking ridiculous questions but then deciding that a deal was a deal. Closing the trapdoor and walking back to the steps that led downstairs, the Iceman paused at the top of the stairs and flicked the light switch that would turn on the light installed in the roof of the little cell thus illuminating Hayley's Geoffries small world.

* * * * *

9:11 A.M.

Parker knocked on the bright yellow door, the cheery color in direct contrast with the mood, both of himself and Wyatt as well as the occupants of the house.

The door opened slowly and a face peeped out at them, drawn and pale with red-rimmed, puffy eyes and wildly messy white hair.

"Mr. Geoffries?" Wyatt asked holding out his badge. "I'm Detective Wyatt and this is Detective Bell. We spoke on the phone earlier."

Hank Geoffries nodded but neither said anything or opened the door further.

"Can we come in?"

Geoffries looked at them as though they were aliens speaking an unintelligible language. Parker and Wyatt had wanted to come over and speak with Hayley's parents immediately after they found out that she was the Iceman's next victim but both her parents had been too distraught. They had given minimal information to the police when they made the report that their daughter was missing and given permission for CSU to go through the house but had been too upset to speak further.

Eventually relenting he and Wyatt had spent the previous afternoon speaking with neighbors, seeking anyone who had seen or heard anything. They had come up empty. Marty had worked on the Geoffries house and unfortunately he too had come up with nothing.

Jerking his head uncertainly Hank Geoffries opened the door allowing them access to the house. "My wife is sleeping," he told them as he closed the door behind them and led them down a hall lined with photos of the happy family, moving from the young married couple, to the birth of their daughter, and into the years beyond. "Our doctor prescribed some sleeping pills, I finally convinced her to take one a couple of hours ago, she was scared to go to sleep in case Hayley came back."

Leading them into a cozy den, the walls of which were painted a deep red, the furniture was nice but well worn, and more happy family snaps filled the walls. Mr. Geoffries sunk into an armchair so taking the couch adjacent to him he and Wyatt sat too. As much as they wanted to be sensitive to the horror that the Geoffries family had been thrown into there was certain information they needed to get if they were going to find their daughter.

"Mr. Geoffries, what time did you and your family go to bed on December first?" Wyatt asked.

Looking at them forlornly he answered slowly, "Maybe ten o'clock."

"Did you hear anything? Anyone walking around in here?"

Tears begun to slide, unnoticed, down his face. "No, we didn't hear anything. Wendy, she snores, I started sleeping with earplugs years ago." Burying his face in his hands. "We were sleeping. While he was taking our baby we were sleeping."

Gently, Wyatt pressed on, "When did you notice that Hayley was missing?"

Drawing in a shuddering breath Hank Geoffries began

disjointedly, "Yesterday morning, when we got up, usually Hayley's up early, but she wasn't there, it was seven thirty, she's always up by then. I went up to her room but she wasn't there, we looked everywhere, then Wendy thought that maybe she went out. I went to look outside and I found the . . ." breathing heavily. "I found the holly on the doorstep. I remembered those other girls. The ones from last year." Desperate eyes bored into them. "He has her doesn't he, the Iceman has my daughter."

"We think so," Parker told him quietly.

As the older man took that in Parker saw how much the terrified father had aged in the last twenty-four hours. A photo on the mantle showed a fit guy, with tanned skin and a full head of graying hair, guessing the man to be in his early fifties, he had looked at least a decade younger. Now he looked every year of his age and more, his blue eyes sunken, his cheeks hollow, he looked weary and tired and old.

"Have you noticed anyone watching your house in the past few weeks?" Wyatt asked.

"No, nothing. No phone calls or anything either, everything has been just the same as normal . . ."

"I saw something."

All three heads swiveled in the direction the thin voice had come from to see Wendy Geoffries standing in the doorway. A beautiful woman, she looked just like her daughter. They had the same dead straight black hair, while Hayley's had been highlighted with red Wendy's was highlighted with streaks of blonde. Even dressed in sweats with a robe wrapped around her tiny frame, the mother looked poised and graceful.

Upon seeing his wife Grant hurried over to her. "You shouldn't be up," he told her as he helped her over to the couch.

Wendy ignored him and pushed away his well-meaning hands to hold out her own hand in front of Wyatt. "I'm Wendy, are you the detectives who are going to find my baby?"

"We're the detectives working your daughters case," Wyatt confirmed as he shook her hand. "Detective Wyatt."

"Detective Bell," Parker said taking the hand offered, a hand that felt as frail as a baby bird and reminded him of Tessa. "What did you see, Mrs. Geoffries?" Admiring the mother's strength and courage he didn't know if he could be as strong if it was his child in the hands of a madman.

"Wendy," she corrected perching on the edge of the sofa. "It was a couple of days ago, maybe more like eight or nine." Apparently her sleep had reinvigorated her she seemed much more focused and together than she had the day before. "I was out for my daily walk and when I came back there was this man coming from around the side of the house. I asked him what he was doing and he said he'd lost his puppy and thought it had gone around the back of our house. He said he knocked and no one answered, and he didn't want to be rude but he really wanted to find his puppy. He seemed nice enough, and genuine, he even had a leash in his hand, but I was a little nervous so I waited outside until I saw him drive off in a white van."

"Did you get a license plate?" Parker asked, momentarily allowing himself to ride a wave of hope.

Her confidence faltering, "No, I uh, I didn't get it, I'm sorry, I didn't really think he was dangerous, just a little creepy. Do you think that was the man who took Hayley?"

"Could you give us a description of the man?" Parker asked, avoiding her question for the moment.

"Not really, I think he was kind of tall, maybe he had brown hair, to be honest I wasn't paying that much attention." Then she repeated her question, "Do you think that was the man who took Hayley?"

"Maybe, but there's no way we can know that for sure," Wyatt soothed.

Wendy nodded uncertainly then stood and walked to the mantle and retrieved the family photo Parker had been looking at earlier. She picked it up carefully as though it might shatter if she held it too tight, tracing her fingertips over the picture as though it were all she had left of her child.

"We're going to do everything we can to find your daughter and bring her home safely," Parker told her. Wendy turned and studied him with deep brown eyes full of a childlike trust that he wasn't sure he deserved and knew he couldn't live up to.

DECEMBER 4TH

10:42 A.M.

"Hey, sleepyhead," Tessa greeted Parker as he slowly rolled over in bed. He must have gotten back early this morning, it had been about two o'clock when she had settled in an armchair in the living room unable to face going up to bed on her own. Exhaustion must have eventually taken over because she didn't remember Parker getting home. He must have carried her up with him because when she had awoken a couple of hours ago she had been asleep in the bed beside him.

"Hey yourself," he mumbled sleepily, raking fingers through his unruly black hair making the ends stand up. "You were really conked out when I got home, didn't even stir when I picked you up and brought you up here." He studied her carefully, "You doing okay?"

Turning away from Parker's scrutinizing stare. "I'm fine."

Grabbing her shoulder he turned her around so that she faced him but she carefully avoided his gaze until he took her face in his hands and forced her to look him in the eye. "I wish you would talk to me," he murmured softly.

"I . . ." guilt almost overriding her fear of sharing about her feelings. "Really, Parker, I'm . . ."

"Fine," he finished for her releasing his hold. "Okay, but I'm here when you're ready, okay?"

Tessa nodded, relieved that Parker was dropping it for now. "How's your case going?"

Parker rubbed tired eyes and rested back against the headboard of the huge four-poster bed. "So far we haven't got a lot to go on."

Settling herself in the crook of Parker's arm. "I thought you had some eyewitnesses."

Tightening his arms around her. "They only got a glimpse from a

61

distance, they gave us a vague description but not enough to do a proper ID."

"Do you think she's still alive?"

"What do you think?" Parker asked her.

"I think that he'll keep her alive until December thirty-first," Tessa answered without hesitation. From childhood she had always had an intuitive ability to read people, to know what they were thinking and what they were going to do.

"I agree," Parker concurred.

"You want pancakes for breakfast?"

"Are you gonna make them from scratch?"

She smiled, growing up Parker's adopted mother had insisted that cooking from a packet was not real cooking and he had become accustomed to home cooked meals, luckily Tessa loved to cook. "I'll make them from scratch while you take a shower. What time is Skylar picking you up?"

Glancing at his watch, "Twenty minutes, so I better get a wiggle on." He gave her a quick kiss on the top of the head and climbed from the bed heading for the bathroom.

Before heading downstairs to start on breakfast Tessa made the bed and straightened up the room. Then in the kitchen she got to work mixing pancake batter, she was just taking the first ones out of the frying pan when Parker entered.

"Those smell great," Parker was practically drooling as he sat down at the table. "I can't even remember when I last ate."

Setting several steaming hot pancakes down on a plate and placing it before him, he started eating as soon as she put them down. Retrieving the glass bowl of batter Tessa was about to pour more into the sizzling pan when the doorbell rung.

"That's probably Wyatt, early as usual," Parker muttered through a mouthful of pancakes.

Scrunching up her nose as she caught sight of the mushy ball of half-eaten pancakes in his mouth. "I'll get it," she told him, heading down the hall, absently stirring the mixture as she swung open the front door.

* * * * *

10:53 A.M.

Devouring the pancakes Tessa had made, Parker preferred them plain without any toppings, everything Tess cooked was always mouth-wateringly good.

Dropping his fork with a clatter at the sound of shattering glass. Sprinting down the hall towards the front door he found Tessa, seemingly frozen in place, as she stared at the man in the doorway.

The man didn't appear to have hurt her, in fact he was doing nothing but standing there returning Tessa's unwavering stare. Fingering his gun Parker put himself between Tessa and the strange man, his feet crunching on the tiny shards of the glass mixing bowl, and leaned over so he was looking her in the eye. "Tessa?"

She said nothing, her eyes staring through him as though he were transparent.

"Tessa," he repeated, shaking her gently.

Still she said nothing.

Turning to the man who was still standing there staring at Tessa. "Who are you?"

The man too said nothing and Parker groaned, he was beginning to feel like he was trapped in a silent movie. Shaking Tessa harder this time. "Tess, snap out of it. Why are you staring at him? Who is he?"

Slowly as though waking from a deep sleep she blinked, her eyes clearing, her mouth moving but no sound coming out.

"Tess," he said more gently. "Honey, who is he?"

"He's . . ." her voice soft and faraway, "He's . . . it's Daniel."

"What?" looking from Tessa to the man and back again. "That's Daniel? Your brother?"

Tessa nodded shakily eyes still locked on the other man.

Now that Parker knew who he was he could see the likeness between Daniel and Tessa. Daniel had Tessa's aqua eyes, the same light spattering of freckles across his nose and cheeks; his hair was as curly as Tessa's but a darker shade of blonde. While Tessa was short, her features delicate like a pixie's, Daniel was tall, an inch or two taller than Parker, his features sharper, more defined, and he was still staring at his sister like he couldn't believe she was standing before him. There was no mistaking that the two were siblings.

Who knows how long they would have stood there in silence staring at one another if Wyatt hadn't shown up. "Parker? Tessa? What is it? What's going on?" Climbing the couple of steps up the small veranda his look flipping from suspicious when he glanced at Daniel to concerned when he looked at Tessa. "Who's he?"

"That's Daniel," Parker told him.

Confused, "Tessa's brother? What's he doing here?"

Snapping back to her senses. "Who cares what he's doing here," Tessa screeched. "Go away, Daniel, I don't want to see you." Turning and storming back into the house, Parker and Wyatt on her heels, Daniel too seemed to come back to life at the sound of his sister's near hysterical voice and he too followed them inside.

"Tessie, wait," Daniel called out, catching up to them and grabbing Tessa's arm.

"Don't touch me," she shrieked yanking her arm free and glaring up at him.

"Hey, buddy, she told you to go," Parker once again inserted himself between the siblings.

"I'm not your buddy and this is none of your business," Daniel shot back.

"If it concerns Tessa then it is most certainly my business," Parker retorted.

Daniel looked from him to Tessa, understanding dawning. Addressing Tessa, "You're dating him?" Pure horror in his voice, "Please tell me you didn't marry him."

Shooting her brother a withering stare. "What I am and am not doing with my life is none of your business."

"Tessie, I'm your big brother, everything you do is my business," looking down at her with imploring eyes.

"You have got to be kidding me," Tessa scoffed. "You gave up any right to call yourself my brother when you ran off on me. Why did you come back now? It's been fourteen years."

"I came back because I heard about what happened with . . . with Dylan Riley," squirming uncomfortably.

Tessa winced at the name but her anger had taken over. "You came back one year after everything that happened, after everything he did to me. How would that help me? Unless you've been hiding away in Antarctica then I think you probably heard about that when it happened. Just go, Daniel, I have nothing to say to you."

"Come on," already Parker didn't like Daniel Micah and was all too happy to throw him out of the house. Daniel had abandoned Tessa when she needed him, left his little sister alone and scared, something Parker just could not understand, nothing could make him desert his own sister. "Let's go," pushing Daniel towards the door.

"Get your hands off me," Daniel shoved him so hard he stumbled backwards, almost knocking over Tessa.

"You left her," Parker shouted getting in Daniel's face. "You walked out on her. After everything that happened you turned your back and walked away. She's your sister, your baby sister, how could you do that? What kind of guy are you . . .?" breaking off as Daniel's fist slammed into his nose, his hands flying to his face as pain radiated out across his head.

"Daniel! What do you think you're . . .?"

"I just want to talk to you, Tess," Daniel begged.

"Well I don't want to hear anything you have to say. I don't want to see you; I don't want to talk to you. Just go."

Clutching at her desperately. "Tessie, please," Daniel beseeched. "I want to make things right between us."

Biting his tongue to keep from jumping in, this was Tessa's fight and Parker knew that she was more than capable of handling things herself.

Shrugging out of her brother's grip once again, now dangerously close to tears. "Daniel, I can't do this with you. Skylar, please just make him go."

"Tess," Daniel protested but Wyatt had got hold of him and was gently tugging him towards the door.

Tessa choked on a sob and leaned against him resting her head against his chest. Keeping one hand pressed to his nose, the other held Tessa tightly.

"Come on, Daniel, don't make things worse," Wyatt told Tessa's brother calmly. "You already punched a cop."

"You guys are cops?" Daniel asked incredulously.

"Is that a problem?" Parker snarled through the pain.

Ignoring him, "Tess, how could you get involved with a *cop?*" Wyatt had him at the door now but he continued to call through to them, "I'm not going away, Tessa. I'm staying at grandfather and grandmother's place. I'm gonna fix things between us, I promise."

Tessa buried her face against him, now crying quietly. "I can't deal with him now, Parker," she whispered through her tears, her voice muffled against his chest.

"Shh, it's okay, he's not going to hurt you again, Tess," he told her with more calm than he felt. If Tessa hadn't been in the room he would have had Daniel Micah on the floor in seconds.

Pulling herself together Tessa looked up at him ruefully, "I'm sorry about your nose." Tugging him towards the kitchen where she retrieved some ice from the freezer and held it gently against his nose. He watched her as she carefully avoided his gaze and when she finally looked up at him her eyes were full of a vulnerability she rarely let him see. "Why did he come back, Parker? Why now? When I'm finally starting to get my life back. Why did he come back?"

* * * * *

12:17 P.M.

Humming away, fingers dancing over the keyboard creating a rhythm.

The Iceman was in a brilliant mood.

Recently returned to work after a visit with Hayley Geoffries, who had apologized for her earlier stupid comments and pleased with this the Iceman had offered her a choice of food or fresh clothes. There had been no indecision, no hesitation, after almost sixty hours of not eating Hayley had chosen food immediately.

She had been quiet and respectful in everything that she had spoken and she had not tried to bargain pointlessly for her release, but the look of pure hatred in her eyes reassured the Iceman that she had not yet given up hope.

It was always so disappointing when the Iceman's special visitors gave up their spirit, when hope finally dissipated it left them nothing but an empty shell. Remembering Kelly Lorris, if Hannah Green had been the favorite then Kelly had been the biggest let down. Despite the initial fight she had put up in her apartment of the thirty-one days she had spent in the aquarium cell, close to twenty-nine of them she had been nothing more than a limp, listless, husk of humanity. She had hardly spoken, had barely touched the food and water, and more than once the Iceman had been forced to climb down into the room to force feed her lest she die too early.

Greta had lasted close to the end, Hannah was still fighting until the second her life ended, but Stacey Woods had been different, she had spent ten months in captivity. In order to preserve her for the entire time the Iceman had employed a different strategy with her. Instead of leaving her alone in the cell, for her good behavior she was rewarded with trips outside, with pictures and videos of her family, with promises that when the time came she would be released unharmed.

Stacey had been the one with whom the Iceman had most identified.

Growing up in a family with indifferent, unsupportive parents, Stacey had learnt at a young age how to rely on herself, this was a lesson that the Iceman too had learnt as a child. Disrespected by her parents and her colleagues, Stacey had a couple of close friends with whom she spent the majority of her time, but on the whole she was a lost soul desperately seeking the attention of those around her.

The Iceman had given her the notoriety that she so longed for.

Crossing to the small office window, the Iceman was thrilled to see that it was finally snowing, soft flakes fluttering through the air, scattering against the street below. The world was beginning to get ready for Christmas, trees in front yards were strung with fairy lights, Christmas trees appearing in house windows, front yards were being transformed into winter wonderlands. Although winter was the Iceman's favorite time of year, Christmas most certainly was not. Christmas was supposed to be a celebration of the birth of Christ not an excuse to support commercialism.

Focusing back on the plan it was time to decide on the next victim, the Iceman had devised a list months ago but it was now time to narrow it down to one choice. It took time to learn the exact movements of each girl, to learn their temperaments and how they were likely to react in certain circumstances. It was the Iceman's rule to always be prepared.

Returning to the computer the Iceman opened up a secret file that was well hidden and password protected. A file that contained all the information gathered on each of the girl's the Iceman had chosen in the preliminary sweep. Now it was time to pick just five lucky girls, one of who would become infamous as the Iceman's next special visitor.

* * * * *

2:45 P.M.

"We want to thank you all for coming out this afternoon . . ." Wyatt's voice a distant hum, Parker was still thinking about Tessa and the confrontation with her brother. The pain in his nose had dulled to a distant throb after downing a couple of painkillers, bruising was already starting to butterfly out from the bridge of his nose staining under his eyes and his cheeks a deep bluey black.

He hadn't wanted to leave Tessa alone but she had insisted, telling him she needed some time by herself, and he could see she was embarrassed that she'd let herself get emotional. And so here he was, in a conference room at the station with Wyatt and the families and friends of the Iceman's previous victims. Hannah Green's mother, Greta Hamburg's parents, Kelly Lorris' father and two of Stacey Wood's friends.

". . . As I'm sure you're all aware the Iceman has struck again with the attempted abduction of Elizabeth Landry and the abduction of

Hayley Geoffries," Wyatt's voice broke back into his consciousness. "We know that you've already talked with the police and given us your statements but we want to go over things with you again. Maybe after time something new will come to mind, something that might help us identify him."

"You still don't have *anything* on him?" Mr. Lorris asked eyeing them accusingly as though they were deliberately stalling in finding his daughter's killer.

"We're moving forward with our investigation but we're hoping that one of you might have remembered something else," Wyatt answered vaguely. "Now I know we've already asked you whether you noticed anything unusual just before the girls were taken but I want you to think back, see if you can remember anything at all."

"I don't really see the point," Greta's mother announced. "We've already told you that none of us saw anything."

"Maybe if you thought about it you might remember something that didn't seem important at the time, but now looking back you think it might mean something," Parker joined the conversation.

"Well we can't think of anything," Mrs. Hamburg huffed indicating herself and her husband and crossing her arms across her chest.

"What about the rest of you?"

"Hannah was gone for months before he took her," Mrs. Green murmured, guilt over what she perceived to be her part in the abduction and death of her runaway daughter had taken it's toll on the woman.

"Mr. Lorris?" Parker asked.

Still staring at them with open hostility, "I don't remember anything new. And quite frankly I'm appalled that it's been a year and you've made absolutely no progress, you are no closer to catching this monster than you were then."

"We're doing everything we can," Wyatt said somehow managing to remain calm.

"What about you guys?" Parker asked Stacey's friends who had remained silent throughout the exchange.

"I'm sorry I can't think of anything else," Pamela Stanton said apologetically, her boyfriend Alvin Kent said nothing but his face was thoughtful.

"Alvin?" Parker prodded gently. "Do you remember something?"

"I'm not sure," he said slowly. "I don't know whether it's connected or not."

"Anything you can think of might help us to find him," Wyatt reminded him.

Alvin nodded and begun. "It was a couple of weeks before Stacey went missing," his voice trembled slightly as he thought of his friend's body being discovered just days ago. "I was coming around to her place to fix her bathroom sink, it kept getting clogged up and Pam told her I would take a look. Stacey was at work but I had a key, and I'd finished work early so I went around. The street was busy so I had to park down the road when I got to Stace's place there was this guy."

"Where was the guy?" Parker asked thinking back to the story Wendy Geoffries had told them.

"He was coming from around the side of Stacey's house, I asked him what he was doing and he said he'd lost his puppy. Said he was driving it home and stopped to let it take a pee at the side of the road only it ran off," Alvin shrugged uncomfortably. "I don't know if it had anything to do with Stacey's abduction, the guy was a little weird but I didn't think he was . . . then I just kind of forgot about it . . . do you think that he was the killer? Do you think he was the Iceman?"

"There's no way to know," Parker said, although he was almost positive that it was indeed their guy there was no sense in making the kid feel like he had let down his friend. "Could you describe the man you saw?"

Hesitating, "Maybe five foot ten, brown hair I think."

They'd got everything out of these people that they were going to get. "Thanks everyone for coming, you've been very helpful."

Their guests grumbled amongst themselves as some officers led them from the room.

"How's your nose?" Wyatt asked once they were alone.

Fingering it tenderly. "It's okay," Parker answered then sighed.

"What's wrong?"

"Nothing seems to be going right with this case," pulling some more painkillers from his pocket. "The Iceman case is going no where, Mr. Lorris is right we are no closer to catching the Iceman now than we were a year ago, how many more women are going to die before we find him?"

"At least we know one of the way's he gets his information on his victims," Wyatt reminded him.

"But that doesn't help us find him and it doesn't help us keep the young women of the city safe," Parker was relishing feeling sorry for himself. As much as he hated to admit it, "The only way we're going to get enough information on this guy is to wait until he grabs another girl."

DECEMBER 5TH

9:47 P.M.

Twenty year old Phoebe Stein was positively dancing down the street, she was sure, certain in fact, that tonight was the night that her high school sweetheart and boyfriend of four years was going to propose. Suspicious from the moment he had asked her out to dinner a week ago, announcing he wanted to take her to this fancy seafood restaurant. He'd told her to dress up and said that he had a surprise for her and after being together for so long Phoebe could read him like a book.

She's been so excited that she'd started getting ready hours ago and even though she wasn't meeting Josh till ten here she was hanging around the restaurant fifteen minutes early. Phoebe loved Josh with all her heart and couldn't wait to marry him and begin their lives together but her nerves were jangled and she could hardly stand still.

Deciding to take a walk to calm herself she certainly didn't want to put Josh off from proposing by acting like a hyperactive preschooler. Rounding the building Phoebe started strolling through the alley at it's back; it was quiet and deserted a perfect place to focus her bouncy mind.

Phoebe was deep in thought walking up and down the lane, planning the perfect wedding when suddenly she was grabbed from behind. About to let out a startled squawk when a strong hand clamped over her mouth and she was shoved up against the cold stone wall of one of the other businesses that backed onto the alley.

"Scream and I'll slit your throat," a hoarse voice whispered in her ear.

Phoebe felt her body freeze in terror. Every self-defense course she had ever taken, every thing she had ever been taught about what to do if she found herself in a situation like this fleeing her mind.

The hand was slowly removed from her mouth and for a second she weighed her options, trying to decide if she should risk calling out but then she caught sight of something glinting in the moonlight. Her attacker held up a long carving knife and Phoebe felt as if she'd been thrown into some B grade horror movie. Wiggling wildly against his arm that crushed against her chest and pinned her firmly in place against the wall.

Placing the blade of the knife against her neck. "I'd hate to have to slice up such a pretty little thing," the voice whispered again. Phoebe could feel his breath against her cheek, smell the alcohol on it, and wondered what this man was going to do to her.

With the blade of the knife pressing into her flesh and his arm keeping her still Phoebe was helpless as the man ran his hand up and down the outside of her thigh, she shivered, from fear and revulsion not the chill in the air. His breath starting to come harder and faster the man pressed up against her positioning his hips against hers, and she could feel him hard between her legs as he rubbed up and down, groaning in delight.

Then in a flurry of activity he was ripping off her coat and dropping it on the muddy ground then tearing at her tangerine satin dress. Squeezing her eyes closed Phoebe tried to imagine that she was someplace else, anywhere else, as he once again traced his fingertips up her thigh, the inside this time. When his hand stopped between her legs Phoebe couldn't take it any longer as panic took over she began to thrash hysterically.

Pressing the knife harder against her neck, deep enough to cut the skin, Phoebe could feel a trickle of blood escape as the man put his mouth against her ear and snarled. "Don't fight it, I know you want it, it's gonna be the best you've ever had," he whispered harshly, then his mouth was on her, devouring her, his tongue forcing itself between her teeth.

Struggling not to throw up and then deciding too late that maybe if she had it would have put him off. Phoebe writhed beneath him, desperately seeking any means of escape. While he continued to kiss her the man's hand strayed back between her legs, Phoebe clamped them together in a vain attempt to slow him down but he was stronger than she was and pushed them apart with ease. His hands were pawing at her, groping all over her body in a frenzy as though he didn't know what he wanted to touch first.

At last, with a moan of pleasure, he pulled his hands away, the knife dropping slightly from her neck as he fumbled with his zipper and Phoebe realized that this was going to be her only opportunity to escape. If she didn't move now he would rape her and once he had taken from her what he wanted he had no reason to keep her alive.

With a sharp jerk Phoebe rammed her knee into his groin, as he went down the knife swung wildly and she felt it scrape across her cheek. As he crumpled to the ground clutching his penis, which was half through his open zipper, groaning from pain this time not pleasure, Phoebe ran.

She ran and ran and ran.

Tears streaming down her cheeks, unaware of where she was going just knowing that she had to get as far away from that man as she could. The end of the alley came into view just yards away. She was going to make it. She was going to get away. Freedom was so close . . . and then she was falling to the ground. Fire shot up her wrists as they broke her fall, the pain travelling up her arm and merging with the throbbing in her shoulder.

"Filthy little scum," a voice breathed in her ear as something slid out of her back and she was flipped over. Struggling to catch her breath Phoebe stared up into her attacker's red-splotched face and realized where she knew him from. He grinned at her and held his knife above her face; it took a moment for Phoebe to realize that something was different about it. It still glimmered in the moonlight but this time it didn't glow white but shone a bright red, this time it was covered with her own blood. "This time I don't think you'll be so feisty," he smirked.

"Still think you *can* do it?" Phoebe mocked before she broke off into a coughing fit.

The cherry blotches on his skin merged together making his face as bright red as the blood on his knife, blood that was slowly drip,

drip, dripping onto her face. Phoebe tried to lift her hand to wipe it away but found that not only did pain swarm her entire body but she also seemed to have lost control of her limbs.

Chuckling the man took her wrist lifting her arm and then letting it go causing the useless appendage to plunk promptly to the ground. Pleased with his trick the man repeated it over and over, and with each time Phoebe felt her panic grow. She was helpless, had lost control of her body, he was the cat she was the mouse and she could see in his eyes that he was going to enjoy playing with her before finishing her off.

Recognizing the resignation in her eyes he smiled malevolently and leaned in close to whisper, "I'm going to enjoy this." With his knife he sliced through first one of her shoulder straps and then the second taking great delight it peeling down the top of her dress.

"Phoebe!"

The man jumped at the sound of the voice but Phoebe felt her heart start to soar with hope and relief. Josh had arrived, he would save her, Josh was her hero, her knight in shining amour, he would stop this man.

Out of the corner of her eye she caught the glint of the blade . . .

* * * * *

10:15 P.M.

"He won't let go, won't let anyone get near."

Parker and Wyatt followed the middle-aged officer through the hubbub of activity in the alley onto which backed two rows of businesses. Parker was not in a brilliant mood, the pain from his nose had travelled to the base of his skull and he now had one killer headache. To make things worse when he had arrived home for dinner Tessa had been relentlessly chipper. Clearly put out by her brother's sudden reappearance in her life and by her rare show of emotions and determined to prove that she was handling things just fine. Not the least bit fooled by Tessa's performance he had wanted to stay with her, try to take her mind off Daniel, but then he'd gotten the call, and now he was here, in the middle of the night, in the snow, investigating what could be another botched kidnapping by the Iceman.

"Any time we try to convince him to let go he just freaks out," the policeman was elaborating. "He's lucky that the guy fled, could have gone after him too."

Wondering whether Joshua Timma felt like he was lucky considering that he'd just witnessed the murder of his girlfriend. Focusing himself, he wasn't the only one who'd had a horrible day. "Any other witnesses? Anyone to contradict the boyfriend's version of events?" Parker was still hoping that this was just a lover's quarrel gone bad and not the work of the Iceman.

"Cab driver who dropped Mr. Timma off heard him scream came to see what was going on and witnessed a man fleeing from the scene and driving off in a white van. Cab driver's the one who called it in."

"He give us a description?" Parker asked although he could already guess the answer.

"Male dressed all in black," the officer shrugged. "It's not much to go on."

"No it's not," Parker mused as they reached Joshua Timma. The young man sat on the muddy ground, eyes bloodshot, face ashen with shock, clothes streaked with blood that spilled out onto the concrete around him. In his arms he clutched Phoebe Stein's lifeless body. The young woman's blood soaked dress was partially pulled down exposing her small white breasts for all the world to see, her eyes open in the hauntingly empty stare that was death. If this was the work of the Iceman then the killer had clearly lost control making him almost infinitely more dangerous.

"Josh?" Parker spoke softly.

The young man looked dully up at them.

"I'm Detective Bell and this is my partner Detective Wyatt . . ."

"I'm not letting her go," Josh cut in warily.

"That's okay," Parker soothed. "How about we just talk for now. Is it okay if I sit?"

Josh nodded uncertainly.

Carefully sitting a short distance away, making sure to disrupt as little as possible so the crime scene techs could later do their job. "Did you see the person who did this?"

Pressing his eyes closed Josh took a shuddering breath.

"Josh, tell me what happened from the beginning?" Parker pressed gently.

"I was paying the cab driver," Josh began shakily, "When I heard something. I thought at first it just a stray cat, but then I heard laughing. When I came around the corner," he nodded his head to indicate the direction, "He was leaning over her. I saw her dress and I realized it was Phoebe," starting to cry Josh swiped a hand at the tears leaving a smudge of his girlfriend blood on his cheek. "I think I called her name and then I was running towards her, he turned and saw me and I swear he grinned at me, then he just . . . he just slit her throat . . ."

"Can you give us a description of the man?" Wyatt enquired.

Distracted, "Uh . . . I think he was kind of tall, kind of thin but it was dark when I saw his face, all I really saw was his smile. I'm sorry that's all I remember."

"You're doing great, Josh. Did you notice anything about what he was wearing?" Parker pushed.

Wrinkling his brow in thought, "He was dressed in black I think. I'm sorry I wasn't paying attention, I was focused on . . ." Josh's gaze returning to Phoebe's body.

"Any gloves?" Wyatt asked

"I don't know."

"Did he say anything to you?"

"No, he just smiled," Josh shuddered at the memory. "It was a really creepy smile."

"Creepy how?" Wyatt asked.

"It was like he was pleased that I was going to see him . . ." once again his gaze went to the gaping red slit in his girlfriend's throat.

Catching sight of Zak Fenton hovering impatiently nearby, patience was not a virtue Zak possessed, Parker stood and took a few steps toward Josh and squatted in front of him. "Josh, its time."

"I can't," Josh whimpered pitifully.

"There's a chance that the man who attacked Phoebe was the Iceman, you've heard of that the case?"

Eyes growing wide Josh nodded.

"There's a chance that he might have left something of himself behind . . ."

"You mean like DNA?" Josh interrupted.

"Maybe, but the only way we're going to know, the only way we're going to find the man who did this, is through Phoebe, and to do that we need to examine her body. Hopefully he left us something that will help us catch him."

"It's my fault," Josh said suddenly his haunted eyes meeting Parker's. "I was the one who wanted to come here for dinner. I was supposed to drive her but I got held up at work and asked her to meet me here. I was going to ask her to marry me," he began to cry quietly.

"Help us find him, Josh," Parker didn't bother to tell Josh that Phoebe's death was not his fault, that was not the way guilt worked and Josh's grief-stricken brain was not in a place where it could think rationally. "Let us take Phoebe, let her body talk to us, tell us what it knows."

Pulling Phoebe's body against his chest, tucking her head beneath his chin and squeezing her tightly, his hand lovingly stroking his girlfriend's matted chestnut hair. Then he gently laid Phoebe's body out on the ground, handling her as carefully as though she were made of glass. With a light hand he closed Phoebe's eyes and pressed a last kiss to her forehead then very deliberately he turned his back on his girlfriend and attempted to pull himself together.

"We're going to need to take your clothes, Josh," Parker told him.

Nodding absently, "I need to tell her parents and . . . and my parents," Josh mumbled.

Gesturing forward an officer who moved quickly to guide Joshua Timma away, as soon as the young man was out of sight Zak pounced on the body. Parker frowned at Zak's lack of empathy and turned to Wyatt, "Do we really think this was the Iceman?"

"J.J. wants us to work it as though it is," Wyatt told him.

"It would mean he's escalating," Parker commented, this was the last thing they needed. If the Iceman was escalating he would become exponentially more dangerous and reckless and more than likely leave a trail of bodies in his wake. "Looking at the dress it seems like he may have been trying to rape her then slashed her throat when the boyfriend showed up . . ."

"Looks like the struggle may have started over here," Marty called out from several yards down the alley. "Got a coat on the ground down here and a few drops of blood."

"Cause of death blood loss, Zak?" Parker confirmed.

"Probably," Zak agreed from where he was perched above the body.

"Then if this is the Iceman he's changing his MO, he's never tried to rape one of his victims like this before . . ."

"That we know of," Wyatt interjected.

"If he did then none of them reported it or told friends or family that they'd been assaulted," Parker reminded him.

"And all rape victims report their assaults?"

"Okay," Parker conceded. "Maybe, but still, he didn't leave any holly, he let the boyfriend live even though he'd seen him, and he killed Phoebe in a frenzy. Does that sound like our ultra methodical killer?"

"Maybe this one was different," Wyatt suggested. "Maybe he felt something for Phoebe, was attracted to her and couldn't control himself, let his thing overrule his brain."

"That doesn't really sound like the Iceman," Parker said doubtfully.

"The crime is in the same area the Iceman's been hitting, the victim is in the same age group, it's wintertime, it's night, the attacker was dressed in black, drives a white van . . ."

"But it's not the first of the month," Parker interrupted. "I'm not saying it isn't him, I just think we should keep an open mind. Because if this is the Iceman and he's really escalating," pausing for dramatic effect, "Then we're all doomed."

DECEMBER 6TH

9:32 A.M.

She'd been asleep when Parker had returned home close to midnight, and when he'd got up this morning she had pretended to still be sleeping to avoid another conversation on how she was doing since her brother's visit. Parker wanted to pull apart the whole situation and address it piece by piece but Tessa didn't want to talk about it, didn't want to think about it, she wished that Daniel had never come back.

Thinking back to what Daniel had said as Skylar had been dragging him from the house, he'd said that he wasn't going to go away, that he wanted to make things right between them. Deliberately pushing thoughts of her brother away, Daniel could say or do whatever he wanted it wasn't going to make any difference she didn't want anything to do with him.

Unable to settle at anything Tessa dropped into a chair in the living room and tucked her feet up underneath her. She was reaching for a blanket that was draped over the back of the neighboring chair when there was a knock at the door. Ignoring it, she didn't really think it would be Daniel, not that it mattered, she didn't feel like talking to anyone right now. Wrapping herself up in the blanket and closing her eyes, groaning when she heard a key in the lock and then moments later her name being called.

"Tessa?"

It was Casey.

"Tessa?" Casey called again, more anxiously this time.

Maybe if she ignored her friend then Casey would simply go away.

"Tessa!"

No such luck, Tessa opened her eyes to see Casey's tall, slender frame filling the living room door.

"Didn't you hear me calling your name?" Casey demanded as she set her coat on the table and stalked over to stand next to the armchair, hands on hips, face screaming annoyed.

"I heard," Tessa muttered.

Expression softening, "Wyatt told me about what happened with your brother."

"I don't want to talk about it," Tessa told her, scrunching up her eyes as she used to when she was a child as though that would make all the horrible things in the world go away. If you couldn't see them then they couldn't exist.

Casey sat on the coffee table in front of her. "Tess, you never want to talk about it and it only makes things worse. You keep bottling everything up and eventually you're going to explode."

Tessa didn't want to talk about Daniel. It was too painful, fourteen years later and it was still too raw. What she wanted was to deal with this in her own way, the way she had always dealt with trouble, by refusing to acknowledge its existence.

"Wyatt said you told him to go, maybe he left town," Casey suggested.

Shaking her head. "He didn't leave."

"How do you know that? Has he come back?"

"No, but I uh, Daniel said he was staying at my place so I went to see if he was there." After everyone had left yesterday she had driven out to the estate, knowing it was a bad idea even as she was on her way.

"He was there?"

"Yeah," she nodded, Daniel was as stubborn as she was and if he said that he was going to stay and try to convince her to forgive him then that was what he was going to do regardless of how she felt about it.

"Tess, I know he hurt you when he left," Casey prodded carefully. "You were what? Twelve? He was eighteen?

Keeping her eyes firmly closed Tessa nodded.

"It was right after your mom tried to . . . to kill you," Casey said gently.

Images flashing across her closed lids like a movie projector in her brain, replaying the events of the night that Daniel left. "He was the first thing I saw when I opened my eyes," she said softly. "He saved my life and then he just left."

Tessa felt a hand on her shoulder and reluctantly opened her eyes to see Casey's understanding face peering down at her. "Talk to me, Tess. Tell me what he did to hurt you so badly. You need to get it out."

She'd never spoken these words to another human being before in her life, but maybe Casey was right, maybe it was time to finally rid herself of any leftover feelings she had for Daniel. Cautiously she begun, "When we were kids we weren't super close but whenever our parents fought we used to hide out together in Daniel's room. We used to talk, play board games, anything to block out the sounds of our parents screaming."

"It's nice that you had each other," Casey said taking her hand and squeezing it reassuringly.

"After Patrick left and Emilie fell apart we moved in with Patrick's parents, our grandparents." Tessa never referred to her parents as mom and dad, they always were and always had been Emilie and Patrick. "I was ten when Patrick walked out on us, and things kind of got better when we moved to our grandparents, until Ellie . . ." voice faltering as it always did when she thought of her childhood friend.

Casey's grip on her hand tightened. "I'm sorry, honey. I didn't mean to bring up that."

Shaking her head to clear it. "No it's okay," she reassured her friend, steadying herself before continuing. "Most of what happened that night is a blur, the drugs Emilie gave me made me so sleepy. I remember her dragging me through the house, I remember her running the bath, but it's all like a dream, bits and pieces. Until she started to . . . I can see it like it's happening right now . . . I remember her holding my head under the water, I remember the feel of her hand tangled in my hair, I remember holding my breath . . ."

"Tess, maybe that's enough for now," Casey spoke over the top of her.

But Tessa wasn't speaking to her anymore, wasn't speaking to anyone anymore; she was merely recalling events on autopilot. "I remember feeling like my chest was going to burst, I remember opening my mouth, I remember the water coming into my lungs and everything going black, then the next thing I remember is Daniel's face hovering above me. He stayed with me while we waited for the ambulance, he'd knocked Emilie unconscious, hit her over the head I think. He didn't go with me to the hospital, I kept waiting for him but he never came, by the time our grandparents took me home he was gone."

Pressing a hand against Tessa's cheek. "You're ice cold, Tessa," Casey announced worriedly, leaving the room to retrieve another blanket from the linen closet.

Alone Tessa found her mind flicking to images of Emilie. The woman had never been a real mother to her children. An alcoholic and a drug addict, suffering from crippling depression, she spent little time with her kids, preferring to spend her days alone in her room, painting. Tessa knew she shouldn't blame Emilie for what she did, she was sick, now in a psychiatric facility, and not fully in control of her actions, but despite all that she *did* blame Emilie for what happened.

"Here you go," Casey draped the blanket over her, tucking the edges around her as though she were a small child. "You feeling okay?"

"I hate talking about this, I hate thinking about it. Daniel was everything to me when we were kids, I loved him so much, he was the only person I ever really trusted. I hated Patrick for abandoning us, I hated Emilie for letting him go, for not fighting for him, I hated her for giving up. And then Ellie died and I had no one, just Daniel. When I came home from the hospital and found out that he was gone I had never felt so alone in my life."

"I'm sorry, Tess."

"If he had of said goodbye. If he had of come to me and said that he was leaving that he hated life at our house, I wouldn't have blamed him, I hated it there too. But he never said goodbye, didn't even leave me a note, he was just gone. In the hospital I kept thinking, he'll come soon, I was just lying there waiting, and he never came . . ." aware she was crying only when Casey reached over and brushed away some tears. "I thought it was me, that everyone kept leaving because of me, because of something that I did, because I was no good . . ."

"No, Tess," Casey leaned over and enveloped her in a hug, stroking her hair soothingly. "That's not true. I don't know why Daniel left but it was not because of you. You have to believe that."

But Tessa didn't believe it. Patrick, Emilie, Ellie, Daniel, Anthony Higgins, Janice, Tiffany, Dorothy, Gina, they were all gone now, people that at one time Tessa had allowed herself to love.

Unsure how long she lay in Casey's tender grip, crying and clinging to her. She didn't hear Parker arrive home, didn't know he was there until Casey gently moved her into his arms and for once Tessa didn't bother to hide her tears. For only the third time in their year long relationship she allowed Parker to see her cry, to see her weak, exposed and vulnerable.

"Shh, it's okay, baby," Parker murmured against her hair, the familiar smell of his aftershave comforting, the steady beating of his heart beneath her ear reassuring. "No one is going to hurt you again. No one is going to take me away from you, okay? You and I are going to be together forever."

Safe in Parker's arms she almost believed it.

Almost.

* * * * *

3:30 P.M.

Walking home from school Winter's mind was still snagged on the same thing that had been occupying her every waking minute for the last three days. Not just her waking thoughts, it was even weeding its way into her dreams.

Sighing, Winter bumped a hand against her temple as though that might dislodge the irritating image.

From the second that she'd had the bright idea to go through her stepfather's drawer and found the paper bag she had regretted it. Not that what she had found was necessarily incriminating but . . .

Chewing on her lip as she paused to cross the street Winter felt like she was stuck in a nightmare. If her stepfather was the serial killer that had been stalking the city for a year, the same killer that had left the body in the ice that Winter had stumbled upon a couple of days ago, then there was no doubt in her mind that she had to do something. The problem was she just didn't know what that something was. Thinking about her options, as far as she could see she really only had three.

One; she could go to the police right now. However she wasn't sure they would believe her and she didn't think she had enough evidence. The police would probably think she was insane if she turned up telling them that she thought her stepfather was the Iceman because he had holly in his backyard and a paper bag full of white women's gloves hidden in a drawer. For the moment this option was out.

Two; she could tell her mother. The problem with this was that her mom was usually too busy with the restaurant to spend any time with her only daughter. Besides her mom still didn't even know that Winter had been the one to discover the Iceman's latest victim. And again she was likely to run into the same problems talking to her mother as she would the police, not enough proof.

The third and final option, and the one that seemed to make the most sense, was for Winter to keep digging. If she could find concrete proof that her stepfather was the killer then she could take it to the police and they would be able to take it from there. She didn't know how she was going to find what she needed but she knew that somehow she would do it, had to do it, she wanted that man out of her house and out of her and her mom's lives.

As preoccupied as she was with her dilemma Winter didn't notice the figure in black that had been following her since she left her school. Didn't notice it slip behind a parked car a couple of houses down as she fumbled for her key. Didn't notice it creep closer as she opened the front door and let herself inside. Didn't notice it as it quietly made it's way into her backyard. Didn't notice the camera it used to snap her picture as she made herself a snack. And she didn't notice it sneak away as silently as it had come.

DECEMBER 7TH

7:38 A.M.

Gently Parker ran his fingers through Tessa's soft blonde curls. With her head resting against his chest she had eventually drifted off to sleep about an hour ago. Yesterday he had been reluctant to leave Tessa alone; it terrified him when she cried because he knew she only did it when she had reached her breaking point. But she had pasted her upbeat face back on and insisted that she was fine, she'd continued the charade until she'd received a certain phone call.

Chest rising and falling gently in her sleep, Tessa whimpered softly and snuggled closer to him, molding her body against his, as he lay and watched her in the thin light of the lamp that Tessa insisted be kept on while they slept.

Brushing his fingertips across her forehead when the phone suddenly let out a sharp ring, startling not just himself but also Tessa who sprang up with a strangled scream, wide eyes darting wildly around the room.

Grabbing her shoulders Parker shook her gently. "Tessa, hey, honey, look at me, it's just the phone."

Locking her eyes on to his she took several shuddering breaths, trying to calm herself.

"It was just the phone," he repeated giving her a reassuring smile and stroking her cheek to help soothe her. "Okay?"

Nodding she closed her eyes and took another deep breath, letting it slowly out, the phone that had ceased ringing started insistently up again. Ignoring it, his attention focused solely on Tessa who opened her eyes and nodded at the trilling phone on the nightstand, "I'm okay, get it."

Snatching it up before the person on the other end could hang up, "Hello?"

"Parker?"

Keeping one eye on Tessa who had laid back down against her pillows and pulled the feather quilt up to her chin. "Marty?"

"Yeah it's me."

The CSU tech sounded uncharacteristically excitable. "What's up?"

"I got a match on one of the hairs from the Phoebe Stein crime scene."

Surprised, "You know who the Iceman is?"

"DNA came back a match to a Jamie Presland. Guess where he works?"

"Where?" Parker asked a little impatiently.

"The restaurant that backs onto the alley."

Impressed, "Wow it's only seven thirty in the morning and you've already made my day, Marty."

"It's been a pleasure. Speak to you later."

"See ya."

Sitting for a moment listening to the dial tone before turning to Tessa who was staring up at him with thoughtful turquoise eyes. "You got a lead in your case?"

"Marty just ID'd the man who murdered Phoebe Stein in the alley a couple of days ago."

"That's great," Tessa smiled at him.

"We think Phoebe's attacker might have been the Iceman," he told her.

Raising an eyebrow at him, "Really?"

"You don't think it sounds like his MO?" he asked. Tessa had an amazing ability to read people and situations and see things that others missed.

Shrugging, "I don't really know all the details."

Studying her for moment, she seemed calmer than she had earlier this morning. "You okay?"

"I'm fine . . . really," she added when she saw the look on his face. "I feel better than I have in a really long time. I know I was a little jumpy about the phone, but really I feel good."

"You're serious?" In her eyes was a calm he had never seen in the twelve months since they had met.

"Maybe talking about what happened with Daniel actually helped," she admitted.

Surprised, "Does that mean you'll consider talking with Beth?" Since the night she had shot Dylan Riley he had been trying to convince Tessa to talk with Elisabeth Bennett. As well as helping with criminal cases Beth was an excellent therapist with her own practice specializing in helping trauma survivors.

After an incident eighteen months ago when he had been forced to shoot a psychopathic teenager who was holding a gun on her newborn daughter he himself had gone to see her. At first he had thought the whole thing was nothing but a waste of time, but it had been part of the conditions of him returning to work so he reluctantly complied and had gone along to the sessions merely to pass away the time. It wasn't until several sessions in that Beth's quiet patience begun to wear him down and he found himself opening up to her in a way he never had before.

Tessa however was a lot more anti-therapist than he had been. Her grandparents had sent her to a psychiatrist when she was eleven and she had witnessed the murder of her friend, and then again after her mother tried to kill her. Both these times she had sat in silence at each and every session until in the end the psychiatrists had given up on her.

"No," she said firmly, narrowing her eyes at him. "Talking about things is not who I am . . ."

"But you just said . . ." Parker started but Tessa cut him off.

"I know what I said. And talking about Daniel helped me to let go any feelings I had left for him. I realized that a part of me was still hoping that he would come back and that things could go back to the way they were, but when I saw him I realized that I felt nothing but anger towards him."

"If it helped to talk about Daniel then don't you think it would help to talk about everything else? Like about Dylan and Eleanor?" he protested even though he could see her mind was made up.

"No I don't think it would help," Tessa shot back evenly. "That's not who I am and you knew that about me when you met me,

Parker. I keep everything inside, I bury things away, I pretend that they don't exist, I'm like the kid playing hide and go seek who covers their eyes and thinks no one can see them. I don't talk about it, I don't think about it, and it's like it goes away. I've been alone most of my life, I've dealt with things alone, and that strategy was working fine when I met you. *I* was doing fine."

Rolling his eyes at that comment. "You were doing fine were you?"

"Yes I was," she nodded adamantly.

"Really? You lived alone in a house that had more security than the Whitehouse. You didn't have any friends, you spent all your time alone writing and painting, and you were being stalked by not one but two killers," letting his words hang in the air. "You weren't doing fine, Tess, you were an emotional mess," he finished softly.

"I was dealing with things in the way that was best for me," Tessa was getting angry now. "Which I am going to continue doing, and if you can't understand that then . . ."

Grabbing hold of her arm as she threw back the covers and started to climb from the bed. "Tess, wait," caving in and deciding to let it go for now. "I don't want to fight with you. If that's the way you want to deal with stuff, fine. If you want to pretend it all never happened, fine. I just want you to be happy."

Gently pulling her towards him she held herself rigid then relented and allowed him to settle her against his chest. "The past is over, Parker," she whispered. "I can't change it and I can't live in it anymore, I won't let it control me. I want to focus on the future, you and me, that's my life now. Patrick, Emilie, Daniel, Dylan, Ellie, they're all gone; they don't have any place in our lives. I'm so tired of thinking about what happened, I'm not going to do it anymore, I can't or it's going to destroy me. I'm ready, Parker, I'm ready to let it all go, I'm ready to be happy."

"I want you to be happy, I want us to be happy, but . . ."

"No. No buts. You think I'm strong but I'm not, not anymore, I can't do it on my own and I don't want to, I need you to help me, and one of the ways you can do that is to let it go. Can you do that? For me? For us?"

Squeezing her tightly. "I'll let it go if you can promise me one thing."

"What?" she asked warily twisting so that she was looking up at him.

"That you won't shut me out," he insisted. Tessa thought that his biggest fear was that the man who'd tried to burn her alive would come back to get her but she was wrong. Parker's biggest fear was that Tessa would simply implode from the heavy burdens she insisted on carrying alone. No one could destroy Tessa faster or more effectively than she herself could. "If you change your mind and you want to talk about it, you'll come to me, you won't let it pull you down. We're a team now, you and me, together. Deal?"

"Deal."

* * * * *

8:30 A.M.

"ICEMAN STRIKES AGAIN!"

With an almighty roar the Iceman threw the newspaper across the room. Unfortunately it was too light to do much damage but at least the motion ebbed a tiny portion of the frustration that was beginning to well up.

Luckily there was no one else at work yet so the Iceman took advantage of the isolation to completely trash the office. Throwing papers on the floor, knocking framed pictures off the walls, overturning chairs and tables, by the end all the Iceman could do was sink to the ground and try to calm ragged breathing.

If there was one thing that the Iceman despised above all else it was when someone brought disrespect to another by claiming credit for his or her work. The murder of the young girl behind the seafood restaurant was not the Iceman's work, and that anyone could possible see any resemblance between the two cases was absolutely preposterous.

It was not the fact that the 'Iceman' had been accused of the murder, after all murder was the Iceman's business, but that anyone could accuse the Iceman of such a sloppy attack. The Iceman was proud of the fact that each and every crime committed was done to perfection. No hairs, fibers, DNA, no fingerprints, shoeprints, no eyewitnesses who saw anything incriminating, were ever left behind.

Not to mention that the police should know by now that nothing, not even two young men jogging in a place they never had before, would force the Iceman to deviate from the plan. If the Iceman had wanted to abduct Phoebe Stein then she would be sitting beside Hayley Geoffries this very second.

The Iceman could never be caught because the person the police were looking for did not exist. Whether out stalking potential victims, performing the abductions or staging the bodies, the Iceman always wore a complete disguise, something that was as far from reality as it was possible to be. So far, more than a year since the first body was discovered, the police had no leads and were no closer to putting an end to the Iceman's reign of terror.

The crime in question was possibly the sloppiest the Iceman had ever seen. According to the newspaper report the attacker apparently had not bothered to cover his face, had not bothered to wear gloves, had allowed himself to be overpowered almost letting the girl get away. Unfortunately for young Phoebe Stein her attacker had managed to recover long enough to slit her throat when her boyfriend appeared. If the Iceman hadn't been so angry about being blamed for the incompetent attack it would almost have been humorous.

The Iceman had worked tirelessly to plan and execute the perfect crime. A crime that had the entire city panicked, that had the police clueless, that had thrown the Iceman into the public eye as a figure to be feared, to be revered, to be respected. The Iceman would not allow all that to be for naught, nothing was going to prevent the conclusion of the plan.

Sighing the Iceman glanced at the clock and saw it would be only an hour or so until others began to arrive at work. They could not see the office in such disarray. So stuffing anger down deep inside the Iceman stood and began to reassemble the room to its usual appearance. When everything else was taken care of, when all the pieces of the puzzle had fallen into place, then the Iceman would make sure that the whole world knew that Iceman was unbeatable.

Then the Iceman would be respected.

* * * * *

11:15 A.M.

"Mrs. Hamilton?"

The woman frowned at them from behind narrow glasses. "Yes?"

"This is Detective Wyatt, and I'm Detective Bell, we need to talk to you about one of your employees."

Tossing her shoulder length brown hair over her shoulder. "I'm really very busy you know. I wasn't allowed in here until late yesterday and I'm still behind with everything that needs to be done," she glared at them as though they were personally responsibly for her inconvenience.

"I'm sorry about that, Mrs. Hamilton," Wyatt soothed. "But actually the murder is why we're here."

Frowning she kept them on the street while one hand held the door half closed. "What does that have to do with me and my restaurant. The attack happened out the back."

"We found a hair at the scene, we were able to get DNA and from that to identify Phoebe Stein's killer as a man who works here. A Jamie Presland."

Recognition flickered in her hard grey eyes but she wasn't ready to relent and let them in just yet. "The paper's been saying that it was the Iceman who attacked that girl."

"We're considering that possibility, Mrs. Hamilton."

"And you think that one of my employees is the Iceman?" she asked incredulously.

"Mrs. Hamilton, Jamie Presland has been identified as the man who brutally murdered a young woman, we're here to take him in for questioning."

"Well that's going to be a problem then," Mrs. Hamilton sighed.

"Jamie didn't turn up at work yesterday, and he's not here today."

"Have you spoken with him?" Parker demanded, frustration making his voice harsh. Nothing in the Iceman case seemed to go easily, just when they thought they were taking one step forwards they were pushed back two.

Shaking her head. "He sent an email."

"Do we have your permission to try and trace the email, see where it was sent from?" Wyatt asked.

Studying them for several moments Mrs. Hamilton finally relented, "Do whatever you want."

"May we come in and talk to you about Jamie?"

Again she studied them and Parker got the uncomfortable feeling that Mrs. Hamilton was looking right inside his head and reading his thoughts. Positive she was about to deny them entrance when eventually she let go of the door and disappeared inside the restaurant.

With a glance at his partner Parker followed her inside and stopped short at the sight of the magnificent aquarium that filled the middle of the room. Tropical fish cruised around inside it giving the room a tranquil feeling, tables and chairs fanned out around the rest of the large space. The ceiling had been painted black, hundreds of glowing fairy lights strung across it making it look like the night sky. The place was spectacular and Parker knew from the second he saw it that this was where he was going to propose to Tessa.

Mrs. Hamilton hovered near the door to the kitchen. "Drinks?"

"Coffee's fine," Parker answered for himself and Wyatt.

"How do you take it?"

"White," Wyatt answered.

"Black," Parker replied with a smirk at his partner. It was a longstanding tradition between the two of them to try and convince the other to drink coffee the way they liked.

Returning promptly with a tray piled high with three steaming cups of coffee and a plate of cakes. Setting them on the table and taking a seat, Parker and Wyatt crossed to sit with her, waiting while she handed out the mugs and cakes, before beginning.

"Mrs. Hamilton, what can you tell us about Jamie Presland?"

"First of all please call me Cece, when you call me Mrs. Hamilton it reminds me of my mother-in-law, not someone I like to spend a lot of time thinking about. And second of all there's not a lot I can tell you about Jamie I'm afraid. He mostly kept to himself, but he was a model employee, always turned up on time, worked hard, almost always available to fill in if someone was away."

"Did you know he had a record as a peeping tom?"

Her hesitation was his answer.

"We're going to need his information," Wyatt told her.

Sheepishly, "The only information I have for him is a PO Box. I don't even have a bank account, I pay him by cheque," Cece admitted.

"Was Jamie working on December first last year, or January and February first this year?" Parker asked.

"That's a year ago," Mrs. Hamilton told them irritably.

"What about December first this year, that's only a week ago," Parker pushed, the restaurant owner was really starting to get on his nerves.

Tapping a perfectly polished bright red nail against her chin as she thought. "No he wasn't working December first," she said at last.

"We really need to know about those other dates," Parker pressed.

"I suppose I could check my old records," Cece said with about as much enthusiasm as one usually musters for a trip to the dentist.

Arching an eyebrow at her and wondering why on earth the woman was being so uncooperative when they were telling her that one of her employees could be a serial killer.

Shooting him a withering glare, Cece Hamilton sighed deeply as she stood and disappeared from the room. While they waited Parker made his way over to the aquarium, ever since he was a child he had loved watching fish, finding the serene way they glided so effortlessly along comforting. When he had first moved in with the Bell's they had had a huge aquarium in their kitchen and he would spend hours simply sitting watching the fish swim.

"No," Cece's announcement made him jump.

"No you couldn't find any records, or no Jamie Presland wasn't working on December, January and February first?" Parker asked, refocusing his mind.

"No Jamie wasn't working on any of those days," Cece clarified.

"Mom?"

They all turned as the restaurant's front door swung open and a pretty teenager peeked anxiously through at them. She had long black hair, long lashed dark eyes and skin as white as snow. "Mom?" the girl repeated.

"What is it, Winter?" Cece Hamilton snapped crossly.

"Uh, nothing. What's going on?" Winter came part way across the room but didn't venture too close.

"I'm Detective Bell and this Detective Wyatt, we're . . ."

"They're investigating the man who killed that poor girl," Cece interrupted.

"We're here about Jamie Presland, do you know him?" Parker asked not about to let Cece Hamilton dominate the conversation.

Winter nodded.

Noticing the way she wiggled uncomfortably, Parker went to her, "Winter, has Jamie ever hurt you?"

Shooting her mother a look, Cece nodded briskly, "Come along, Winter. If you know something tell the police."

"Sometimes I see him watching me," Winter began tentatively.

"Has he ever touched you?" Parker pressed gently.

When her daughter hesitated Cece barked, "We don't have all day, Winter."

"Winter, has Jamie ever done anything that made you feel uncomfortable, has he ever done something that you didn't want him to do?" Parker asked softly.

Winter held his gaze, "A couple of times he asked me out. I said no, I'm fifteen and he's like thirty," she said thirty as one might say ninety. "And sometimes when we're alone he tries to kiss me," she shuddered. "He's always drinking. He thinks he hides it but I've seen him do it, and his breath always smells of alcohol."

"Why didn't you say anything?" Cece asked unsympathetically, and Parker wondered about the relationship between mother and daughter.

Shrugging, "It was no big deal, I dealt with it myself."

"Run along, Winter, I'm sure you have homework," Cece commanded dismissively.

Winter started towards the back of the restaurant but Parker stopped her, "Winter, do you have any idea where Jamie might be?"

She shook her head and without another word hurried from the room.

As the door closed behind her daughter Cece stood and began to shepherd them towards the front door. "I'm sorry I couldn't be more helpful," she announced, not sounding the slightest bit sorry.

"I'll leave you my card," Parker held it out but Cece didn't take it so he set it down on the table instead.

"Someone will be around to collect your computer," Wyatt reminded her.

Nodding, "As long as it doesn't disrupt my work," Cece conceded.

"If you think of anything else about Jamie that might be helpful please give us a call," Parker said to her.

"I don't think I know anything else about him. I didn't even know he was harassing my daughter," Cece replied.

"Thank you for your time," Wyatt was saying but Cece Hamilton was already closing the door behind them.

"She is one odd woman," Parker commented.

"She certainly didn't seem to care that Jamie Presland, a man who might be a serial killer, has been hassling her fifteen-year-old daughter," Wyatt shook his head disgusted, there was nothing in the world Wyatt wouldn't do for his kids, nine-year-old Sam and five-year-old Stacey. "I'll put in a call get someone to track down a home address for Jamie Presland."

"If he hasn't already skipped town."

As Parker and Wyatt drove off down the street and Cece Hamilton returned to her office young Winter crept back into the room retrieved the card Parker had left on the table and slipped it into her pocket.

* * * * *

11.38 A.M.

"No, no, no," Hayley screamed at the monitor that mocked her with images of freedom, so close and yet so unreachable.

"No, don't go," she screamed again, more desperately this time.

The monitor stubbornly continued to show her an image of an empty room.

They were gone.

The police officers were gone.

She hadn't realized they were police officers at first, but then she had seen the badges, and the guns.

For one blissful second her heart had soared, her mind filled with images of rescue, of home, of her parents, she was going to be saved. But then she had realized that the police had no idea that she was there.

One of the officers had stood right in front of the aquarium, watching the fish, staring right at her and yet unable to see her.

Now they were gone. And she was alone. And it was too much for any person to bear.

Before she knew what she was doing she was screeching at the top of her lungs, tears streaming down her cheeks, hands clawing at the hard, unyielding concrete wall.

Exhaustion got her in the end. And she dropped to the floor, curling up in a tight ball, breathless, fingernails ragged, hands bloody.

And Hayley Geoffries knew that she was never getting out of here alive.

DECEMBER 8TH

1:06 P.M.

Tessa was busily baking cakes when she became aware of the presence behind her. Not so much because the intruder made a noise but because she had spent most of her life being paranoid and had honed the ability to sense when danger was lurking.

"You know that's breaking and entering," she commented as she set the cake into the oven then turned around. "I told you I didn't want to see you."

"And I told you I was sticking around," her brother shot back.

Ignoring him Tessa continued with her baking, taking one cake from the oven to cool and beginning to ice another that had already been cooling. Decorating the cake with perfectly formed letters in preparation for Casey and Skylar's wedding anniversary for which they were having a party here a few days before Christmas.

"You still hate chocolate cake?" Daniel asked, breaking the silence with an olive branch.

Intending to disregard his question but then yielding, "Yes. I'm making this one for Parker, chocolate's his favorite."

Frowning, "Your police officer boyfriend."

Frowning right back at him. "That is none of your business."

"A cop. Tessie, how could you date a cop?"

Refusing to be drawn into an argument about this now.

"Tessie, when did a cop ever help you? After Eleanor? After everything that Dylan Riley did to you and your friends?"

"I am not going to have this conversation with you again," she bit out through clenched teeth. After Ellie had died it had been Daniel's theory that the police should have done something about it, conveniently leaving out that she was the only one with information about that crime and she hadn't told anyone what really happened that night. "That was your theory, not mine, Daniel," she reminded him.

Her two dogs took this opportunity to bound in from the laundry room where they'd been busy napping, they halted their headlong pursuit towards her when they spotted the new person in the room. Buttercup, a golden retriever, and the shyer of the two dogs, stopped and hung around Tessa's legs, Ladybug, a Dalmatian, on the other hand went straight to Daniel. Following Ladybug's lead Buttercup also headed over, both dogs nuzzling at her brother's hands, eager for more attention.

Daniel bent down to them, rubbing their heads and laughing as Ladybug licked his face. "They're adorable, what are their names?"

"Buttercup and Ladybug," Tessa told him grudgingly then turned to the dogs, "Hey you two are supposed to be on my side you know, not cuddling up to the enemy." The dogs cocked their heads and looked at her with clearly puzzled expressions but obediently came trotting over to her side, licking her hands as way of apology. Busying about getting dinner for the dogs when she became aware of Daniel's hurt, puppy dog expression, she did her best to ignore it and returned to her baking.

"Do you really see me as the enemy?" Daniel asked at last.

Once again Tessa didn't answer, didn't trust herself to answer, she may be angry with her brother but unfortunately she didn't want to hurt him further.

"Tessie, please look at me," Daniel crossed the room but wisely refrained from putting his hands on her. "Come on, Tessie, you know that I love you, you know that I would never intentionally hurt you."

Hating the pleading sincerity in his voice, the way it made her resolve waver. Forcing herself to remember how alone she had felt that first night after she returned home from the hospital. "Don't, Daniel, don't try and wash over what you did. You left me alone after everything Emilie did, you knew what that house was like and you still left me alone there."

"I did what I thought was the only thing that would keep you safe . . ."

"You wanted out, I get that, we both hated that house, but you didn't even say goodbye you were just gone. Even if that's true, even if you left because you thought you were keeping me safe, why didn't you say goodbye?" to her annoyance Tessa could feel tears welling up behind her eyes.

"I wanted to, Tess, it broke my heart to leave you like that but I didn't think I had a choice," reaching out a hand to her.

Deciding anger was the better route to go Tessa let herself get worked up, yanking her arm away from Daniel. "All those years and you never once thought to contact me . . ."

"I sent you a card every year on your birthday," Daniel interrupted.

"Oh well thanks, Daniel," she jeered. "That makes everything all better. I was all alone in the world but you sent me a birthday card once a year, wow what a great big brother I have."

Looking wounded. "Tessie," he began.

Too riled up to stop now Tessa continued, "What about when I was fifteen and I was in the hospital, when I had pneumonia and almost died, you didn't think that would be a good time to make a reappearance? Why did you come back now, Daniel? When I've finally moved on why did you have to come back?"

"I told you I came back because I heard about what happened with Dylan Riley."

"You just heard about it even though it happened a year ago?"

"Where I've been staying, we don't get a lot of news, but someone sent me a letter with a newspaper article in it, an article about you, about what happened."

He sounded so genuine but Tessa was too skeptical to believe a word that came out of her brother's mouth. "Someone sent you a letter?"

"I thought it was you, reaching out to me," now Daniel looked confused.

"I never sent you any letter," she told him.

"What about that . . . guy. Your . . . boyfriend?" he could hardly force the words out.

"Parker," she glared at him. "He wouldn't have sent you anything, even if he knew where you were, he knew that you hurt me and he wouldn't want you around."

"Then I don't know who it was but that's why I came, Tessie, and I would have come right away if I'd known, you have to believe me," his eyes, identical to her own, bored into her so earnestly.

"Daniel," she sighed, "I can't fix things up with you. You left me and I was so scared and alone, but I'm not anymore. I finally moved on, I have Parker now and I can't go back. I can't keep living in the past."

Disappointment written all over his face. "Please, Tess, one more chance to prove myself to you."

"I'm sorry, Daniel, I can't. Please just go," turning her back, she couldn't bare to watch him leave, as angry and hurt as she was by him he was her big brother and she still loved him.

He stood, unmoving, behind her for several minutes then she felt hands on her shoulders, "Tessie, promise me something."

When she didn't answer he apparently took it as a sign of assent and continued, "I want you to remember, no matter what happens, that everything I did, everything I've ever done was because I love you." Kissing the top of her head, "I love you, Tessie," and then he was gone.

Listening to him retreat down the hall and the clunk of the door closing behind him, the aroma of burning chocolate cake filling the room, Tessa brushed at the tears threatening to spill down her cheeks.

"I love you too, Daniel."

* * * * *

3:41 P.M.

"He's gone."

"Hopefully just not too far," Parker sighed.

They were standing in the front yard of Jamie Presland's near derelict house, a single storey weatherboard. Originally painted a pale green and trimmed with a darker, richer green, now the only paint left had been turned grey by years of wind, sun, rain and snow. The yard where they stood contained a single dead tree and a few scattered tufts of half-dead grass.

Now that the house had been cleared he and Wyatt made their way inside, about to embark on a search for anything that might lead them to Jamie or tie him to the Iceman case. While J.J. was continuing to push the Iceman angle Parker still wasn't one hundred percent convinced either way.

The inside of the house was as dismal as the outside. The walls were covered with peeling wallpaper, revealing decades old paint underneath that was also peeling away to reveal even older layers. The carpet was worn through to the floorboards in places and what was left was nothing more than rough, ripped rags. The furniture too looked like it had seen better days, a mismatched jumble of things Jamie had probably found at the tip or on the streets.

The house contained a living room, kitchen, two bedrooms and a bathroom, not many places to hide a victim. They had already ruled out the possibility that Jamie was holding Hayley Geoffries here if he was indeed the Iceman. Dividing up the rooms, Wyatt would take the master bedroom and the kitchen, while Parker would search the other bedroom, living room and bathroom.

Deciding to start with the living room, Parker was met with an enormous stack of newspapers by the door. Other than the papers the room contained two battered couches and an old TV set on a milk crate, not many places to hide potentially incriminating evidence.

Starting with the couches Parker pulled out the cushions and felt around the springs and frame, finding nothing. Next he checked out the TV, remembering an old case where a young man had shot two innocent bystanders in a drug buy gone wrong. The killer had escaped the scene but witnesses gave a detailed description of him. After identifying the killer and tracking him down to his perfectly neat apartment police had torn apart the place in a search for anything incriminating. Eventually one of the young officers had thought to check inside the back of an old television set and been rewarded by finding the gun the killer had used.

Pulling off the back of the set revealed nothing besides the TV's wires and electronics, so Parker left it where it was and started circling the room tapping on the walls, checking for any little hidey-holes.

Kneeling beside the stack of papers, Parker found something on the very first one. "I think our guy's a scrap-booker," he yelled through to Wyatt.

His partner's head popping around the doorway moments later. "He's keeping articles?"

"He sure is," Parker held up several newspapers where articles had been removed. "I'm gonna bet these were about the Iceman." Picturing in his head Jamie Presland sitting in this very room gloating over each and every detail of his heinous crimes.

"He might have taken it with him if he's run," Wyatt suggested.

"But if he left in a hurry he might not."

As Wyatt returned to his search of Jamie's bedroom, Parker moved onto the spare bedroom. It didn't take long to search the room since it contained only a desk, drawers were empty, and a computer over which someone appeared to have poured a bucket of water in an attempt to destroy it. About to call through to Wyatt that they would need to get someone from the crime lab to go through it when his partner called out to him.

Entering the master bedroom he saw Wyatt hunched over a box that he'd pulled from its hiding place buried deep in the wardrobe. "What've you got?"

"Gloves," Wyatt grinned up at him.

Bending down beside his partner he saw several pairs of white women's gloves, identical to those worn by the Iceman's victims. "I think he may be our guy, I wasn't sure at first, but the gloves, the newspaper articles, I think Jamie Presland is the Iceman."

Leaving Wyatt to finish checking out the bedroom Parker went to search the bathroom. Finding nothing useful as he rifled through the drawers and cupboards, and nothing as he rifled through the pile of junk under the sink he was about to call it a day when he noticed something unusual in the wall. Like the rest of the house the bathroom was a mess, the black and white tiles that covered the walls and floor were chipped, in places huge chunks of them were missing.

Attention drawn to the far corner of the room where the grout around the tiles was a bright, fresh white, not grayed from years of neglect like the rest of the grout in the room. Retrieving a pair of scissors from the drawer he worked away at the grout, breaking through it in less than a minute, the tiles falling away in his hands. Hidden behind was a narrow, but deep, rectangular space, about to reach inside he froze. Lying in the dark hole was a scrapbook, which Parker would bet his career held the missing newspaper articles, but hidden underneath the book was something even better.

"Hey, Wyatt," he called out.

Waiting until his partner appeared. "What'd you find?"

Carefully reaching into the hidey-hole Parker pulled out what would be the last metaphorical nail in Jamie Presland, a.k.a the Iceman's, coffin.

When Wyatt saw what he had found his face broke into a wide grin. "We got him."

Returning his partner's smile, in his hand Parker held the knife that the Iceman had used to slit Phoebe's Stein's throat. Apparently Jamie had been so confident that the police would never find him that he had not even bothered to clean it before he hid it away as it was still coated with Phoebe's blood.

DECEMBER 9TH

7:52 A.M.

"Here you go," Tessa set a steaming cup of coffee next to Parker's plate of waffles.

"You're not eating?" he asked through a giant mouthful.

"I'm not hungry," she replied pulling a bottle of chilled water from the fridge and sitting beside him at the table.

Rolling his eyes at her. "You have to eat, Tess, you're so skinny."

Frowning and punching him in the shoulder for emphasis. "Hey!" She might be small but she was also strong, she visited the gym a couple of times a week and ran every day, rain, hail or shine.

"Sorry," he smiled and kissed her cheek, leaving a sticky residue of syrup, which he tried to wipe off with an equally sticky finger.

"How's your case going?" she asked, with Parker's weird hours she was often asleep before he got home.

"We got enough evidence to bury him," Parker was beaming like a kid on Christmas morning. "His house was like a treasure trove. We found a scrapbook full of newspaper articles about the Iceman, we found a packet of women's white gloves, and we found the knife he used to kill Phoebe Stein still covered in her blood."

"Did you find anything to help you locate him?" she asked.

Smile faltering a little, "No, we didn't."

"You'll find him," she reassured as she moved to stand, but Parker grabbed hold of her wrist and pulled her back down. "What?"

"What's wrong?" narrowing his eyes at her.

"What do you mean?" she asked innocently.

"I mean that you don't seem too pleased that we found him."

Not wanting to burst his bubble, she shrugged, "I am pleased," standing she began to gather dishes and load them into the dishwasher.

Parker watched her while he finished off his coffee. "You don't think Jamie Presland is the Iceman do you?" he asked finally.

Sighing, she didn't want to get into a discussion about this. "You said you found a lot of evidence that pointed to him being the killer."

"That wasn't an answer."

Twirling her hair around her finger and trying to find a way out of the conversation without having to say anything. Tessa didn't want to become involved in this case, and she certainly didn't need more to feel guilty for or more to blame herself for if she got caught up in this and because of her things didn't work out.

When she said nothing Parker came and stood behind her, hands on her shoulders, gently massaging. "Come on, Tessa. Tell me what you're thinking."

"I don't want to get involved," she pleaded.

Cajoling, "No one is better at reading people than you are, no one is better at knowing what's going on inside someone else's head."

"Last time I had an advantage," she reminded him.

"Tess?"

Biting her lip, "Okay, but you're not going to like what I have to say."

Turning her around so that she faced him. "I don't care."

Leading him by the hand back to the table and looking him straight in the eye. "Jamie Presland is not the Iceman."

Shaking his head, "I thought that too at first, but everything we found at his house, the scrapbook, the gloves, the *knife*. If he's not the Iceman then why would he have that?"

"Look," she began in her most rational voice, which she always used when arguing her point. "I'm not saying that Jamie Presland didn't murder Phoebe Stein, I'm saying that . . ."

"That the two cases are not related," Parker finished. "I thought that too at first, but why would he have the gloves? The scrapbook?"

"I don't know, maybe he's a fan, or a crime buff, whatever, it doesn't matter, it's not relevant, Jamie attacked Phoebe that makes him a killer, it doesn't make him a *serial* killer. He did not kill those other women and he is not the one holding Hayley Geoffries hostage."

"Why? How do you know the same man didn't commit both crimes? How could you possibly know that?"

"Because it's not logical," she answered simply, expanding when Parker looked ready to protest. "Think about it, the Iceman is highly organized, he plans everything out perfectly. He wears gloves to every crime scene, he doesn't leave anything behind, even when the abduction of Elizabeth Landry was thwarted it didn't slow him down he simply moved on and took another girl. If he had wanted to take Phoebe then nothing would have stopped him, and he certainly wouldn't have allowed her to attack and overpower him."

"He did catch up to Phoebe and kill her," Parker countered defensively. "Maybe there was something different about Phoebe, maybe he felt something for her that he hasn't felt for the other victims," he suggested.

Raising a doubtful eyebrow. "Even if that were true," she continued, "Why would he change his MO? This is a killer who killed his victims on a particular day, the same day each month, he was well enough in control to stop killing for ten months then begin again on the exact same day. Does someone who is that calm and methodical strike you as the same guy who attacked Phoebe in such a wild, frenzied manner?"

"Maybe he's escalating," Parker shot back; apparently he had an answer for everything this morning.

"This is not the kind of killer who suddenly starts escalating at this speed, and not like this," she was starting to feel drawn into the case and struggled to remain detached.

"What about the ID we got from Elizabeth and the two men who saved her? And Josh Timma and the cabbie. Jamie Presland fits that description."

"What the ID that said the Iceman was a tallish white man? Parker, most of the population fit that description, *you* fit that description."

"Well I disagree. I believe that Jamie Presland is the Iceman."

"Fine, believe whatever you want," leaving the table to start the dishwasher. "You know you're the one who asked for my opinion. I told you I didn't want to be involved," setting her mouth in a stubborn line and tilting out her chin determinedly.

"You're right," Parker sweet-talked trying to hide a smile at her indignation. "I'm sorry, thank you for your input."

Not quite ready to make peace she huffed, "You know I am a genius."

"You're right," he said again. "You're wonderful, great, brilliant, amazing, magnificent, breathtaking . . ."

Laughing she batted him on the arm. "Okay, okay, okay." Then growing obstinate once again, "I'm telling you, Parker, I'm positive that the Iceman is not Jamie Presland, he's still out there and he's going to keep killing until you stop him."

* * * * *

9:19 A.M.

"Alright status report please," J.J.'s voice boomed through the room.

"Cause of death was exsanguination from the wound to her throat, she also had a punctured lung from the knife wound to her back," Zak summarized briskly.

"It looks like there was an initial attack and somehow Phoebe managed to get away. She made it part way down the alley before Jamie threw the knife at her, either he knew what he was doing or he fluked it but he got her right in the back," Wyatt explained further. "That gave him his opportunity to attack her, he was probably going to rape her before Josh Timma showed up, so he improvised and killed her then managed to get away. We searched Jamie Presland house, everyone knows about what we found right?" Wyatt asked.

All heads bobbed.

"Where are we on the computer?" J.J. demanded.

"Turns out it wasn't as badly damaged as it seemed," Marty filled everyone in. "One of my guys took the hard drive out, put it in another computer, it was full of pornography."

"Are we thinking that's his motive? Sexually dominating his

victims." J.J. suggested.

"None of the other victims were raped," Zak reminded them.

"Why is that?" J.J. demanded as though he couldn't believe that any violent criminal would pass up the chance to rape a young girl when the two of them were completely alone. "Is he a homosexual? Or maybe there's something wrong with him, maybe he's impotent."

"Rape isn't about sex," Beth reminded him patiently. "It's about control. He doesn't need to rape his victims to be in control of them."

"Then why leave them naked?" J.J. asked, bewildered.

"Too humiliate them," Beth replied.

They all turned to look at her.

"It's why he's doing all of this, making things as melodramatic and shocking as possible, he wants to be noticed, he wants *us* to notice him," Beth continued waving a hand around the room to include them all. "And to revere him. He wants his victims to know that he is in control, that it is he who decides if they live or die. He didn't rape any of the victims and he didn't torture them physically, he just wanted to control them."

"Anything from the knife, can we confirm it was the one used in the Stein murder?"

"Still waiting for DNA to confirm," Marty told them. "But fingerprints on the handle match the ones on file for Jamie Presland."

"What do we have on Jamie Presland?" J.J. queried.

"A couple of peeping tom charges five years ago, no time served, then nothing until this," Wyatt replied.

"At least nothing he got caught for," Beth interjected.

"Does he have access to holly?"

"He didn't have any in either his front or back yard, not that there was much of anything," Wyatt told him. "But," he continued quickly upon seeing J.J.'s face flush with anger, "His next door neighbor had a huge holly bush in his yard. And his boss confirmed that he wasn't working on any of the days when the Iceman posed his victims and kidnapped his next."

"Parker, you're unusually quiet today," J.J.'s brown eyes boring into him. "What's up?"

"Tessa doesn't think that Jamie Presland is the Iceman," he announced. As much as he wanted to believe that Jamie was the killer so they could find him and put an end to all of this, what Tessa had said made perfect sense.

"Last I checked Tessa's not a cop and she's not working this case so her opinion is irrelevant," J.J. growled.

"I know that," Parker countered. "But this is Tessa. We all know she's brilliant and we all know how accurate she is at reading people."

"People's she's met," J.J. countered. "And as far as I know Tessa has never met the Iceman."

"She's concerned that the sudden change in MO doesn't add up with everything we know about the Iceman."

"What about all the evidence we found at . . ."

"Actually," Beth piped up, "The change in MO has been worrying me too."

"What?" J.J. turned to glare at her.

"Tessa's right, it doesn't fit with what we know about the Iceman. Everything about the first crimes points to the killer being a highly organized, thrill killer. This categorization would explain why he is able to wait long periods between kills, and also why there's been no sexual component. Thrill killers usually commit their crimes against strangers, and they believe that they will never be caught, but they usually also refine their killings, becoming *more* successful as time goes on."

"Meaning they don't usually go backwards and commit a frenzied attack?" Parker asked.

"It's highly unlikely," Beth answered.

"What about some sort of trigger, something to set him off," J.J. suggested.

"Maybe," Beth said doubtful, fingering the scar on her cheek. "You can never really know for certain what's going on inside someone's head."

"If Jamie Presland is not the Iceman then why would he be keeping a scrapbook chronicling the Iceman's crimes?" J.J. pressed.

"Tessa thinks maybe he's just a fan," Parker provided with a look to Beth for confirmation.

She shrugged, "Maybe, it wouldn't be the first time a 'novice' criminal has followed the work of someone they admire."

"How do we know he's not?"

"Not what?" Parker asked confused.

"How do we know the Iceman's not raping women in between the murders? Lots of women don't report rapes," J.J. put forward.

"I guess we don't know, but I don't think it seems very likely," Parker answered.

"Okay, but we're forgetting the ID," J.J. reminded. "Elizabeth and the two men who saved her, Wendy Geoffries, Joshua Timma and Alvin Kent all gave the same description of the Iceman."

"Tessa thinks that since the description was so vague it could fit anyone."

"Are you trying to bother me?" J.J. groaned wearily. "Do you agree with Tessa? Do you think we have the wrong man?"

"No, I believe that Jamie is the Iceman, I'm just playing devil's advocate," Parker felt at least ninety percent sure that this was true, that Presland really was the serial killer haunting the city.

"What about the scar?" Wyatt asked. "Elizabeth Landry said that the man who attacked her had a weird scar on his wrist."

Pouncing on this, J.J.'s eyes lit up, "Do we know if Jamie Presland has any such scars?"

Flicking through the file in front of him, stopping when he reached something that could be the answer. "It says here," Parker looked up to find all eyes focused on him. "That when Jamie was fifteen he attempted suicide, slashed one of his wrists before his sister found him and called an ambulance."

"So Jamie Presland has a scar on his wrist just like the Iceman, perfect," J.J. looked convinced, as did Wyatt, Marty and Zak, even Beth was wavering. "Now where are we on possible locations where he could be hiding out?"

"We're still searching, looking for old addresses, family's addresses, anything, but so far we haven't found anything that looks good," Wyatt told him.

"We're also looking for anywhere he might have stashed Hayley," Parker added. "Anything with a remote location."

"All right people, let's move out, Jamie Presland is the Iceman, if he thinks we're never gonna catch him he's dead wrong," J.J.'s eyes were sparkling wildly. "We are going to put an end to his game once and for all."

DECEMBER 10TH

5:17 A.M.

It felt like months had passed since she'd first been brought here.

Forcing her sluggish mind to focus, Hayley knew that couldn't be true. The Iceman killed his victims on the first of the month so if it had been December first when she was abducted, and the Iceman kept her somewhere else that first night, bringing her here on the second, then the third was the day of the first visit, of which she'd now had seven, then today must be the tenth.

On the first visit she'd taken water and light, on the second she'd opted for food, then a bucket that she could use as a toilet, on the fourth she'd taken a book to read, and then a change of clothes, and on the sixth water to clean herself. On yesterday's visit she'd upset the Iceman. Hungry, thirsty and exhausted, her body quickly wasting away to nothing, and still worked up from the police officer's visit to the restaurant, she'd lost it when the trapdoor opened. Begging and pleading for her release, she had screamed and cried and banged her still battered hands against the concrete walls.

The Iceman had not been impressed with her outburst.

After giving her a long lecture on respect the Iceman had told her as punishment she would not receive a gift that day. The Iceman also made her give up everything that she had, lowering a bucket down into her cell the Iceman had demanded that she give up the book, the bucket and any food and water she had left. As incentive to do as she was told the Iceman had pulled out the gun and shot several rounds into the floor, one narrowly missing her foot, another whizzing so close to her arm she could feel the rush of wind as it went past.

To further increase the punishment the Iceman had also turned out the lights, once again plunging her into darkness. This last penalty proving too much, Hayley had burst into hysterical sobs as the Iceman closed and locked the door. Trapped all alone in the pitch-blackness too much to bear, she had cried until her whole body ached and she could hardly breathe.

Now hours later she had calmed back down, her spirit and desire to escape flaming anew as she plotted how she could get herself out of this. Earlier, she couldn't quite remember which day; she had tried hauling all the furniture to the edge of the circular room closest to the hatch lid. Then maneuvering the table onto the bed, and balancing the chair on top of the table she had climbed up in the desperate hope that she might be able to reach the top. What good it would do she wasn't sure, since the Iceman always kept her locked in. Her tower made it nowhere near the roof and building it had sapped most of her remaining strength.

Hearing the soft sounds of the Iceman's arrival, since her ability to see had been taken away by the lack of light her other senses had sprung further to life. Hayley wearily pushed herself to her feet, her head swimming and for a second she felt dangerously close to passing out. Pressing her eyes firmly closed as she heard the Iceman lift the small door, knowing that the sudden light would send her eyesight into disarray. As it was even with her eyes closed the light shone brightly against her lids.

When she felt that sufficient time had passed Hayley opened her eyes to see the Iceman peering curiously down at her. Sometimes the Iceman seemed quite sane, for a serial killer anyway, but sometimes it was pure madness in the eyes that studied her as though she were some sort of foreign specimen.

Today though she knew what she had to say if she were going to keep herself alive, the Iceman was always babbling about respect and it's importance and the lack of it in modern society. If respecting her captor would provide her with enough food and water to survive another day then respect is what she would offer.

"I'm sorry," she called up, her voice had changed over the last ten days so that she almost didn't recognize it. "About yesterday."

The Iceman said nothing, simply stared down at her.

"I shouldn't have become so emotional, it was disrespectful."

Upon hearing her words the Iceman's eyes lit up.

"I don't know what came over me," Hayley continued. "You have given me food and water and so much more than I deserve. I should have been more grateful. I'm very, very sorry."

For one terrifying second Hayley thought that the Iceman wasn't going to buy her phony apology and leave without giving her anything. Vivid images of her own dead body, bones protruding from starvation, sprung to mind and she almost lost control of her emotions, managing to reign them back in at the last second.

But then the Iceman spoke, "I am please to hear that you recognize your mistake. You are looking thin, I will give you food and water, but to make sure that you appreciate just how important it is to be respectful, I will not give you light."

Controlling a wince, Hayley knew that she could live without light; she could not however live without food and water. "Thank you," she forced the words from her mouth.

The Iceman lowered down the bucket containing a single bottle of water, a loaf of bread and small jar of strawberry jelly. Removing the items from the bucket and placing them on the table as the Iceman pulled the bucket back up.

"Until tomorrow," the Iceman said as way of a goodbye and with a thud let the trapdoor slam shut.

Hayley listened as the lock slid into place and almost welcomed the darkness that hid reality from her eyes. Finding the food and water she grabbed hold of it and took it with her back to the bed. After eating a slice of bread and drinking a couple of mouthfuls of water she pulled the blankets over her head and tried to be happy that she would live to see another day.

* * * * *

7:28 P.M.

Winter figured she had a half hour before her stepfather returned home. Thirty minutes to find something that would convince the police that Grant Hamilton was the Iceman. She had seen the news, seen the papers, seen that they were claiming that Jamie Presland from her mom's restaurant was the killer but Winter wasn't convinced.

Jamie was disgusting, it was true, she hated him, hated being around him, hated the way he drooled all over her, always pressuring her to have sex with him. She could believe that he might have killed that girl in the alley in a rage because she fought back, but there was no way she could believe that he was a vicious and meticulous serial killer. To be honest she knew he wasn't smart enough to have committed the intricate crimes; the planning and execution of them seemed too far above him.

Now more than ever she needed solid proof if she was going to convince the police that they had the wrong guy. Winter didn't know why she felt so positive that her stepfather was the serial killer, it was just a feeling that she couldn't shake no matter how hard she tried.

Down on her knees in the small den at the back of the house, a room used only by Grant, Winter was desperate to find what she needed. A huge flat screen TV covered most of one wall, a couch and two recliners aimed at the screen. A desk sat at the back of the room, an empty space on top where Grant's laptop usually lived. Getting to work on the top drawer, which appeared to be full of old receipts and credit card bills, deciding there might be something incriminating on one of them Winter pulled out a handful and started to skim through them.

Half way through the sack when a hand grabbed her sweater at the back of her neck, yanking her off the floor and pressing against her windpipe.

"What do you think you're doing?" a voice boomed in her ear.

Clawing at her neck, trying to draw in a full breath, before she could she was flying across the room, crashing into the wall and crumpling to the ground, pain racketing through her body. Grant loomed over her, his face a contorted mask of rage, fury vibrating from every fiber of his body.

"What do you think you're doing," he roared again, slamming his boot into her ribs.

"I . . . I . . ." Winter couldn't think of a convincing lie.

"You were snooping through my things," he supplied for her, delivering another blow to her already aching chest.

"I'm sorry," each breath she drew felt like fire burning in her lungs.

"What were you looking for?" yanking her back up to her feet and pinning her against the wall, lifting her so that she couldn't touch the floor.

"Nothing," she whimpered, trying to wiggle free from his grasp.

Backhanding her across the face. "You're lying. Tell me."

Determined not to let him break her. "Nothing, I wasn't looking for anything."

Ramming a fist into her stomach and letting go of her, the air knocked from her lungs, Winter dropped to the floor like a sack of rocks. Vision fading in and out, pulse drumming in her ears, fighting the urge to throw up, eventually the world came back into focus and she realized that Grant was no longer there.

Unable to stand Winter dragged herself across the carpet towards the door, halfway there when her stepfather returned, stamping a foot against her wrist with such force she was sure she felt the bones crunch.

"Going somewhere, darling," he drawled as he grabbed hold of her leg and dragged her back to the wall, heaving her to her feet and holding her up against it. Her injured arm hanging limply by her side, Grant pinned her other arm to the wall with a hand clamped around her wrist and pressed his hips against her preventing her from striking out with her legs.

"You're gonna tell me what you were looking for," Grant snarled. "Or things are going to get real messy."

That was when Winter caught sight of the bright blue boxing glove that encased his right hand. Grant loved boxing, he loved doing it, he loved watching it, he loved talking about it, and unfortunately for her he was good at it, knowing just how to deliver a well-placed blow.

"Please, Grant," she wheezed, trying vainly to get free, but her stepfather was surprisingly strong considering he was so lean.

Without a word he pulled up her sweater exposing the smooth

white skin on her stomach, resting the glove against her. Moving it up and down, the smooth material gliding easily across her flesh, then he pulled his arm back and plowed it into her stomach. The world span, and she threw up, spluttering and coughing, as she tried to draw in enough air to fill her lungs.

Bringing the glove to his lips he kissed it then leaned in close and at first Winter thought he was going to try and kiss her, but instead he whispered in her ear, "I always get what I want."

Forcing away the pain. "It was nothing," she whispered.

Moving the glove to the side of stomach, just above the bottom of her ribcage, Grant delivered another blow to her ribs, then another and another until Winter could feel her bones cracking and splintering under the pressure.

Eventually she couldn't take it any longer. "Alright," she screamed.

Grant stopped, a sinister smile flicking across his face. "Go ahead," he said cordially.

"Alright," she repeated, biting her lip to keep from crying out in pain. "I was trying to look for proof."

"Proof of what?"

Breathing harshly, "Proof that you're cheating on my mother."

Staring at her in shocked silence for a moment, then Grant burst into peels of laughter. Releasing his grip Winter slumped back against the wall, struggling to stay upright, as her stepfather doubled over, snorting.

Finally calming down Grant stared into her eyes, Winter wanted to look away but it was like her stepfather's eyes were magnets, drawing her in against her will. "You will never touch my things again, do I make myself clear?"

Winter bobbled her head.

With a quick snap of his wrist he punched her one last time in the shoulder then stalked from the room.

Watching him go Winter slid slowly down to the floor, cradling her broken wrist, each breath feeling like her lungs were full of thumbtacks, spitting blood from her mouth as she tenderly fingered her bruised abdomen. If there had been any doubt in her mind before it was now completely eradicated, her stepfather, Grant Hamilton, was most certainly the Iceman.

DECEMBER 11TH

8:49 P.M.

"Guess what?" Tessa said to Parker as he pulled the car into the parking lot.

"What?" he cast her a sideways glance before maneuvering his SUV between two others.

"I called her back," knowing Parker would understand who she was talking about.

"You did?" unable to keep the surprise from his voice.

Laughing, "Michelle was just as surprised as you are."

"You really called her back?" he asked as he turned off the engine.

"Mm hm."

"Why? What made you change your mind?"

"I told you I wasn't going to let the past rule my life anymore, so I called Michelle and we talked. It was great," she said more to herself than Parker. "Just like old times."

Michelle was one of her friends from school, one of the few friends left alive after Dylan Riley's bloody rampage. After the night she had been forced to shoot Dylan, overwhelmed with guilt about the death of her friends and the part she felt she had played in it, it had been too difficult to deal with those who were left. And so she had refused to see them, talk to them, email them, or contact them in any way. At first Michelle and the others had rung regularly but thanks to the magic of caller ID Tessa knew when not to answer the phone.

Michelle had been the most persistent, and it was her last phone call that had changed Tessa's mind. After Daniel had arrived in town she had felt like she was loosing control again, all the loneliness and terror and helplessness she had felt as a child came rushing back and then Michelle had called. That night as she'd lain awake in bed, as she had so many nights before, she realized just how much she was missing out on by letting the past rule her present and her future. Then, of course, she had felt guilty for turning her back on her friends when they had needed her the most, it had taken several days to build up enough courage to return Michelle's call.

"That's great, Tess," Parker smiled.

"I don't know if things can ever go back to the way they were before, but at least we're talking again, and we'll take things slow and just see what happens," Tessa felt a peace settle over her that she had never felt before at any time in her life.

Climbing from the car Tessa noticed it was snowing, not a lot, just soft flurries that seemed to hang in the air before tumbling quietly to the ground. When she was a child she had loved nothing more than to be out in the snow, running through it, rolling in it, letting it cover her in a thick white blanket. It had been something she and Daniel used to do together, before he left.

Refusing to think about her brother tonight, she tilted her face to the sky, closed her eyes and let the snowflakes softly settle there.

"What are you doing?" Parker chuckled as he came around to her side of the car.

"I love the snow," she replied. "It's so soft, so white, so perfect, so beautiful." Enjoying the tingling in her cheeks that each snowflake left behind as it melted.

Taking her face in his hands, Parker gently kissed away the last lingering snowflakes, and then his mouth found hers, his kiss soft and unassuming. Tentatively, taking a big chance for her, she opened her lips and let his tongue enter. If he was surprised he didn't show it, one hand moving to the small of her back and pressing her tighter against him, his other tangling itself in her hair. Her own hands started to move, one resting lightly against his buttocks, the other sliding under his sweater and tracing the lines of his chest through his shirt. In that moment they were just a young couple in love. There was no serial killer on the loose, there were no haunted pasts, no fear or trepidation, just pure love.

"Come on," Parker pulled away, his breathing heavy, eyes hot and bothered, he took her hand and began to tug her towards the restaurant.

Tessa knew that Parker was up to something. He had been nervous and jumpy for days now, even more so since he had made the reservation at this seafood place a couple of days ago. Tessa was pretty sure she knew what was keeping him so on edge but she didn't want to ruin what he obviously wanted to be a surprise.

"It's amazing," Parker was saying.

"What is?"

"The aquarium at the restaurant. It's so big," Parker was wound up tighter than a kid at a fairground. "And it has so many fish in it. Gorgeous ones, I wonder where Cece Hamilton found them, as far as I know there's no tropical fish shops around here." Parker loved fish, loved catching them and eating them, and most of all he loved watching them; he found it soothing.

"Maybe you could ask her," Tessa suggested, Parker had been talking for months about getting an aquarium for his house.

Cringing, "I don't think I'm one of her favorite people right now, especially since her computer is still at CSU. She's already called a dozen times in the last couple of days asking when she can have it back, reminding everyone that she needs it for work. Each time she calls she's like a hundred times more worked up than she was the time before."

"Doesn't she realize that her computer is part of an active police investigation into a serial . . .?" she trailed off as she felt the change in Parker's demeanor. "What?"

Hand straying to his gun. "Over there," he murmured with a tilt of his head. "I think there's someone there. Someone watching us."

"You think it's . . .?"

"Maybe," Parker answered before she finished. "Stay here."

Releasing her hand he started towards the side of the building where he thought he had seen the figure lurking.

"Parker," she called softly after him. "If it is the Iceman then you shouldn't go after him alone." Tessa knew she couldn't handle it if anything happened to Parker.

"I'll be fine, if I wait he might be gone, this could be our one chance to catch him." Starting off at a jog and calling over his shoulder, "Go inside and wait for me."

As she watched him disappear around the side of the seafood restaurant something moved in her peripheral vision. Spinning around Tessa was positive she saw someone slinking along the edge of the car park, keeping care to stay low.

Hesitating for only a split second Tessa took off after the figure, she knew Parker would be furious with her for following a potential suspect on her own, but right now she didn't see another choice. Reaching inside her purse for her cell phone, if she could stay out of sight but keep on the man's trail then she could lead Parker straight to him. If indeed it was the Iceman.

Creeping closer, and just like the man she was pursuing taking care to stay low and use the cars for shelter, she saw that the figure was dressed all in black, was close to six foot and lean. Heart thundering as she realized the man did indeed fit the description of the serial killer.

Glancing down to dial Parker's number when she looked back up the figure in black was gone. Startled she stood up straight and quickly scanned the parking lot but saw no sign of the man she had been following. Annoyed at herself for losing sight of him she decided the best course of action was to call Parker and tell him what she'd seen. Who knows maybe he had been following the killer and she had been simply following a restaurant patron returning to their car.

As she was bringing the phone to her ear it felt as though she were struck by a bolt of lightening, the phone flew from her hand, she tumbled down into the snow, and knew no more.

* * * * *

9:03 P.M.

With a muttered curse Parker had to admit that he had lost whoever it was he'd been chasing. Usually Parker never swore, while living in the last foster home he'd ever stayed in his foster parents

128

had been adamantly against it. Deficient in teaching their only biological son not to torture children, and yet resolute in insisting the children in their care not curse. Any child that uttered anything even vaguely considered a 'swear word' would receive a swift punishment, usually consisting of no dinner, a mouth washed out with soap and a night spent alone in the basement.

Returning his gun to its holster and backtracking to the restaurant disappointed that he had not been able to apprehend what he believed to be Jamie Presland. He'd followed the figure into the alley but once he got there the man he'd been following seemed to simply vanish. Making his way up and down the entire alley, onto which backed at least forty businesses, he had checked behind every dumpster, tried every door, but had ultimately come up empty.

Parker was becoming tired of losing to the Iceman. Yesterday had yielded another fruitless search at Jamie's mother's old house, and they were still no closer to locating him or Hayley Geoffries. The press had somehow discovered Jamie's name, splashing it across the front page of all the papers, screaming it in the headlines of every news program. Jamie had to know that they would be hunting him down, leaving no stone unturned in their search for him and his victim. Soon he would lose his ability to move about freely, he would also eventually lose his hideout, they would track it down and whether he was there at the time or not sooner or later they would find him. As Wyatt had pointed out yesterday the problem was if Jamie felt like he was backed into a corner then he might panic and kill Hayley before the first of the month.

J.J. was right. The Iceman could think he was invincible, could think all he wanted that he was smarter than the police and that he could evade capture indefinitely. But that would be the source of his undoing; that would be what would lead them straight to him in the end, his arrogance, his underestimating them.

On the plus side Parker felt his body heat as he thought about Tessa's uncharacteristic display in the parking lot. In the end he'd had to pull away quickly before he reached the point of no return, he could hardly throw her down on the snowy ground in a public lot, rip off her clothes and do it right then and there. Knowing Tessa's history he had been making sure to take things slow with her, and was rewarded as bit by bit she opened herself up to him. Things hadn't progressed much past kissing and some careful roaming, Tessa usually tensed up when things went much further. Even with her earlier display Parker still wasn't convinced she was ready to take the next step, and as much as that subsequent leap thrilled him, Tessa was worth the wait.

As he swung open the restaurant's doors he felt the butterflies come back. Tonight was the night he'd been planning for the last six months, dreaming of for years, and spent most of his life believing would never come. Parker was almost positive that Tessa had an inkling of what he was going to do tonight but she hadn't said anything.

Scanning the inside of the restaurant he saw no sign of her and his nervous butterflies quickly turned to worms of dread. Surely Tessa wouldn't have gone after the man he'd seen herself, but then he reminded himself whom he was talking about. Tessa Micah was nothing if not impulsive, and she most certainly would have followed the figure, even though she knew there was a chance he was a serial killer, without a second thought.

"Uh, Detective Bell."

"Mrs. Hamilton."

Somehow she read the panic in his face, her own becoming immediately anxious. "What's wrong?"

"Have you seen a young woman, she would have come in about five or ten minutes ago. She's got really white blonde hair, curly, she's short, wearing a blue dress, white coat, blue scarf." Seeing no recognition in Cece Hamilton's grey eyes, "You haven't seen her have you."

"No, I'm sorry," shaking her head. "I'll check with the other staff though, maybe someone else has seen her."

Calling over his shoulder as he headed for the door, "Thanks, I'm gonna check outside, let me know if she comes in."

Once outside Parker scanned the area, but saw no signs of life, the whole world seemed to have gone quiet. Maybe, he thought, Tessa realized she had left something in the car and gone back to get it, deciding that was at least a place to start he took off at a fast jog for the parking lot. He was almost positive, he assured himself, that Tessa would have called him if she saw anything suspicious, and if she had seen the man he'd been chasing and decided to follow him then she would definitely have let him know.

Forcing himself to keep calm, Tessa would be fine, she was always fine, and she'd probably be mad as hell that he'd been worrying about her, she hated when he did . . .

Halting abruptly as he caught sight of a body lying facedown and motionless in the snow.

Dread pooling in his stomach as he took a few steps closer.

The body was small and white, blending in with the snow.

Another step closer revealed a puddle of pink snow around the unnaturally still body. Nearby lay an open cell phone, a shredded white coat, and a blue purse.

Tessa's purse.

Springing into action with a horrified gasp, Parker ran to her and dropped to his knees in the snow at her side, quaking fingers reaching for her neck seeking a pulse. Almost passing out with relief when he felt it fluttering weakly beneath his fingertips. The brief respite from his panic when he realized Tessa was alive ended quickly as he begun to check her for injuries.

Easing her carefully onto her back he saw a deep, and heavily bleeding, knife wound in her arm, quickly running his hands up and down her body he found no other injuries. Grabbing for her scarf, which was still coiled around her neck, he wrapped it tightly around her bleeding arm. Blood quickly soaked through the thin blue material so Parker unwound his own thicker woolen black and white striped scarf and tied it firmly over the top of Tessa's.

Keeping one hand pressed to the wound he fumbled with his other for his cell phone. Beginning to dial when he heard a noise behind him, dropping the phone to reach for his gun, unlikely as it was that Tessa's attacker would return he was taking no chances.

The face that appeared from around the corner of an SUV was not that of a killer but Cece Hamilton's. "Detective Bell, did you find . . ." she trailed off and stopped short at the sight of the scene before her.

"Call an ambulance," Parker yelled to her, his attention reverting to Tessa, whose skin was starting to become tinted with blue, she was as cold as the snow in which she lay. Parker was furious at himself that because of his phobia of wearing a jacket he had nothing to wrap her in.

Turning to Cece Hamilton who was still frozen in place, her face as white as Tessa's. "Mrs. Hamilton," he called trying to keep his voice calm as he noticed blood seeping through the scarf. "I need you to stay focused okay, I need you to call an ambulance and I need something to warm her up."

"What . . . what happened?" unable to take her eyes off Tessa's unconscious body as she stumbled forward, slipping off her jacket as she came.

"Someone attacked her," taking the jacket from Cece's outstretched hand he wrapped it around Tessa as Mrs. Hamilton dialed her phone, her gaze still riveted to Tessa.

"Mmm," Tessa moaned beneath him.

"Tessa? Honey, can you hear me?"

Tessa nodded.

"Sweetheart, I need you to open your eyes for me," stroking her cheek.

Eyelids fluttering slowly open, she looked dazed and disoriented.

"Hey," he soothed. "I'm right here, everything's gonna be okay, an ambulance is on it's way."

"What happened?" she mumbled weakly, struggling to sit up.

Keeping her still with a firm hand on her shoulder. "Stay still, you've lost quite a bit of blood," he said the word before he thought about it and immediately Tessa's eyes widened, her head turning towards her injury as though noticing it for the first time.

"Blood?" she stammered her breath started to catch in little wheezing gasps; Tessa was terrified of the sight of blood.

Catching hold of her face with his free hand he angled it so she was looking at him. "Don't look at it, honey," he tried to calm her. "Just concentrate on me."

Trying to restore her ragged breathing, with a slight nod at her injured arm she asked, "How?"

"You were attacked, you don't remember?"

Scrunching her eyes closed as she thought. "I was following someone," she began haltingly. "I tried to call you but something hit me . . . it was like . . . like being struck by lightening . . ."

Pulling her shaking body into his arms, supporting her against his knee and holding her tightly, for his own sake as much as hers. "Shh, it's okay, it's okay," he whispered against her hair.

"I think I saw his face . . . but I can't . . . I can't remember . . ." she was becoming agitated again. "I can't remember what it looked like."

"It's okay, it's okay," he soothed. "Just try to rest," he pressed her face against his chest and stroked her hair.

Tessa reached with the hand of her uninjured arm and pulled his arms tighter around her. Her small hand wrapping around his thumb the way a newborn's little hand curled around it's mother's finger, and held onto him as though her life depended on it.

They remained this way until the wailing sirens signaled the approaching ambulance and police cars. As the ambulance came to a stop beside them Parker stood and gently lifted Tessa, who had now fallen silent, into his arms and carried her to it, setting her on the stretcher that the paramedics pulled from the back.

"I'm gonna be right back, okay?" he told Tessa giving her hand a reassuring squeeze.

Eyes still closed she nodded, and he left her in the capable hands of the EMT's to go speak with Wyatt who had just arrived.

"What happened?" his partner asked, not bothering to lock his car as he came running over and tried to catch a glimpse of Tessa. "Is she okay?"

Now that Tessa wasn't here Parker let the panic that had been bubbling just beneath the surface spill over. "Someone attacked her."

"What? How?"

"We were walking from the car to the restaurant, I thought I saw someone, over by the side wall," he gestured wildly. "I told Tessa to wait for me inside while I went to check it out, I thought there was a possibility that it could be Jamie Presland, but you know what

Tessa's like. The guy must have snuck around the building when he saw me coming, tried to get away through the parking lot, Tessa said she was following someone and then it was like she got struck by lightening."

"Struck by lightening? Maybe she was Tasered?" Wyatt asked.

Parker wasn't listening. "I left her alone, Wyatt, and he hurt her, I found her unconscious and bleeding in the snow," he couldn't shake the picture from his mind.

Wyatt put a hand on his shoulder. "She's gonna be okay, Parker," he reassured. "Did she see who attacked her?"

Rubbing his shaking hands across his face he saw that the hand that had been keeping pressure on Tessa's wound was stained with her blood. Deliberately putting his hands behind his back and thinking of Tessa's fear of blood a fresh wave of terror over what could have happened to her washed over him. Calming himself with difficulty, "she said she couldn't remember what he looked like."

"But she saw him?"

"Yeah she did."

"How sure are you that it was Jamie Presland who attacked her?"

"I only saw him from a distance but . . ."

"But you think it was him?"

"I'm almost positive."

"So he's still in the . . ."

"Detectives?" one of the paramedics called out.

Heart in his throat Parker bolted for the ambulance. "What is it? What's happened to her?"

Tessa's eyes were closed, an oxygen mask covered her face, an IV in her arm, the paramedics had removed Cece Hamilton's coat and covered her with a blanket.

"It's alright, she's okay," the medic assured him soothingly. "We gave her a mild sedative, but she's okay. Really."

Taking a calming breath as he reached for Tessa's hand. "What is it then? Why'd you call us?"

Exchanging looks the EMT's hesitated.

"What?" Parker repeated panic building quickly at the looks on their faces.

"The wound on her arm," one of them begun. "We didn't see it at first, it just looked like a knife wound, but then when we cleaned it up and stitched it . . ." he trailed off.

"What?"

"Maybe it's easier to just show you," the other medic suggested with a sigh, and with a gloved hand he gently removed the bandage from Tessa's arm.

Both he and Wyatt gasped when they saw what it was the paramedics were talking about and Parker automatically squeezed Tessa's hand, a gesture she returned weakly.

In the flesh on her arm the Iceman had carved them a message.

A warning.

Three letters.

I C U.

DECEMBER 12ᵀᴴ

3:11 A.M.

Tuning out the mumbling voices from the front seat, Tessa tried to clear her mind and think, attempting to recall the face of the man who had attacked her. It had been a familiar face, one she had seen before but that she couldn't remember when or from where.

Her head felt like it was full of cotton wool and her arm was throbbing with a beating pain that not even the drugs the doctor had given her seemed able to dull. Add to that the fact that it had been a long night and she was finding it almost impossible to focus on anything for more than a second.

After the paramedics had stitched her arm, as per her instructions so that she could avoid a trip to the hospital, she had tried to convince Parker to take her home but he had insisted that she be checked out properly at the hospital. So they'd ridden there in the ambulance, and she'd sat patiently while a doctor had looked her over. However when Parker, Skylar, the doctor, plus Casey and J.J. who had both showed up upon hearing what had happened, had all ganged up on her to try to convince her to spend the night she had told them they could either drive her home or she'd catch a cab.

Currently they were in Skylar's car, a few minutes away from Parker's house, and the promise of a hot drink and bed were tantalizingly close. Parker and Skylar were babbling away in hushed voices in the front seat, while Tessa closed her eyes and tried to rest. She knew that they were talking about the Iceman case, Parker was positive that it was Jamie Presland who had attacked her in the parking lot, and that they didn't want to worry her by including her in the conversation.

Fingers of her left hand reaching across to lightly trace the wound on her right arm. It had taken a lot of cajoling to convince Parker to tell her about the message carved in her skin. Shivering violently at the thought of someone using a knife to write in her flesh as she lay unconscious in the snow, shaking harder as she thought about the message. I C U. I see you. Apparently the Iceman wanted them to know that he was nearby and that he was watching them.

Trembling as she thought of the killer still out there, continuing to hurt people until someone stopped him, and she was more convinced than ever that the Iceman was not Jamie Presland. She couldn't explain how she knew she just did. Parker kept assuring her over and over again that they would catch the Iceman before he hurt anyone else. Marty himself was working the scene where she had been attacked and Maisy had stopped by the hospital to collect her clothes.

"Tessa?"

Opening her eyes to see Parker's worried face studying her, and saw that they had reached home.

"You okay?" he asked her as he pressed the back of his hand to her forehead. "You look a little flushed, the doctor said we had to be careful that your arm doesn't get infected."

Irritably pushing his hand away. "I'm fine, Parker, just tired."

"Come on, goldilocks, lets get you inside," Skylar jumped in, taking her hand and gently pulling her out of the car.

Swaying unsteadily on her feet, the effects of the Taser and the drugs that she'd been given had taken their toll, leaving her completely drained. Luckily Skylar was beside her and wrapped a steadying arm around her waist, keeping her upright.

"Tessa!" a voice screeched from behind them as a car door slammed and feet pounded the pavement. "Are you okay?"

Daniel appeared before her grabbing at her and almost sending her toppling to the ground.

Before she could answer Parker demanded, "What are *you* doing here?"

Ignoring him, "Tessa, what happened?"

"I'm fine, Daniel," she told him wearily, pulling Skylar's coat tighter around herself, the hospital scrubs they'd given her to wear gave no protection from the icy wind.

Giving her a once over he raised a suspicious eyebrow and turned on Parker. "Where were you when she got attacked?"

"Where was I?" Parker echoed, fury crackling from every pore. "I was chasing down a murderer! I told Tessa to wait inside . . ."

"So you're saying it's my sister's fault that she got attacked?" Daniel queried angrily.

"No, I'm saying I was trying to catch a man that's already killed five women and is holding another girl hostage. Anyway," Parker snapped warily, "How did you even find out what happened?"

Tessa too had been wondering how Daniel had learnt of her attack, but right now she was too tired to care. Starting towards the house, Skylar at her side, Parker and Daniel stopped their bickering long enough to give chase.

"Tessie, wait," Daniel called, following them up the steps to the door.

"Hey, buddy, you're not welcome here," Parker blocked his entry.

"Get out of my way," Daniel shoved past him and followed her and Skylar down the hallway.

Dropping onto the couch Tessa let herself sink down into its softness and rested her head against the back pillows, it was heaven.

"I'll make you some tea," Skylar told her as he disappeared into the kitchen.

"They said that he, the man who attacked you, that he cut some sort of message into your arm," Daniel winced as he dropped to his knees beside the couch.

"Who told you about what happened?" Parker asked again.

"Who cares," Daniel yelled at him. "Tess, are you okay? I was so worried when I heard, I went to the hospital but I just missed you so I came straight here."

"Have you been stalking us?" Parker grabbed Daniel's arm and yanked him to his feet. "Following us around? Is that how you found out?"

"What? No. Of course not," Daniel looked outraged at the suggestion. "I used to know one of the paramedics who treated Tess, when he realized she was my sister he called me."

Trying to block out their voices, which were only adding to the headache that was slowly taking over her brain. Skylar draped a soft, woolly blanket over her shoulders, handed her a steaming cup of tea and started to rub her shoulders. Taking a sip of the tea, the feeling of the hot liquid sliding down her throat started to warm her cold, aching body.

"How could you let this happen?" Daniel snarled at Parker. "I thought that you loved her, but you leave her alone to go running off after a serial killer? How stupid are you?"

"How stupid am I? What was I supposed to do, let a killer get away? How could I know that he was going to go after . . ."

Cutting him off, "If you really loved Tessa then you should have been protecting her . . ."

Now it was Parker's turn to cut Daniel off, "And if you really loved Tessa then you never would have left her."

Throwing his hands in the air in frustration. "How many times do I have to tell you that the reason I left *was* to protect Tessa? It was the only way I knew to keep her safe."

Unable to take anymore of the boy's squabbling Tessa turned to Skylar, "Please make them go away," she begged.

"Come on, guys," Skylar inserted himself between them. "She needs to rest not listen to you two behaving like preschoolers. Maybe it's time you left," he suggested to Daniel.

"Why should I go? Tessie's my sister," Daniel frowned.

"Because it's my house," Parker replied smugly.

"Well I'm not going anywhere until . . ."

"Please, Daniel," her voice dangerously close to a whimper.

Face softening and crossing over to her Daniel pressed a gentle kiss to her temple. "Okay, I'm going, but I'm going to call later to check on you," he declared determinedly, casting a challenging glare Parker's way. Pausing at the living room door he fixed Parker with a stare, "If you let anything else happen to her . . ." leaving the threat hanging unuttered in the air.

Parker ignored Daniel and waited until they heard the front door close before he came to her. "I'm sorry about that, Tess," he said as he brushed at the hair on her forehead.

"So you should be," she told him, pulling away. "I don't like to see you like that, Parker. Daniel was worried, you didn't have to make a scene."

"And he didn't have to come back here after you told him to stay away," Parker said in a voice bordering on a whine. "I'm sorry, Tess," he said more seriously. "But I was terrified tonight. Seeing you lying there in the snow, unconscious, and then finding out what he did to you." Exhaling deeply, "Daniel was right, it was my fault, I shouldn't have left you alone."

Reaching for his hand. "It wasn't your fault," Tessa encouraged. "I should have waited inside like you asked me to." Too tired to say more Tessa let her eyes slide closed, feeling sleep crashing at the edges of her mind like waves at the seashore.

"I'm going to go too, I'll see you later," she heard Skylar announce quietly.

Then Parker was scooping her up into his arms, her head drooping sideways to rest against his shoulder as he carried her up to bed. Managing to hold onto consciousness as Parker laid her down and whispered that he loved her, she thought she murmured back that she loved him too, but an image popped into her head. Tessa tried to catch hold of it before it vanished but exhaustion took over and before she knew it she was fast asleep.

* * * * *

6:38 A.M.

Every bone and muscle in her body felt like it was full of pins.

Everything hurt. Breathing, swallowing, lying, sitting, moving, being still.

Winter thought the pain would have subsided in the thirty-six hours or so since her stepfather had beaten her up.

As the saying went there was always a silver lining to every cloud and hers was no exception. The idea to lie to Grant and tell him that she was looking for proof that he was cheating on her mother had come to her at the last second. If she hadn't thought of saying that then Winter was positive she would not be alive at this second.

As it was he had left her badly injured.

After Grant had left her barely conscious on the den floor, she had dragged herself to the phone and called an ambulance. Not her mother. Winter and Cece had never been close and now Winter didn't know how to explain everything to her mom so for the moment she thought it was best to say nothing. In the end it had been the hospital that called her mom not Winter.

Instead of telling the paramedics, who had arrived shortly after her stepfather left, the truth she had told them that she'd tripped and fallen down the stairs. Winter wasn't positive that they believed her nor was she sure the doctors at the hospital believed her story. She was pretty sure that they thought she had been beaten, and most likely by someone she knew, probably a family member or boyfriend. The doctor who had treated her had insisted she speak with a social worker before he would allow Winter to go home with her mother.

Lying to her mom and the doctor's felt weird. Her other stepfathers over the years had all been losers but none of them had ever laid a hand on her, and as emotionally detached at her mother was she had never resorted to physical violence, so Winter had never had to keep a secret such as this.

Grant's attack had left her with a broken arm, a broken cheekbone, two chipped teeth, several cracked ribs, and a badly swollen abdomen. At first the doctors had been worried about internal bleeding, had spoken about surgery, but an ultrasound had shown that nothing was ruptured, just bruised, the only lucky break she'd had in the whole situation.

If she was going to prove beyond reasonable doubt that her stepfather Grant Hamilton was the Iceman and not Jamie Presland then she had to keep searching. Nothing was going to stop her. Grant's attack had only strengthened her resolve, made her more determined than ever to wipe that smug smile off his face and turn him in as the Iceman.

Although Winter had to admit that even aside from being beaten up the plan wasn't going so well so far. She had the gloves and the fact that they grew holly but that was it. Before her stepfather's arrival her search of the den had been completely fruitless, she hadn't found anything even remotely helpful.

At least she was alone again. Yesterday even her apathetic mother had made an effort to be nearby and as loving as was possible for her to be. Cece had spent the day at home, fielding only a half dozen or so phone calls from the restaurant, she hadn't fussed as mothers were apt to do but at least she had made the effort. When he realized that she didn't intend to turn him in, Grant had thought it best to make himself scarce, and late last night he had headed off to work.

Yesterday Winter had enjoyed having her mom around but today she was grateful to have some peace and quiet and another opportunity to search the house. An idea had occurred to her while she'd been lying in a hospital bed waiting to be examined; maybe she was going about this all wrong. She kept trying to find proof that her stepfather had committed the murders of four young women but maybe there *was* no proof that tied him to those crimes. But Winter had been forgetting something. Something important.

The Iceman was currently holding his next victim captive.

Where? No one knew.

But Winter had an advantage. She knew Grant and if she could figure out where he was holding Hayley Geoffries then she would have all the proof she needed to prove to the police, to her mother and to the world that Grant Hamilton was the Iceman.

* * * * *

10:41 P.M.

"Are we sure he's in there?"

"Witnesses say he went in and never came back out. So unless the guy has magical powers and can turn himself invisible, then yeah, he's in there," J.J. explained.

Parker was tense. Everyone was tense.

The Iceman case had been going on for over a year. Five women were dead, two others had been attacked, one was still being held captive, and this was the first time they had actually come close to catching their guy,

They were all on edge.

It had been a really long day. Parker had hardly slept at all after they arrived home from the hospital. Once Daniel and Wyatt had left and he'd carried Tessa upstairs she had practically passed out from exhaustion after whispering that she loved him. He on the other hand had lain awake for hours, unable to shut off his brain. Unable to stop the images of Tessa in the snow, of what Jamie had done to her, of what he could have done to her, of what *he* would do to Jamie when he finally got his hands on him.

Tessa had slept for hours, awakening at eleven, screaming, from the grips of a nightmare. He'd been dozing at the time but had become instantly awake at the sound of Tessa's terrified shrieks. She'd told him that the nightmare was not like the ones that usually plagued her dreams, but an exact replica of one that she had dreamt only once before.

In the dream she had been stuck inside a giant puzzle, the pieces falling from the sky, her job had been to join the pieces together before someone died. Or more accurately, before someone was killed. For each second that it took her to complete the puzzle one person would be killed, the dead bodies left to leer at her, accusing her, blaming her. The puzzle was a face, a face she knew but couldn't remember, a face she had seen before but couldn't recall from where. A face that she was forced to put together to save innocent lives, but couldn't because she didn't know what it looked like.

Parker had listened intently, soothed and reassured her, told her that the dream was just a manifestation of fear from the attack and her guilt at not remembering his face. But Tessa was not to be consoled. She was positive that the face she was supposed to know needed to be recalled if they were to stop the Iceman serial killings. She was still convinced that Jamie Presland, while guilty of the murder of Phoebe Stein, was innocent of the deaths of Hannah Green, Greta Hamburg, Kelly Lorris and Stacey Wood.

Once again concerned about leaving Tessa alone, because of her injuries, because of Daniel, because of Jamie and his message that he was watching them, Parker had delivered her into the watchful care of Casey. Hoping that as well as keeping Tessa out of trouble it might also help to cheer her up, her resolve to focus on the future starting to crack after the attack.

A sharp jab in the ribs brining him back to the present as Wyatt gestured with his head at the house behind them. A house that belonged to Yvonne Waters, an ex-girlfriend of Jamie with whom he managed to stay close to over the years, although Parker suspected it was more like pity on Yvonne's part. At the moment Yvonne was overseas, but according to an acquaintance of both Jamie and Yvonne, she had given him a key to her place and an open invitation to stay there whenever he wanted.

Discretely canvassing the neighbors they had learnt that there was indeed a man fitting Jamie Presland's description staying in the house. Apparently he had first been seen two days ago, coincidently the day after they had found his last hideout at his mother's old house.

Earlier this evening knocking on Yvonne's door had yielded no response but neighbors assured them that they had not seen Jamie leave the house since he had arrived back there this morning.

Therefore he had to still be inside.

They hoped.

Silently they made their way towards the house. A huge, double-storey brick structure, with lots of big windows, the ones on the ground floor had flower baskets hanging from them. The front yard was small but immaculate, well fitted with thick, leafy hedges bordering the front fence, a couple of tall elms, and flowerbeds along the front of the house. Obviously Yvonne Waters took pride in her home.

With perfectly co-ordinated precision they entered the house, some through the front door and some through the back. Sweeping through the house room by room, covering one another, every trained eye surveying the area, looking for any signs of movement.

In the end they found him cowering in the shower in the upstairs bathroom, desperately holding the curtain closed as though it were a reinforced steel door that could keep out anybody. Parker was still downstairs when the call came out that Jamie Presland had been found and detained, and it took every ounce of his self-control not to run madly up the stairs and beat the guy to death for what he'd done to Tessa. Instead, along with Wyatt, he calmly made his way upstairs and into the bedroom where Jamie still lay on the soft cream carpet, hands cuffed behind his back.

Marching over to the man he stood for a second looking down at him. Wondering how such an insignificant looking person could cause all the terror and heartache that this monster had managed to inflict on his victims, their families and the community as a whole. As he pictured the man leaning over Tessa's limp body, carving his sick message into her skin, watching her bleed, he was overcome with hatred and before he knew what he was doing he was hauling the man to his feet and throwing him against the wall.

Feeling the eyes of his colleagues watching his every move, knowing what had happened and wanting to give him space, but ready to step in if the need arose, not wanting to see that case thrown out if Jamie later claimed his confession was beaten out of him. Pulling back a fist Parker was about to slam it into the guy's terrified face, when Tessa's face flitted before his eyes and he knew he couldn't do it.

Letting the fist drop to his side he studied Jamie's face. Light brown eyes, pupils dilated with fear, nose crooked probably as a result of a previous encounter with a fist, thin lips around yellow teeth, a high forehead and receding brown hair. His face was dotted with sweat, nostril's flared with each anxious breath, his whole body was quaking.

"Why did you do it?" Parker finally asked.

Jamie's eyes flicked around the room as though one of its other occupants might supply the answer. "I . . . I . . ." he stuttered.

"You killed five women, there has to be a reason why you would do that," Parker repeated.

"I had to," Jamie murmured, gaze dropping to the floor.

"Where's Hayley Geoffries?" Wyatt asked, coming to stand beside them.

Without looking up, "I don't know," Jamie answered.

"Of course you know," Parker lectured as one might to a recalcitrant child. "You mean you won't tell us."

"I don't know," Jamie repeated.

"You may as well help your case as best you can, show some compassion," Wyatt began reasonably. "You killed five women, you're getting a life sentence no matter what you say or do, at least be a man and tell us where she is. Don't make it six dead women, Jamie."

"I don't know," Jamie said again as though he were a CD stuck on repeat.

"Whether you tell us or not, we're gonna find her," Parker told him. "And she's going to identify you as the man who abducted her. Just like Elizabeth Landry is going to identify you as the man who tried to abduct her."

"I didn't," Jamie spoke in his monotone voice, completely devoid of emotion and remorse.

"Yes you did," Parker was surprised at the calm that had washed over him. "And you attacked my girlfriend last night, carved a message in her arm as she lay unconscious on the street after you Tasered her. You wrote on her arm like she was nothing more than a means to an end for you. I C U, I see you, well guess what now the whole world is going to see *you*. The whole world is going to see what a monster you are."

"Tell us, Jamie, tell us where Hayley is, don't let her die," Wyatt spoke softly, almost hypnotically.

"I don't know," Jamie said again.

"Are you trying to build an insanity defense?" Parker asked him disbelievingly, wondering why the guy couldn't just give it up. "It's over, Jamie. We've got you. Your little self-promoting reign of terror is over. You're going to spend the rest of your life in jail. We've got your little scrapbook, we've got the packet of white women's gloves you kept in your house, we've got the knife you used to slit Phoebe Stein's throat when your attempt to rape her was thwarted, and it has her blood on it. And we've got this . . ."

With that Parker spun him around and yanked his arms up, causing Jamie to grunt in pain. With the sleeve of his dirty green sweatshirt pulled up the scar on Jamie's wrist was plainly visible. "This scar, it ID's you as the man who tried to grab Elizabeth

Landry from an alley, an alley where you left your calling card. Your game's up."

As he started to lead Jamie away the man leant over and whispered in his ear, "It isn't over."

Parker laughed, "For you my friend everything is over."

DECEMBER 13TH

9:53 A.M.

Walking down the street, careful to remain inconspicuous, the Iceman was following one of four potential next victims. The girl, a seventeen-year-old named Belinda Merrington, was not the Iceman's first choice but most likely the back up in case anything went awry. The Iceman had already picked out the perfect next victim; she was young, pretty, tenacious and utterly and undeterredly determined.

Despite a slight hiccup in the plan with the police thinking that pathetic Jamie Presland was the Iceman, everything else was trundling along just as it should be. Hayley Geoffries was still tucked away and for the moment still fighting for every second of her life. She had also learnt her lesson, going out of her way to be respectful on the last couple of daily visits. The recognizance stage of the plan was also trundling along well; the Iceman already had a firm grasp on the next batch of potential victim's personalities and their daily habits and movements.

The Iceman had also taken care of Jamie Presland.

If the police wanted to think that he was the serial killer then they could think it, as long as it kept them out of the way. The Iceman had tracked down Jamie Presland's house before the police and planted plenty of evidence to convince them that they had their man. It hadn't been hard to do, Jamie had kept the knife he'd used in the attack on young Phoebe and hadn't even bothered to clean off the blood. The Iceman had added a scrapbook of newspaper articles about the crimes and a spare packet of white gloves that had been lying around.

It hadn't taken the Iceman long to find Jamie's hiding place, a quick survey of the house and the first thing that had stood out was the fresh white grout in the otherwise filthy bathroom wall. Prying open the space with the intention of hiding the scrapbook, the Iceman's own, inside it had been an unexpected bonus to find the blood-splattered knife. Leaving the stack of newspapers in the living room in the event that the police hadn't been able to find the hidey-hole then they would at least be hooked with the papers that were conspicuously missing every article about the Iceman murders.

At first the Iceman had been furious that someone else was going to take credit for everything but on closer consideration had decided that it might work for the best. It meant that the Iceman could continue on with things without having to be too concerned about drawing the police's attention. As long as Jamie was out there and the police were focused on finding him, then no one would be expecting the crimes to continue. Even if the police did manage to locate the ever-idiotic Jamie there was no way the guy was going to confess to a string of murders he hadn't committed.

As Belinda veered off into the library the Iceman snapped back to attention and also veered off and followed her inside, taking careful note of where she went before choosing a book and settling down to read. The library was bustling, quiet and warm it offered a welcome respite from the icy day that many had embraced. Elderly men and women read newspapers in the corner, poor college students tapped away at the computers, harried mothers with their toddlers poured over picture books.

Skimming the pages of the book, the Iceman thought back to the night at the restaurant. The attack on Detective Parker Bell's girlfriend was a stroke of genius. Completely unplanned, when Detective Bell had spotted what he thought, correctly albeit not the person he expected, was the Iceman and raced off to the alley, the Iceman ducked away and doubled back around to the front of the building. Hoping to sneak away quietly and was almost to the road before sensing a presence, the Iceman had dropped quickly to the ground and looped back to surprise her from behind.

Tessa Micah had sensed the Iceman's presence a split second before she was Tasered. Standing over her unconscious body, lying like an angel in the snow with her blonde curls catching the moonlight, the Iceman had been tempted to throw her in the back of the car and drive away with her. However knowing that to kidnap the lead detective on the case's girlfriend would incur the wrath of the entire police department the Iceman had settled instead for a plan B.

With a small penknife the Iceman had cut away her coat, taken hold of her thin white arm and carved a little message for the police. Her arm was too small to write much on, but the Iceman thought that the note left was highly effective. I C U, a reminder that the Iceman was still out there, that the Iceman was still in control of the city, that the Iceman could not and would not be ignored, brushed away, or silenced.

Wondering whether Tessa or the police had picked up the hidden message inside the obvious one. Research done on the players involved in the Iceman saga had revealed that Tessa Micah was a genius with an IQ of 178, if anyone was going to figure out the loosely veiled communication it would be her.

Startled the Iceman caught sight of Belinda making her way to the library door, a stack of books in her arms. A glance at the clock on the wall revealed they had been here just over an hour; time certainly flew when one was having fun.

Returning the book to its place on the shelf, then following Belinda out onto the street, catching sight of her heading in the direction of her home. Belinda lived with her parents, her two little sisters and three younger brothers, the Iceman was almost disappointed that she was not going to be the first choice, it would have been fun trying to get her out of that house undetected.

Still nothing could beat the girl that was next in line to join the Iceman's legacy, a legacy that would remain unsurpassed for all eternity.

* * * * *

2:26 P.M.

"How's Tessa?" Wyatt asked as he clicked his cell phone off.

"She's doing okay," Parker answered hesitantly, the truth was that

Tessa was doing all right but he wasn't sure he was. He couldn't seem to shake the image of Tessa bleeding in the snow, that he was the one who put her there, that because of his investigation she could have been killed.

"But you're not," Wyatt seemed to read his mind.

Deciding how best to answer, then figuring that since Wyatt always knew what he was thinking anyway there wasn't much point in trying to hide it. "I don't know," fiddling with the things on his desk, despite the hour the station was unnaturally peacefully. "Maybe I'm just tired."

"Maybe," Wyatt said agreeably. Whether interviewing a suspect, dealing with a victim, or helping his friends, Wyatt never pushed instead he always gave people space to talk when they were ready.

Parker knew that he had a tendency to blame himself for things that were completely out of his control, something Tessa tended to do as well. It was one of the things they had in common and one of the things that had attracted him to her, her amazing capacity to empathize with those in pain.

"I don't know," he said again, wearily rubbing his face. "I guess I'm just not used to my job having such an impact on someone I care about."

"Has Daniel shown his face again?"

"No. He called to check on Tess like he said he would but he hasn't come back."

Wyatt must have read something in his voice because he raised an eyebrow, "What is it?

Not sure how to verbalize what he was feeling. "Don't you think it's odd that Daniel turned up now?"

"Wait," Wyatt looked at him as if he'd suddenly grown five heads. "You're not suggesting that Daniel Micah, Tessa's brother, is the killer,"

"No! No," Parker repeated more calmly. "Jamie Presland is the Iceman, but . . . I don't know, maybe Tessa's paranoia is starting to rub off on me. It's just, why would he come back now, he said it was because he just found out about Dylan Riley, but that was a year ago. I just don't trust him."

"Or," Wyatt spoke gently, "Maybe it's just that you don't like him."

Frowning at his partner. "Of course I don't like him, he broke Tessa's heart and left her all alone, but it's more than that, I don't know how to explain it." Puffing out a breath of air in frustration, "He came to see Tessa the other day, and apparently he told her that the reason he came back was because someone sent him a newspaper article about her. About what happened with Dylan Riley."

"Who sent it to him?"

Shrugging, "Daniel said he doesn't know. He thought at first it was Tessa, then he thought it might have been me. The timing is just off, and the way the guy found out about Tessa being attacked . . ."

"I thought he explained that," Wyatt interjected.

"He did, but I don't know, I just don't trust him," sipping distractedly at his coffee which had been sitting untouched on the desk so long it was now stone cold. "It's like if something doesn't sense then it's probably not true, and what Daniel told us definitely doesn't make any . . ."

"Wyatt, Parker, we're ready to go," J.J. boomed at them from across the room.

They'd been waiting for more than twelve hours for a chance to interview Jamie Presland. Unfortunately the guy was smart enough to invoke his right to counsel, and so they had been forced to wait for his court appointed lawyer to arrive before they could begin questioning him.

As they stood and headed for the interview room housing Jamie, Wyatt shot him a look, silently asking if he was going to be okay to do this, Parker nodded that he would be and carefully boxed away his feelings.

Entering the tiny interrogation room, which contained only a table and four chairs, two on either side, Jamie Presland and his fresh out of law school public defender, Judy Hammer, already occupied the seats on the far side of the table. He and Wyatt took their time getting settled, fiddling with the tape recorder, finishing their cups of coffee, arranging their seats.

Both Jamie and his attorney watched their every move with nervous eyes. Jamie paying particular attention to their drinks, licking his lips at the sight of the coffee, Judy Hammer just looked plain stressed.

After letting them squirm Parker caught Jamie in a harsh gaze and begun, "The evidence against you is strong, Mr. Presland, but it might help you if you tell us where you're hiding Hayley Geoffries."

Looking at him blankly then glancing at his lawyer. "You don't have to answer that," Ms Hammer told him.

"I don't know where she is," Jamie declared adamantly, brow furrowed with false concern.

"You're being charged with five counts of kidnapping, five counts of first degree murder, one count of attempted kidnapping, and one of assault," Wyatt reminded him. "The only thing you can do to help yourself is to tell us where Hayley is."

"I don't know where she is," Jamie replied stubbornly.

"What about the scrapbook we found in a hidden compartment in your bathroom? I suppose you have no idea how that got there," Parker asked sarcastically.

"You don't have to answer that," Judy chipped in.

"Actually I don't. I didn't make the scrapbook and I don't know how it got there," Jamie shot back as his lawyer tried to get him to stay quiet.

"And the stack of newspapers in your living room, the ones with all the Iceman murder articles cut out, I guess you don't know how they got there either?" Parker jeered. Surprised that Jamie wasn't more smug and self congratulating, champing at the bit to share every detail of his crimes, how he had outwitted the police time and time again.

"I'm advising you not to answer that," Ms Hammer said again.

"I don't read the paper," Jamie said with a completely straight face, ignoring his lawyer.

"And I suppose there's a reasonable explanation why you have a packet of women's gloves in your spare room?" Wyatt asked with a raised eyebrow.

"You don't need to . . ." Judy Hammer started.

"Shut up," Jamie snapped at his lawyer. "I don't have anything to hide." Turning back to him and Wyatt, "I didn't put the gloves there, I didn't even know they *were* there."

"Jamie, we found the knife, right where you left it," Parker reminded him. "It has Phoebe's blood on it, it puts you at the scene of her murder." Marty had called them with the results of the test just an hour ago, the blood from the knife matched Phoebe Stein's.

At this Jamie's demeanor changed, he was no longer calm, no longer in control, taking advantage Parker pushed, "She really did a number on you, Jamie. What did she do to get away? Kneed you right in the groin while you tried to rape her? I bet that really hurt, did you see a doctor? I hope she hasn't left you with permanent problems down there . . ."

Taking the bait, Jamie's face was now bright red. "The little whore attacked me," Jamie screeched, lunging from his seat, his lawyer trying desperately to hold him back and looking like she wished she were anywhere but here. "She got what she deserved I'm only sorry that her boyfriend turned up before I could have some fun. My thing's all red and black, swollen real bad too," hands moving to his zipper like he was about to pull down his pants and show them his injury.

"Jamie, it was self defense," Wyatt kept his voice calm and even. "She was trying to get away from you because you were going to rape her."

"She got what she deserved," Jamie snarled as though that were the only way he could have received the justice he believed he deserved and sunk sullenly back into his seat.

"Then you're admitting to the murder of Phoebe Stein?" Parker asked smugly.

Pouting at them as he realized he'd been tricked. "Yeah I killed her, but only because she attacked me, she tried to humiliate me. But I didn't do none of that other stuff, honest," Jamie's eyes flitting between Parker and Wyatt.

"I'm sorry, Jamie, but the evidence says otherwise," Parker told him. "Your next door neighbor has a huge holly bush, so we know where you got your favorite calling card from. And the scar on your wrist from the time you tried to commit suicide, will be identified by Elizabeth Landry as the one she saw on the man who tried to abduct her. It's over. You lost. Whether you admit to your crimes or not, we know you did it, we know that you're the Iceman."

"At least show us that you have a shred of humanity by telling us where you're keeping Hayley. Now that you're in custody she won't have food or water, she's going to die," Wyatt prodded.

"I couldn'a killed those girls," Jamie began, smug once again. "They were all killed and set up on those roads on the first of the month, right?" Smiling at them triumphantly, "Well I was working on those days."

Shaking his head in annoyed disbelief, "we know that's not true, Jamie," Parker rebuked. "We spoke to Cece Hamilton, she told us you weren't working on any of those days."

"She's lying," he protested wildly.

"Why would she do that Jamie?" Wyatt asked reasonably.

"I don't know," he threw up his hands in frustration. "Why do women ever do the things they do?"

"You remember exactly what you were doing a year ago?" Parker asked him doubtfully.

"Yes," a little flustered this time, then more confidently. "I was working, I'm always working."

"Tell us where she is, Jamie," Parker spoke quietly, desperately, Hayley's time was quickly running out.

Shaking his head as though baffled by their stupidity, "I keep telling you," Jamie spoke slowly as though that would help them to understand him. "I don't know where she is. I didn't kidnap her. I didn't kill those other girls. I am not the Iceman," thumping his fist on the table to accent each word.

"Fine," Wyatt stood and walked to the door, Parker followed. "If you're not going to tell us anything then this interview is over and you can head over to arraignment. I don't like your chance of getting bail, Jamie."

Just before the door swung shut Jamie called out, "Whether you believe me or not it doesn't change things. I'm telling you the Iceman is still out there and he's gonna keep on killing people until you realize you made a mistake and find the right guy."

DECEMBER 14TH

8:42 A.M.

At least she had light back.

That was the first thing Hayley thought after the Iceman's daily visit.

Now though, after days of living in the dark like a mole, Hayley felt odd in the light. Out of place. It felt weird to be able to see around her tiny little cell, the bed, the chair, the table, her bucket.

Burrowing under the woolly, beige blanket, pulling it up over her head, like she used to do when she was small and there was a thunderstorm roaring outside. Being snuggled up like that made her feel like she was a tiny caterpillar curled up inside a cocoon.

As a child Hayley had been fascinated with caterpillars, moths and butterflies and for a while she'd even kept some as pets. She'd had a box full of silkworms, and had spent hours watching the tiny eggs hatch into tiny, stripy caterpillars. Then they gobbled down enormous amounts of leaves as they grew and grew until they were at least two inches long. She had loved watching them spin their silky cocoons, then would sit for hours, entranced, watching the silk moths slowly and determinedly, with enormous perseverance, break free.

When she was growing up Hayley had always felt lonely. She loved her parents, loved the way they supported her and encouraged her in anything that she set out to do, but being an only child and not having many friends she'd always felt alone. It was why she loved reading so much, when she was younger she'd read anything and everything that she could get her hands on, now between work, her studies and her writing she couldn't find as much time for reading as she would like.

For a while Hayley had resented her parents for not having more children, resented them for all the trips they used to take together, leaving her with grandparents, or when she got older, home alone. She'd been angry with herself too, for never encouraging friends to stick around. Over the years she'd had lots of friends but they never lasted more than a year or two at the most. Hayley, preferring her own company more than that of others, always managed to somehow push them away. She used to think there was something wrong with her because she'd rather be on her own than with others.

Now Hayley would give anything to be safe in her mother's arms . . .

Waking with a start, fresh from a nightmare, chest heaving, breath catching, gulping down mouthfuls of air in an effort to calm herself. Almost every time she slept she was plagued by bad dreams. Images of waking with the Iceman beside her, of the Iceman on top of her, hurting her, pictures of all the terrible things that the Iceman might do to her flashed through her mind in a montage. Then came the faces of the other girls, the Iceman's other victims, girls who slept in the same bed she now lay in, they joined together with the Iceman to exact their revenge upon her, as though she were to blame for their fate.

Uncurling herself from her little shell when she realized it was a pounding in her stomach that had awakened her. Tentatively she stood, two weeks of living in this little jail had left her weak and malnourished. The Iceman supplied her with food and water every day, to keep her alive not to be nice, but Hayley had found that she was barely even hungry anymore, only thirsty. On each visit the Iceman left just half a gallon of water, so she had to be careful to ration what she had so as not to run out.

Wobbling her way across the room to her bucket, during her stay in the Iceman's cell she had become an expert at using a bucket. Lowering her pants, she no longer had underpants, the Iceman had taken them the day she chose clean clothes, and never given her another pair. Squatting over the empty bucket, the Iceman gave her a new one with each visit, she did her business, cleaned herself up, using the last of her toilet paper, and pulled her pants back up. Hayley no longer felt like an animal using the bucket, now she was just glad she didn't have to go on the floor.

Food and water seemed to pass through her body in no time at all, and had become one of the only ways to tell the passing of each day. The Iceman usually visited in what she guessed to be early morning, after the visit she'd eat, then spend most of the day dozing and waking, dozing and waking, after waking she usually visited her toilet, drank some water and went back to sleep.

Today however Hayley had set herself a new goal, on this morning's visit the Iceman had offered her some fruit or a pen and paper. Without a second thought Hayley had opted for the pen and paper. She had decided to write a note to her parents. Hayley was almost positive that she wasn't going to get out of this alive, unless the police somehow managed to discover her location, something that was becoming more and more unlikely with each passing hour.

She had learnt her exact location a couple of days ago, the Iceman had decided to reveal a little more about where she was being kept. The display on the monitor that had shown the enormous aquarium encasing her little cell had changed to show a fancy seafood restaurant. Sometimes at night, or what Hayley assumed to be night, the Iceman would show her videos of the happy, carefree people out for a night of fine dining. Going about their business blithely unaware they were in the presence of a monster, and only feet away from Hayley's prison.

It was, she had decided, more likely that the police would discover this place some time after her death. Maybe days, maybe weeks, months or years, but whenever that day came, and Hayley was positive that come it would, then the police would find her letter. A letter detailing everything she knew about the Iceman, and saying goodbye to her parents.

Easing down into the hard wooden chair, she had lost so much weight her bottom had become bony and it hurt to sit on hard surfaces, Hayley begun her letter. It didn't take her long to write down everything she could think of about the Iceman, which wasn't a lot, and all that had been done to her. It was when she started to think about what she wanted to say to her mom and dad that she started to falter.

Dear mom and dad,

I'm sorry for all the times I've hurt you, for all the times I should have said I love you and didn't. I'm sorry that I didn't tell you enough what wonderful parents you've been, of how much I appreciated your love and support. I want you to know that you mean the world to me, and that I love you more than words can say.

From your loving daughter

Hayley

A tear splashed onto the page, smudging the words, as she felt the floodgates threatening to burst she quickly pushed the paper away, rested her head against the table and let the tears flow. When she was finished she firmly tucked away any thoughts of home and her family, picked up her letter and took it with her back to the bed. Dropping to her knees, Hayley hid the note away in the springs of the mattress, somewhere where, hopefully, the Iceman would never find it. Then she heaved herself back into bed, pulled the covers up over her head, squeezed her eyes closed and waited for sleep to take over.

* * * * *

11:20 A.M.

"Hey, Tessa, how's the arm?" J.J.'s voice boomed above her.

"Not too bad," she told him, trying to hide a wince as he engulfed her in one of his giant bear hugs, sending arrows of pain down the arm in question.

Eyeing her shrewdly, "You still think we got the wrong guy?"

Tessa nodded, tilting her head back to meet his eye, J.J. was almost two feet taller than she was. "Sorry, J.J., but I don't think that Jamie Presland is the Iceman. It just doesn't make sense."

"Lets hope we get more open-minded citizens on the jury then," J.J. smiled down at her and patted her on the head, despite his tendency to treat her like a child she really liked Parker's boss.

About to point out the, at least in her opinion, glaring holes in the case when she caught sight of a pretty young girl with long auburn hair come round the corner, escorted by a young female officer. "Is that Elizabeth Landry?" she asked J.J., studying the girl, who was pale and shaking despite the overbearing heat in the office.

"Yes, but you know you can't talk to her until after you see Jamie," he reminded her.

"I know," she assured him. She was here today to see if she could identify Jamie Presland as the man who had attacked her, Elizabeth Landry was also going to be here for the line up. Tessa wanted to talk to the woman, to see how she was faring, but she was already aware of the fact that she couldn't talk to her until after they'd each gone in to try to ID Jamie.

"I'll be right back," J.J. told her heading off in the direction of Elizabeth.

Dropping down into Parker's chair, Tessa began to fiddle with the neat piles of papers on his desk. Idly flipping through the stack when she came to a dead stop, taking hold of a photo and sliding it out from between the others. Staring at it with wide eyes, she hadn't seen it before, had imagined what it looked like and seen it inside her head, but never the real thing.

"Hey you shouldn't be looking at that," J.J. said softly, reappearing at her side, his giant hands covering hers and gently extracting the photo, placing it facedown on the desk. "Don't do that to yourself, Tess."

When he released her hands she picked the photo back up but didn't turn it over. "I kept seeing it in my head," she murmured.

"Come on, Tess, they're ready for you," J.J. reached for her hand, but Tessa pulled away.

Turning the photo back over she took one last look at it, unable to draw her eyes from the picture of the message that had been cut into her arm. Although Parker had told her about it, and she knew what it said, her arm was still bandaged up and this was the first time she had seen it.

"Look at me, Tessa." When she didn't J.J. sat on the edge of the desk and hooked a finger under her chin, tilting her head up so that she could no longer look at the photo. "Tess, if you're not up to doing this, I understand."

Knowing how hard it was for him to say that, she shook her head to clear it. "That's sweet, J.J.," she told him and thought she saw the big man blush, as tough as he could be with those who deserved it, inside he was a giant marshmallow. "But I can do it," allowing him to pry the photo from her hand and pull her to her feet.

"You know Parker can't be in there with you," J.J. reminded her as he led her to the room where Jamie Presland was waiting.

"It's not my first time dealing with the law," she replied with a wry smile.

"It is your first time doing it with the police though and not on your own," he shot back.

Rolling her eyes at him, Tessa felt her heart beat harder as they stopped at the door. This wasn't the first time she'd confronted someone who'd hurt her but last time she'd thought she had nothing to live for and nothing to lose, this time she had everything to lose and everything to live for. Reminding herself that this was not the same as when she'd gone to Dylan, now she was in a police station, Jamie Presland was going to be behind glass, and she didn't even think that he was the one who had attacked her.

Noticing her hesitation J.J. asked, "You want me to go in with you?"

"No, that's okay," she answered automatically, after years of dealing with stress on her own it was a hard habit to break.

"Come on," J.J. rolled his own eyes and reached for her hand again and before she could back out had the door open and was tugging her through it.

Inside the small room was the ADA who would be working the case, Jamie Presland's lawyer and Skylar. Curtains were drawn across the huge glass window that covered one wall.

"When you're ready, Miss Micah," began the middle aged ADA, whose name Tessa couldn't recall at the moment. "We'll open the curtain. Take your time and take a good look, if you see the man who attacked you," his eyes straying to her arm even though the bandage was hidden beneath her mint green sweater. "Just tell us the number he's holding."

Nodding distractedly she made her way to the window, J.J. at her side, and glanced at Skylar to let him know she was ready. Slowly the curtain opened and Tessa stared at the six men on the other side, all were tallish, thirties, with brown hair, and blank faces. As she studied each of the faces carefully Tessa could feel the tense anticipation in the room around her but none of the men looked familiar.

About to tell J.J., Skylar and the ADA that she was sorry but couldn't identify any of the men as the person who attacked her, when an image suddenly flashed into her mind. The nightmare that she'd had the night of the attack, a dream where she had to put together a puzzle of a face she didn't know or else people would die, where people did die. She'd told Parker about the nightmare upon waking, screaming, but at the time she couldn't recall when she'd had that dream before.

Now she did.

It was the night after Ellie had been murdered.

The face was one she'd seen only once before.

But that was impossible. It couldn't be. There was no way. That face couldn't have been there that night and there was no way it could have been the face of the person who attacked her. No way it could be the face of the person who would use a knife to cut a message into her arm.

The blood rushed from her head like water down the drain when you pulled the plug. She must have swayed because she felt J.J.'s arm wrap around her waist as he pressed her against his chest.

"She's white as a ghost," Tessa heard him say, his voice sounding as though he were miles away instead of right behind her.

"I'll get a doctor. Is Beth here?" Skylar's voice also seemed to float above her.

"No," Tessa pushed the face from her mind. "I'm okay." She tried to stand but J.J. only tightened his grip.

"No you're not, you're shaking," J.J. contradicted.

Feeling a little better as blood resumed its usual course around her body. "Really, I just felt faint for a moment, I'm okay now." Turning to the ADA, whose name she just remembered was Brian, "I'm sorry I don't recognize any of those men. I'm alright, J.J.," she assured him as his worried eyes gazed down at her.

Tentatively he released his grip on her, holding out his arms to catch her if she fell as one did for a toddler learning to walk. "Come on," he took her elbow and guided her towards the door, watching her carefully as though she might break at any second.

"I'll send Parker out when we're done," Skylar told her, she shot him a grateful smile as the door swung shut, once outside she pulled free from J.J.'s grip and headed straight for the bathroom.

"Tess," he called after her, but she ignored him, right now she needed to be alone.

Entering the bathroom, Tessa leaned her hands on the basin and stared into the mirror meeting her own anxious eyes. Turning on the faucet and splashing cold water over her face as though that could wash away the face from her mind. If Tessa was right about whom the face belonged to then things were going to get a lot worse before they got better.

* * * * *

11:40 A.M.

Parker had wanted to be in the room with Tessa when she tried to pick Jamie out of the line-up, but he'd reluctantly agreed that the defense could claim that he somehow communicated the correct answer to Tess. Instead he'd agreed to let J.J. go in with her while he'd stayed with Elizabeth Landry, trying to keep her as calm and relaxed as possible under the circumstances.

He'd been passing the time by telling Lizzie a story about the time he and Wyatt had been attacked by a flock of geese while searching for a missing witness in a case that turned out to be a hoax. But he trailed off when he caught sight of Tessa and J.J. leaving the room, Tessa looked terrible, pale and trembley, and it took every ounce of his self-control to keep from running over to her.

Lizzie followed his gaze then shot him a sympathetic look. "Is that your girlfriend? I heard she got attacked too."

"Yeah she did," he mumbled distractedly as he watched Tessa head to the bathroom.

"Is she okay?"

"Tessa's the toughest person I've ever met," Parker told Lizzie, about to make an excuse so he could go and check on her when Wyatt opened the door and waved them over. "You ready, Elizabeth?" he asked, focusing his attention back on the trembling girl who sat in his desk chair.

Elizabeth Landry looked like she was falling apart. Already slim, she'd lost weight since he'd last seen her, her brown eyes were dull and stood out in her thin face. Her auburn hair, which before had been shiny and thick, now hung limply down her back and she was dressed in sweats, not tight-fitting jeans and turtleneck like she had been the night of her near abduction.

As they made their way towards the door Lizzie reached for his hand, gripping it so tightly her nails dug into his flesh, squeezing it back reassuringly he paused at the door to smile down at her. "I'm gonna be right there with you okay? All you have to do is look and see if you can see the man who attacked you. Once you've done that it'll be all over."

Leading her inside the room where Wyatt, ADA Brian Letrem and Jamie's lawyer Judy Hammer were waiting. Brian gave his spiel to Elizabeth about how things would work then Parker guided her over to the window. If it were possible her grip on his hand tightened as the curtain opened and the six men on the other side came into view.

Eyes flitting quickly from one face to another, bouncing backwards and forwards until at last she looked up at him helplessly. "I don't know, he was behind me the whole time, I never saw his face, only his arm. The scar," she added. "That was all I saw."

They'd planned in advance for this and had added realistic scars to the right wrists of each of the decoys. Each slightly different, each similar to Jamie's but none identical. Hopefully Lizzie would be able to ID him through his scar.

Wyatt stepped up to the intercom and instructed the men to pull up their right sleeves and step forward holding their arm out with palm facing skyward. The six men complied and moved closer to the window as they held out their arms for Lizzie to examine.

This time Elizabeth studied each scar with even more care; eventually she turned to him, a triumphant spark in her eyes. "Number three," she announced confidently, then checked each of the faces in the room, "Did I get it right?"

No one answered, but Parker tugged her towards the door. "You did great, Lizzie," he told her as they left the room.

"Did I get it right?" she asked again as the door closed behind them.

Taking a deep breath, "Number three was Jamie Presland," he confirmed.

Face glowing with pride, the spark in her eyes growing. "What happens now?"

"Now, he'll try to apply for bail . . ."

"He's not going to get out is he?" her voice flipping from proud and excited to panicked and terrified in one hundredth of a millisecond.

"Calm down," he soothed. "I'm sure he won't get bail. Then we just have to wait for the case, you'll most likely have to testify."

Taking all of this in. "He's denying being the Iceman?"

"He's admitted to Phoebe Stein's murder but nothing else."

"He didn't tell you where that girl is? The . . ." voice faltering, "The one he took instead of me?"

"No he hasn't," looking over to where Tessa was standing, looking more herself, and caught her eye. She shook her head in answer to his silent question asking whether she had been able to identify Jamie, then nodded in answer to his next question about whether she still wanted to talk to Elizabeth. "I think that Tessa wanted to talk to you, if you think you're up to it," he told Lizzie who followed his gaze to look at Tessa and returned her wave.

"Thanks, Detective Bell," she gave him a watery smile and went to join Tessa, while he headed off to collect Joshua Timma, hopefully they could make it two out of three.

* * * * *

12:15 P.M.

"What happened?"

Tessa had been standing in J.J.'s office staring out the window, lost in thought, when Parker came up behind her, wrapping her up in his arms and resting his chin against the top of her head. Snuggling back against him and closing her eyes, she felt drained after talking with Lizzie. Tessa hoped that she had somehow managed to convince the traumatized girl to never give up hope, but she wasn't convinced she had.

"Tess?" Parker prodded when she didn't answer.

"Nothing," she didn't want to get into a discussion on what had happened earlier until she'd had a chance to process things herself. Instead she asked, "Did Josh ID Jamie Presland?"

"Yeah he did, Lizzie too."

"I know, she told me," that and a whole list of things that were weighing heavily on the girl's mind.

"J.J. and Wyatt said you almost passed out, even the defense lawyer was worried about you," Parker took another shot at trying to get her to talk, he was nothing if not persistent.

Wiggling around to face him Tessa was about to answer when she saw he was wearing a jacket, surprised she hooked her fingers onto the lapels. "What's with this?"

His cheeks reddened slightly, from stress not embarrassment Tessa knew. "I thought if you could lay your demons to rest then I could do the same."

As a small child Parker had lived in foster care, where the biological son of his foster parents in the last home he'd ever lived in before being adopted, had tortured the younger children mercilessly.

One of the boy's favorite things to do was wrap the children up in a straightjacket and stick them in a closet. As a result of this Parker couldn't wear jackets and he couldn't stand small spaces like elevators.

"That's great," she smiled.

Parker eyed her shrewdly. "You still aren't convinced that Jamie Presland is the Iceman are you?"

"I believe he killed Phoebe," she offered a partial answer.

"But not that he did everything else?"

"No, I'm sorry, Parker," Tessa was positive that Jamie Presland was not the Iceman, but if she was right about the face she had remembered then she wasn't attacked by the Iceman either.

"Even after Lizzie ID'd him?"

Nodding, "something feels wrong," Tessa couldn't explain exactly how she knew that Jamie was not the serial killer, she just knew. "Has he admitted to anything?"

"Only Phoebe's murder," he told her and she could see that despite his conviction that they had the right guy he was bothered by the fact that Jamie hadn't admitted to his crimes. Usually a killer who went to these lengths to hold the city at ransom would be jumping at the chance to prove how smart he was.

"You're not going to tell me what you remembered are you?" Parker asked with a wry smile.

Resting her head against his chest. "No, not yet anyway." Allowing herself to feel safe and secure in Parker's arms, maybe she was wrong about the face, she'd never actually seen it before, never met the person to whom it belonged. It wasn't possible anyway that she'd seen it either of those times, she was wrong, she had to be, and if she was wrong about that then maybe she was wrong about Jamie. Tessa hoped that she was wrong because otherwise a lot more people were going to die.

DECEMBER 15TH

4:26 P.M.

"What do you want to do now?"

Tessa shrugged. "whatever you want."

They were curled up together in one of the armchairs in the living room, it was snowing furiously outside, a fire was roaring in the fireplace, and they'd just finished watching a movie. Tessa had hung around with him at the station yesterday afternoon, and they hadn't arrived home till late, they'd slept in this morning and taken it easy on his day off. Tessa was used to his strange hours, herself being someone who often slept weird hours, Parker wondered how things would change once they had kids.

If they had kids, he reminded himself, he was already planning their future even though he hadn't yet proposed.

"You want to go out for dinner?"

"I'm really tired," Tessa told him, closing her eyes wearily for emphasis.

"How about I cook you dinner here?" he suggested.

Opening her eyes and scrunching up her face. "You're gonna cook?" she asked doubtfully. "Maybe I could cook you dinner."

"No," he protested. "You always cook and I wanted to do something for you."

"That's okay," she smiled at him. "I don't mind. What do you feel like?"

"I don't want to trouble you," he told her, he'd been hoping for another opportunity to asking Tessa to marry him.

"Really, Parker, it's no trouble."

Relenting, "Lasagne." There was nothing he adored more than Tessa's homemade lasagne.

"Okay, I'm gonna take a shower then I'll start," Tessa climbed from his lap, gave him a quick kiss on the cheek and headed upstairs.

As he watched her go he wondered what it was that Tessa knew that she wasn't telling him. He was positive that she had remembered something from her attack, something she thought was important but something she wasn't prepared to share with him. He was almost positive that if it was pertinent to the Iceman case then she would have told him, but from past experience he knew that Tessa would keep information from the police if she thought she was protecting someone.

The only person that Parker could think of that Tessa would want to protect was her brother Daniel.

Although things were messed up between Tessa and Daniel he knew that Tessa still loved her brother no matter how much he'd hurt her in the past. The same way Parker felt about his twin sister Matilda.

After going to live with their adopted parents life for Parker had improved dramatically, but the scars of what had happened to them in foster care ran too deep for Matilda. While he had blossomed Mattie had remained withdrawn, trapped in a world of pain and fear. The day after they graduated from high school Mattie had left, disappeared completely, he hadn't heard from her since. But while Daniel had left Tessa without a word, Matilda had left a note, a note Parker still had tucked away, that when he wanted to feel close to his sister he would get out and read again and again.

Parker knew that even thought he hadn't seen Mattie in thirteen years he would go to almost any length to protect his sister and he knew that Tessa would do the same for her brother. He also knew that there was no way that Daniel Micah was the Iceman; they had the killer in custody. If Tessa was trying to protect someone then it wasn't her brother, who else it could be he had no idea.

As he heard the shower turn off upstairs the doorbell rung, yawning tiredly as he made his way down the hall, his good mood evaporated immediately when he saw who was on the other side.

"What do you want?" he demanded.

"What do you think?" Daniel answered trying to push past him into the house.

Blocking Daniel's entry with a raised arm. "I *think* that you're not welcome here. How many times do you have to hear it before you accept it? Tessa doesn't want to see you."

"This has nothing to do with you," Daniel shot back.

"Try to understand this," Parker spoke deliberately slowly. "Tessa and I are together, everything that involves her involves me too."

"You're really annoying, you know that?" Daniel frowned.

"I do my best," Parker smirked.

"What's going on?" Tessa asked, coming up behind him and slipping under his arm. "What do you want?" she asked when she saw her brother.

"To talk to you," instantly changing from annoyed to desperate.

Shaking her wet curls. "Daniel, I can't keep doing this."

Parker's phone chirping from inside his pocket cut off Daniel's response. "Hold on," Parker said, shooting Daniel a warning glance to be gone by the time he was finished.

"Hello?"

"It's Wyatt," his partner's excited voice said on the other end of the line.

"What's up?" he asked eyeing Daniel who hadn't moved an inch.

"Jamie Presland's ready to talk," Wyatt told him.

"Really?"

Catching the excited tone in his voice Tessa turned to watch him.

"How long till you can be here?" Wyatt asked.

Glancing at his watch and then at Daniel and Tessa, he wanted to be there for Jamie's confession but he was apprehensive about leaving Tessa alone with her brother. "Hold on a second," he told Wyatt.

"What's up?" Tessa asked as he lowered the phone.

"Jamie is ready to confess," he told her.

"The serial killer?" Daniel interjected.

Casting him a withering glare then reverting his attention to Tessa, "Wyatt wants me to go in but . . ."

"Go," Tessa assured him. "I'll be fine here."

"Are you sure?" he double-checked. Tessa shot him an irritated frown and nodded, she hated it when he treated her like she was made of glass, Parker returned to his phone call. "I'll leave right now, be there in ten minutes."

As he hung up the phone he finally felt at peace with the whole situation. They had the killer, he'd confessed which would spare Lizzie and the victim's family's the pain of a trial, now, hopefully, Jamie would tell them where Hayley Geoffries was, and then all of this would be over.

* * * * *

4:57 P.M.

Waving as Parker drove off down the street, Tessa wondered whether she had been wrong, maybe Jamie Presland really was the Iceman. She still didn't feel it, but maybe she was starting to lose her ability to read people and rely on her gut. She couldn't think of a legitimate reason why Jamie would lie and say he was a serial killer if he wasn't. It made no sense, and as Parker loved to say, if something didn't make sense then it probably wasn't true.

Sighing when she saw Daniel patiently standing behind her, she was getting tired of having to deal with him. About to ignore him and go inside when he grabbed her arm and roughly turned her around.

"Don't, Daniel, let go of me," wiggling and trying to pull her arm free, feeling her chest tighten in panic when he didn't let go. Tessa hated feeling out of control.

"No, not until you listen to me," his eyes were wild, desperate.

"Please, Daniel, let me go," she begged softly, he must have noticed how much he was upsetting her because he released his grip.

"Tessie, you have to know that I would never hurt you," he pleaded.

"But you did, Daniel," she whispered. "You did hurt me."

"Tessie, please, I need to tell you why I left," reaching out a hand to grab her but thinking better of it.

"I don't care why you left, Daniel. It's in the past, its gone and over. I don't care why Patrick left, I don't care why Emilie did what she did, I don't care why you left and I don't care why you came back." Looking Daniel straight in the eye, eyes that mirrored her own, Emilie's eyes. "I'll ask you one question and if you tell me yes then I'll listen to you. Deal?"

"Deal," Daniel nodded.

"If Patrick came back with an answer as to why he abandoned us, would you listen, would you take him back like nothing ever happened? Would you accept him and that new wife of his back into your life, would you accept his kids, our half brother and sister into your life, make believe you were a family?"

Once when she was fourteen, four years after he left, three years after Ellie's death, and two years after Emilie tried to kill her, Patrick had come back. Shown up one day out of the blue, tried to convince her to move to Paris to live with him, Brigette, her stepmother, and their two children, Patrick Junior and Serena. Tessa had refused to speak to him.

"Well, Daniel?" she prodded. "If Patrick came back right now would you listen to him, would you pretend like nothing had happened?"

Studying Daniel's face as it fell and he shook his head. "No. If Patrick came back I couldn't pretend like none of it ever happened."

Smiling sadly as he gave the answer she'd known he would, but somehow hoped he wouldn't. It was the end, the final chapter, the last goodbye. Feeling a closure to any lingering sense of attachment she felt towards her dysfunctional family, to any dream she had they could one day be happy together.

"Goodbye, Daniel," closing the door behind her.

* * * * *

5:32 P.M.

Humming nervously as he waited.

Wondering what was taking so long.

It had to have been hours since he told them that he was ready to confess, and yet they seemed to have done nothing about it. Jamie was still sitting here alone, waiting.

Alone in his prison cell Jamie had come to a decision.

Clearly no one was going to believe that he wasn't the serial killer, the police were convinced that he did it, and so were the media. It was over for him, they had a stack of evidence and one of the Iceman's supposed victims ID'd him as her attacker. Jamie had decided that if he was going to go down for a crime he didn't commit then he may as well take the credit for it.

Growing up his parents had never believed in him. Before his father's death, when Jamie was nineteen, both his parents had been surgeons. Unfortunately young Jamie had never lived up to their expectations, he wasn't smart, he wasn't good at sports or music, he didn't have many friends, and he wasn't good with girls. It was his younger sister who was the golden child, the one who could do no wrong, the one who was going to follow in their parent's footsteps.

Keenly aware of what a disappointment he was to his family Jamie had never bothered to accomplish anything. Dropping out of school when he was fifteen after a failed suicide attempt, he had spent his life jumping from one bottom wage job to another.

Jamie had to admit that when his father died and his mother fell apart, losing first her job, then her home, her self-respect and finally her life, he had felt a sense of poetic justice. His parents had thought he was worth nothing and now may be the only chance he had to prove that he could do something that would make people stand up and take notice. If he took credit for being the most diabolical serial killer the city had ever seen then he would show his parents, no matter that they were no longer alive to see it, just what he could do.

Whether he plead guilty or not the police had him, and they weren't completely wrong, he had tried to rape Phoebe Stein and had the bruises to show it. He had slit her throat when her boyfriend had interrupted them, and they had the knife to prove it. Rubbing his still painful groin, Jamie was satisfied that he had made the right choice, the only choice he could under the circumstances.

And so here he sat waiting for those detectives to show up.

Just then the door opened and there they were, Detective Bell and Detective Wyatt.

"Hello, Jamie," Detective Wyatt said mildly, his emerald eyes completely calm, his partner on the other hand looked furious, and Jamie remembered that the Iceman had attacked his girlfriend.

Taking a steadying breath, if Jamie was going to do this then he had to do it right. "Hello, detectives," he said calmly.

Jumping straight into things Detective Bell took a seat on the opposite side of the table, palms pressed against it as he leant in close. "Where is she?"

This was the only thing Jamie was worried about. The missing girl. He had no idea where the real Iceman had stashed the girl. His only option was to pretend that he knew but wouldn't say. "How about we start with something else," he suggested.

"How about we start with Hayley since her time is running out. She's been alone for three days now. Unless you left her with a supply of food and water then she doesn't have long left," Detective Bell snarled.

Jamie could see that the detective was honestly most distressed about the girl so hoping to placate him for the time being he offered up assurances. "Hayley will be fine. I left her with plenty of stuff to last her for a couple of weeks," he lied. "So that I didn't have to sneak off and check on her every day."

That seemed to pacify the detectives for the moment. "So you're admitting to each of the crimes that you were charged with?" Detective Wyatt asked him.

Nodding, "yes I did it all. Last year I kidnapped and killed those girls and this year I tried to kidnap that other girl, but those men showed up," he remembered hearing about that on the news. "So I took that other girl instead."

"They have names," Detective Bell told him, if looks could kill then Jamie would have been dead ten times over.

"Not to me they don't, they're just a means to an end," Jamie told him emotionlessly.

Detective Bell was about to lunge across the table at him when his partner put a calming hand on his shoulder. "He's not worth it, Parker."

"Did you attack Tessa? Use a knife to . . . to . . . ." struggling to get the words out past his anger. "To cut a message into her arm?"

"Yes, I'm sorry. I wanted you to know that I couldn't be stopped."

Smiling mirthlessly, "But you were," Detective Bell reminded him. "You were stopped by a twenty-year-old girl. How is your injury?" he asked with mock sympathy.

Reminding himself not to be sucked in, Jamie simply stared back at him without a word.

Laying a pad of paper and a pencil on the table between them. "Write it all down," Detective Wyatt told him.

Knowing that he didn't have enough details to fool the police, he knew only what the papers had revealed. Eyeing the pad, "I'll write only that I kidnapped and killed the girls, I won't write any details."

"Do whatever you want," Detective Bell snapped, turning to his partner, "I'm done, Wyatt. This guy isn't going to tell us where Hayley is. Are you?" he addressed Jamie, when he shook his head Detective Bell frowned at him and pushed back his chair. "I'm leaving."

"Why did you want to see us?" Detective Wyatt asked. "If you're not going to give us any other information, if you're not going to tell us where Hayley is then why did you ask for us to come and see you?"

"Because I could," was the only answer Jamie could think of.

"It's really just a game to you," Detective Wyatt seemed genuinely baffled by his apparent cold-heartedness. "All those women you killed, all those families you ruined, all those people you hurt, and it was just a game. A way for you to pretend that you were in charge, that you were controlling everyone around you. Well you're not in control anymore Jamie, and you never will be again," he stood and followed his partner to the door.

Pausing, Detective Bell turned to look at him, "What made you change your mind? Why did you decide to confess?"

Looking into the man's glowing amber eyes. "Because it's the only way I can get the respect that I deserve," Jamie told him, the only honest answer he'd given since they entered the room.

And with that the door slammed closed and Jamie Presland had no choice but to live with the decision he had made whether he wanted to or not.

DECEMBER 16TH

It had been a busy morning.

This was the first chance the Iceman had had to sit down and read the daily papers. As much as it would be wonderful if the Iceman could spend all day working on the plan, reality required that appearances be kept up so that no one became suspicious. So the Iceman took whatever opportunities came along to take time out of the boredom that was life to revel in the excitement of the plan.

A cup of steaming tea sat on the desk, the office door locked, everyone had instructions not to enter, and the Iceman was sitting back ready to read the daily updates in the paper about the case.

Settling in, taking a long drink of tea and then reaching for the paper at the top of the stack, unfolding it to idly peruse the front page, then reading the headlines the Iceman froze.

Walking in a Winter Wonderland
Iceman confesses to Icy Crimes

The Iceman sat in shock, unable to look away from the picture of Jamie Presland that accompanied the article, as pure fury made the words swirl together. The article went on to detail each of the crimes, including the attack on Tessa Micah with a summary of her previous appearances in the papers. It also explained how Jamie Presland had made a full confession that he was the serial killer.

The Iceman had never been so livid before.

That Jamie Presland would take credit for perfectly planned and immaculately executed crimes that he did not commit was unconscionable.

It had been a risk, a calculated one on the Iceman's part, to allow the police to continue to think that they had got their man. The Iceman had decided to do this to temporarily allow the city to feel like they were safe so that when the next body was found, on schedule, their ensuing terror would be all the sweeter. The Iceman had also allowed the police to think that Jamie was the killer because there was no way the guy would ever confess to crimes he didn't commit.

But he had.

And the Iceman could not figure out why he had done it.

Letting out a muted roar the Iceman tossed the paper across the room then picked up the whole stack and threw them too. As they flew through the air they knocked a framed photo from the desk, sending it plummeting to the floor, the glass shattering into millions of tiny glass raindrops.

Moments later a knock sounded at the door.

The Iceman was fuming but put on a mask of pleasant curiosity and opened the door.

"Yes?" the Iceman asked.

"Is everything okay?" asked the young woman on the other side, who was trying to peer into the office.

"Yes. Why?"

"I thought I heard something breaking and I just wanted to check on you," she smiled a winning smile.

"That was thoughtful," smiling back politely.

"What happened?" she persisted.

"I accidentally deleted a whole spreadsheet," smiling ruefully. "I'm afraid I lost my temper and knocked one of the photos off my desk," pointing to the broken photo frame on the ground.

"Oh, well as long as everything's okay," the girl smiled and turned to leave.

"Thanks," the Iceman called after her then closed and relocked the door, letting out a silent growl.

Picking up the shards of glass the Iceman vowed to make sure that Jamie Presland and the idiotic police who believed him would pay for taking away the glory that belonged solely to the one and only true Iceman.

* * * * *

12:16 P.M.

"Sorry we're late," Casey said as Tessa opened the door.

"No problem, you do have to get these two terrors ready." Tessa smiled down at Sam and Stacey, "Hey, guys." The kids were an amazing composition of their parents, they had their mother's black corkscrew curls, their father's goofy grin, their eyes were a greeny grey, their skin a milk chocolate brown, they were also the politest, sweetest kids Tessa had ever met and she loved them dearly.

"Hey, Tessa, look what I got," Stacey thrust a toy pony in her face.

"That's cute," she replied. "What's her name?"

Offering a shy smile, the little girl twirled her finger around her thick black braid. "Her name's Tessa."

"Wow, just like my name."

Stacey beamed.

"What's to eat?" Sam demanded.

Rolling her eyes, "Sam," Casey admonished. "That's rude."

Laughing, "that's okay, Casey," Tessa told her, then to the kids, "There's snacks in the kitchen and Parker and your dad are out back barbequing."

As the kids cheered and ran for the kitchen Casey apologized again, "He must be about to have a growth spurt cos that kid is always hungry."

They followed the kids to the kitchen and helped them sort out their snacks before fixing their own and taking a seat at the table. Once they were alone Casey begun her interrogation, "How's your arm?"

Stretching it out to demonstrate. "It's still sore but it's okay."

"Are you?" Casey asked with a raised eyebrow that communicated she wanted an honest answer.

"Yes, and I really wish people would stop fussing over me," Tessa told her, she loved Casey but she also loved her space.

"We fuss because we love you," Casey reminded her.

"I know, but it still annoys me," she shot back.

Grinning, "Have you heard from Daniel since yesterday?"

"How did you hear about that? No, no," Tessa answered her own question, "Let me guess, Parker blabbed to Skylar, who blabbed to you."

"Correct," Casey's grin grew wider. "And have you?"

"No, and I don't think I'm going to hear from him again," remembering the look on Daniel's face as she'd closed the door on him.

"You've told him to go before," Casey warned.

"I know, but this time I know I got through to him," Tessa knew that she had seen her brother for the last time.

"Wyatt also told me that you don't think that Jamie Presland is the Iceman," Casey moved on to the next topic on her examination list.

"Skylar has a big mouth," Tessa retorted.

Casey merely raised an eyebrow.

Exhaling, "I don't think Jamie is the killer, I could be wrong . . ."

"Well there is a first time for everything," Parker interjected with a smirk as he came into the kitchen with a huge platter of barbequed meat.

"First time for what?" Skylar asked coming in behind him with another heaped plate.

"For Tessa to be wrong," Parker told him.

"Tessa? Wrong?" Skylar asked with mock shock horror. "Not possible."

"I've been wrong before you know," Tessa pouted, and was about to continue when the kids came barreling into the room.

Sam bounced over to her. "Here you go, Tessa," he said handing her a white envelope stained brown with dirt.

"Where did you get this?" she asked, a pool of dread growing in her stomach as she inspected the writing on the front.

"It was outside, near your fence at the back, it has your name on it," Sam pointed to her name.

"Thanks, Sam," she smiled reassuringly at him.

As the kids hurried off again Tessa slowly turned the envelope over, the back wasn't properly sealed, the two sides just tucked together. Opening it as Casey hovered over her shoulder, Parker and Skylar were busy organizing the food. As she slid it open a photo tumbled out, dropping facedown onto her lap, when she turned it over both she and Casey gasped.

"Guys," Casey called.

Catching the urgency and scarcely concealed panic in Casey's voice they came immediately.

"What is it?" Parker asked.

They both stopped short when they saw what Tessa was holding.

Skylar grabbed her wrist and lifted it up so he could see the photo better without further contaminating it. "Where did you get this?" he asked.

Opening her mouth to answer but no sound coming out.

Casey answered for her, "The kids found it in the yard, it was in an envelope with her name on it," gesturing at the envelope that still sat on Tessa's lap.

"Who touched it?" Parker asked.

"Tessa, Sam and maybe Stacey," Casey told him.

"I'll call Marty," Skylar released his hold on her arm, which dropped back into her lap, and went for the phone.

"It has my name on it," Tessa said eventually her voice coming out strained. "He sent it to me. Why would he do that? Why me?"

Casey put a hand on her shoulder; Parker crouched beside her, taking hold of her chin, forcing her to look away from the photograph of Hayley Geoffries. "The same reason he left that message on your arm," he told her, "Because he wants to mess with your head."

"I told you Jamie wasn't the Iceman," she told him her voice raising an octave. She pulled her face free from his grip and returned her gaze to the photo of the sleeping young woman.

"We don't know that, Tess," Parker reminded her gently. "Look at the envelope, it looks like it's been in the yard a while. He probably left it while he was still on the run, before we caught him."

"Marty's on his way," Skylar interrupted them.

"You better hope that Jamie Presland is the Iceman," Tessa told them and unable to look at the photo for another second she replaced it roughly inside its envelope. "Because if he's not then the real killer knows where I live, he's leaving me notes, and there's nothing stopping him taking things to the next level."

DECEMBER 17TH

4:41 A.M.

Hayley woke with the uneasy feeling that she was being watched.

As her sluggish brain slowly roused itself she realized that she was indeed being watched.

The Iceman was sitting at the top of the room, legs dangling down, gun in lap, and Hayley knew instantly something was wrong.

Standing on legs as wobbly as a newborn foal, Hayley didn't want to risk the Iceman's wrath by asking what had happened so she simply waited.

At last the Iceman spoke, "someone else is claiming responsibility for my crimes, someone who is so far out of my league that they are out of sight. I do not like that kind of behavior, it is disrespectful."

Like everything the Iceman said it always came back to respect. From experience Hayley didn't comment.

For a long moment the Iceman stared at her and Hayley was sure that she was not going to get her daily ration of food and water. She was already running on empty a day or so without anything to eat or drink could wipe her out.

When at last the Iceman spoke Hayley detected pure rage, "Unfortunately my dear, you are going to be the one to take the brunt of my anger. Today is the seventeenth, usually I would not have put you through this injustice so early, but if I do not do something to alleviate my fury then I will ruin the plan. That is unacceptable."

Hayley trembled but said nothing.

Fiddling with the gun the Iceman continued, "I want you to remove your clothing. I will send down the bucket, you are to remove the clothes put them in the bucket along with your toilet, any toilet paper or other luxury items remaining down there. When you have done that I will pull the bucket back up and send you down today's food and water. If you do not comply with my instructions then I will not be back. I will simply wait for you to die and then put you inside the ice on January first. It is your choice."

Staring up blankly, the words seeming incomprehensible, she couldn't do it, couldn't give up her clothing, the book, the paper and pen, her toilet. If she did she would have nothing left, she would simply be an animal in a cage, no she thought, even the animals at the zoo were given toys to play with. Looking into the Iceman's empty eyes was like looking into a bottomless well, she knew that if she didn't do it, then she would surely die, if she did it there was still a chance the police might find her in time.

"I don't have all day, Hayley," the Iceman admonished. "What is your choice. Life or death?"

There was no choice; as long as she was alive there was hope. Besides she didn't think she was strong enough to simply sit here alone and slowly die of dehydration and starvation. She nodded.

"Good," the Iceman nodded approvingly. "I will send down the bucket."

As the Iceman watched Hayley removed her sweat pants and sweater, shivering as her naked body was exposed, wanting to use her hands to cover her private parts but the Iceman was urging her on.

"Now collect up everything else you have, come along."

The book, the pad and pen, the last of the previous day's toilet paper, the soap, all went in the bucket with her clothes.

Tsk-ing at her, "The toilet, Hayley," the Iceman reminded as though she were a recalcitrant child.

Reluctantly attaching her precious toilet bucket to the rope, Hayley couldn't stop her tears as the Iceman began to wind the rope back up. When the bucket returned the small bottle of water, couple of slices of bread and apple didn't seem like a fair trade, but Hayley took them anyway at least they would provide her sustenance for another day.

Hayley closed her eyes as she waited for the familiar clunk of the trapdoor closing, when she didn't hear it her eyes popped open and then wished they hadn't.

The Iceman was standing now, the gun was pointed at her. "I'm sorry, Hayley, it wasn't enough."

With that the Iceman pulled the trigger and Hayley felt a burning sensation rip across her thigh and then the door slammed shut and she was alone.

Pressing a hand to her leg, surprised for some reason when it came away sticky with her own blood. The Iceman had shot at her, hit her, but whether intentionally or not, had not injured her badly. The wound on her leg was bleeding quite heavily, but the bullet was not inside, nor had it passed through, it had simply skimmed the edge on its journey into the wall.

Whether it was a life-threatening injury or not it still burned like fire. With a hand pressed to the leg to stem the blood flow, Hayley limped to the bed, lowered herself to the floor, and with the last of her nails begun to tear at the sheet to fashion a makeshift bandage.

Exhaustion washing over her, after what felt like hours worth of work she managed to break off a strip of the sheet. Pouring most of her drinking water over the wound in an attempt to ward off infection, then wrapping the material around her leg, which seemed to have stopped bleeding anyway.

Too nauseous to eat Hayley curled up as best she could with her sore leg, and decided maybe she should have gone with the Iceman's other option. Maybe if she had chosen not to follow orders then the Iceman's anger would have been severe enough that the shot would have been one to kill instead of one meant merely to injure and prolong her suffering.

A quick death seemed to be becoming a blessing Hayley could only dream about.

DECEMBER 18TH

1:49 A.M.

This was her last shot.

And it was a long one.

Winter had spent the last week desperately trying to find time alone so that she could search for places where her stepfather may be hiding Hayley Geoffries.

So far she had come up with nothing.

This was going to be her last chance, after this she had nowhere left to search, and even this was a stretch.

She was sitting in her car outside her mother's restaurant, the only place vaguely related to Grant where she had not yet looked. The more she thought about it the more excited she became, it would be diabolically clever for Grant to keep Hayley at his wife's workplace.

Deciding she had nothing to lose, if she found nothing here then she would go to the police and hope for the best. Letting herself in the back door, Winter took solace in the quiet of the empty restaurant, her mother had been paying extra attention to her since her 'accident' and Winter was starting to find it very wearing. A week after Grant attacked her and she was starting to feel better, her arm no longer really hurt, the cast had quickly become an irritating burden. Her ribs still hurt when she drew a deep breath, or laughed, not that there was much cause for that, and her stomach still ached, especially when she used the bathroom, but the pain was certainly ebbing.

Giving a peripheral search of the kitchen, the storeroom and the main restaurant room, not really thinking that any of those places were likely to yield anything helpful. The building didn't contain a basement but it did have an attic, Winter decided she would check the office and then head up there.

Her mother's office was small and sparsely furnished, a desk, containing a couple of framed photos of the two of them together, a leather chair, a bookcase, a filing cabinet and a huge cupboard. Skimming the desk drawers and the filing cabinet, then moving onto the bookcase, taking care to shake out and flip through each of the books to see if anything was hidden in between. Finding nothing Winter was at the door when she realized she hadn't checked the cupboard, almost deciding to skip it and go to the attic when she decided she had nothing to lose, who knows maybe there was a secret door to a hidden room back there.

Heading over to the cupboard she rifled through a couple of changes of clothing her mother kept in case she got held up at work. Reaching up to feel around on the top shelf she accidentally knocked off a pair of shoes sending them tumbling to the floor. One bounced straight down but the other fell sideways with an unusual clunk. Frowning Winter dropped to her knees, throwing the shoes behind her and tapping at the floor, noticing a difference in sound depending on where she hit.

There was a hollow space down there.

Realizing the only reason there would be a secret compartment down there was to hide something. Clearing the floor, Winter rolled back the carpet and found a small finger hole. Knowing this could be the break she'd been waiting for, she felt a tingling of excitement as she slid her finger into the hole and awkwardly maneuvered up the trapdoor to find a big black garbage bag.

Pulling out the bag and shuffling a little way away from the cupboard, the top of the bag was tightly knotted and Winter struggled to undo it one handed. Finally, with a grunt of triumph the knot slid undone, and when she tipped it upside down a pile of clothes fell out along with a bundle of photographs, joined together with an elastic band.

Going for the photos first, Winter wiggled the tie off with her good hand and flipped over the first picture.

Gasping as she looked at a photo of Hannah Green, lying in the back of a van, unconscious, her wrists and ankles bound. Breathing hard as she turned over the next one and saw that it depicted exactly what she thought it would, Greta Hamburg. Kelly Lorris came next and then Stacey Wood, each girl in the same pose, unconscious and tied up in the back of a van. The last photo was Hayley Geoffries.

Dropping the pictures into her lap, Winter grabbed for the clothes on the top of the pile, a two-tone pink striped silk sweater, one she'd seen before. Ruffling through the pile of photos until she found the one she was looking for, grabbing it she held it next to the sweater. The item of clothing that lay on her lap was the same as the one that Greta Hamburg wore in the photo.

Quickly laying the photos out on the floor, Winter arranged the clothing so that it went with its corresponding picture. In the end she'd matched the outfits that each girl had been wearing when they were abducted with their photo. Even Hayley's clothing was there.

On a high from her find she decided that the best course of action was to return everything to the bag and replace it in its hidey-hole at the bottom of the cupboard. If Grant came back here to check on his stuff then she didn't want to tip him off that she had him.

Just as she was replacing the lid and rolling back the carpet she heard a noise from somewhere in the restaurant. Scurrying to the desk she slid underneath and prayed that whoever was here hadn't heard her and therefore had no reason to be looking for anyone. Holding her breath when she heard the office door swing open and footsteps coming towards her, from her hiding spot Winter could see a pair of big black boots circle the room before receding.

Scared to move, scared to breathe, after remaining where she was for close to half an hour, Winter eventually decided that whoever it was who'd been here had left. Creeping out from under the desk, checking that the office looked just like it had when she had arrived, she snuck back through the restaurant, pausing at the aquarium. Winter loved watching the beautiful colored fish swim peacefully around the tank, it was like watching a living, breathing rainbow.

Resolving to head straight to the police station from here, she remembered that she still had the card that the detectives had left behind the day they visited her mom. After they had left and Cece had returned to her office Winter had snuck back into the room and retrieved it, stashing it away for when she was ready to use it. Detectives Bell and Wyatt, she recalled. They had both seemed nice, caring, they'd been kind and gentle to her, and she had known, looking deep into their eyes, that she could trust them.

Turning to leave Winter thought she caught sight of a moving black figure out of the corner of her eye, but then stars exploded over her head and the world slid into darkness.

DECEMBER 19TH

8:09 A.M.

"Nothing," Parker told his partner as he glared at his iPhone as if it were responsible for the bad news he had just received, and replaced it in his pocket.

"That was the last one we could come up with," Wyatt sighed dismally.

"I know," Parker sighed back, another strike out in the frantic hunt for Hayley Geoffries.

They had been investigating any place they could come up with that had any relation to Jamie or his past. They'd already searched both his childhood homes, a couple of places where he and his family had vacationed regularly, and around each of the places he'd worked in the last fifteen odd years.

A team had just finished searching their final chance, the home where Jamie's parents had lived, after he moved out at age fifteen and until his father's death four years later. It had taken them a while to locate the property's owners, since the house had changed hands several times since Jamie's mother had lost it after she had an emotional breakdown following her husband's death. The huge mansion had had five owners in the last ten years, the current ones were overseas on an extended family vacation, hence the fact that they were just now able to check out the house having obtained the owners permission.

Frustrated Parker felt like giving up.

Remembering Jamie's words, that he had left enough food and water to last her a couple of weeks, Parker knew they couldn't trust anything that came out of the mouth of a serial killer. While she's still out there then there's hope, he gave himself a pep talk, knowing that while there remained even the slimmest of chances that Hayley was still alive then he would never give up.

Rousing himself from the despair that was settling over him like the thick grey clouds that had settled over the city, obscuring any hopeful rays the sun might give out. "J.J. said Marty finished checking out the photo," he told Wyatt, who momentarily looked up from the file he was aimlessly thumbing through as though it might suddenly start spouting out answers.

"And?" his partner prodded.

When Marty had arrived at his place that night to collect the photo and its envelope, he had also taken samples of Tessa, Sam and Stacey's fingerprints, which the kids had thought was hilarious, to eliminate them and hopefully find a set of Jamie's fingerprints so they could prove definitively that he left the envelope. "And the only fingerprints on it were Tessa and Sam's," Parker told him. Yet another dead end in a case that seemed to move everywhere and yet nowhere, they had their guy but as long as Hayley was out there suffering it didn't feel like a victory.

"Did he find anything else?"

"No, nothing else, looks like he wore gloves when he was handling the photo and the envelope, and the writing on the front was typed, so there's no point doing a handwriting analysis. And since the photo simply shows Hayley on a bed so far it's not helping to point us in the right direction as to where he's holding her." Parker had been hoping that Marty would be able to find something that tied the photo to Jamie because Tessa was now more convinced, and more paranoid, than ever that she had been right and Jamie Presland was not the Iceman.

"The prisoner is ready," a young officer interrupted as he called out to them from across the room.

J.J. had insisted that they take one more shot at Jamie Presland in the hope that he might change his mind and actually tell them where Hayley was, but Parker couldn't help but feel defeated before they even begun. "I don't know why we're bothering, he's never gonna tell us where he has her," Parker caught the whine in his own voice but couldn't summon enough energy to care.

"Maybe we'll get lucky," Wyatt smiled half-heartedly; Parker could see the toll the case was taking on his partner. Wyatt looked tired, his eyes seemed a little sunken, and it looked like there were some white tips in his sandy blonde hair.

"You never know I guess," he said as brightly as he could as he followed Wyatt to the interrogation room.

Inside the prison's small, windowless room, usually reserved for prisoners to talk with their attorney, Jamie sat at the table, shackled, and dressed in his orange jumpsuit. Apparently faring none the worse for prison life, he looked chipper and upbeat like they were old friends.

"Hello," Jamie beamed at them.

Frowning in return Parker took a seat opposite him asking, "Did you leave the envelope?"

"What envelope?" Jamie asked with convincing confusion.

"The one with the photo of Hayley. The one that you addressed to my girlfriend. The one that you left lying around for children to find in the garden at my house," he snarled, he was in no mood for games. "Did you leave it?"

"Oh, that envelope," Jamie nodded enthusiastically as though until that moment it has slipped his mind. "Sure I did that."

"Why?"

"Why what?"

Exhaling deeply, "Why did you leave it?"

"To mislead you, make you think that I wasn't the killer," Jamie said gravely.

"But you confessed," Wyatt reminded him, sliding into the seat beside Parker.

"Right," Jamie nodded as if he'd forgotten about that. "It was just to spook you. It worked right?"

Disgusted, "Are you gonna tell us where Hayley is or not?" he asked.

"Actually, there was something I wanted to tell you about that girl, Hayley," he added apparently remembering Parker's anger when he had refused to acknowledge them as human beings at their last meeting.

A bad feeling building. "What?" Parker asked warily.

"I lied."

"About what?" the feeling was growing.

"She's dead. She always was. When you figured out who I was I decided to kill her before you caught me. I just never got a chance to finish it off properly, you know in the ice and stuff," he was speaking calmly, rationally as if he were relating an interesting cake recipe.

Closing his eyes and shaking his head, Parker heard Wyatt's quiet moan of distress. "Tell us where the body is," he commanded. "So her family can have closure."

Caught of guard, "Uh no can do my friend," Jamie stammered. "It's a secret."

"What do you gain by not telling us," Wyatt demanded.

"I get to keep my notoriety, my fame, my respect," Jamie told them as though it were obvious.

Without another word Parker turned and indicated for the guard to let them out, Wyatt hot on his heels. Once they were in the hall he rammed his fist into the wall, relishing the pain that flew up through his fingers and up through his arm.

"It's over, Parker, there was nothing more we could have done," Wyatt reminded him calmly.

"Yeah there is," he insisted softly, all he wanted was to go home, take Tessa in his arms and hold her and never let her go. "We could have noticed when Hannah Green went missing and caught him before he got a chance to do all this."

If there was any justice in the world then all of this would die down quickly and the Iceman would fade into the past then Jamie Presland would be denied the one thing he wanted most; attention.

DECEMBER 20TH

10:13 P.M.

"What're doing up here all by yourself?"

"I was just checking on the kids," Tessa answered from the window as Parker came up behind her.

"You came up here to do that twenty minutes ago," he reminded her with a soft chuckle, as he began to rub her shoulders.

She had left Casey and Skylar's anniversary party that was raging away downstairs to come and check on Sam and Stacey, who were still fast asleep in Parker's old room. Then she'd stopped to grab something from her and Parker's room, what exactly that was now alluded her, and paused at the window getting caught up in watching the flurry of snowflakes outside. Obviously she'd lost track of time as she'd stood there looking down at the bright, sparkly world. Fairy lights were strung across trees in every front yard, including their own, which Parker had somehow managed to find the time to decorate. Christmas trees shone from windows, the snow reflected the light all around it as it made its journey from sky to ground. After days of nearly constant snowing the ground was covered in a thick winter mantle of fluffy white.

"It's beautiful," Parker's voice rumbled by her ear.

"Yeah it is," she agreed, still unable to tear her eyes away from the magical sight. As a child they had never celebrated Christmas much. They'd had a Christmas tree, but one of the house staff had erected it, they had presents, but it was always some over the top extravagant gift, when all little Tessa had really wanted was her mom and dad to spend the day with her. After the gift exchanging on Christmas morning her parents would disappear, too busy with their own lives to spend time with her and Daniel.

Her most memorable Christmas was the one when she was seven.

199

Fiercely independent, even at that age, and angry at her parents disinterest, Tessa had snuck into the back of one of the maid's car and travelled with the old lady back to her house. Watching from the front window while Maria celebrated Christmas with her extended family Tessa felt a deep yearning to one day have what that lady had. Eventually she had been spotted and after a scolding from Maria had been allowed to stay and join in the festivities. By the time Maria had taken her home, late Christmas night, Emilie and Patrick had not yet even realized that she was missing.

Never again would she spend another Christmas alone, this year, like last year, she had Parker, and he had promised her that he would never leave her, and shocking even herself, she was starting to believe it.

"Honey, you're crying," Parker turned her around to face him. "What's wrong?"

"Nothing," she told him honestly. "I'm just happy."

Smiling and brushing away her tears with his thumb. "I'm glad," he said as he gently kissed her forehead.

"I have something for you," she announced suddenly. "I was going to give it to you for Christmas, but . . ." retrieving the wrapped gift from the cupboard, the only present left that wasn't already downstairs under the Christmas tree.

"Thanks," Parker took the gift from her outstretched hand and methodically began to open the paper, careful not to tear it. When it was unwrapped he stared at it with surprise, "It's a scarf like the one I . . ."

"Like the one you used the night I was attacked to try and stop the bleeding," she pulled the scarf from his hand and wound it around his neck.

"It won't remind you of . . ." he begun worriedly.

"It will remind me of how much you love me," she told him determinedly, taking hold of the ends of the scarf and pulling him down so she could kiss him. Her resolve to not let anything shake her had wavered slightly after she was attacked but she'd decided that this was not going to break her. Giving Parker the scarf was her way of metaphorically putting it behind her, although she hated how much that sounded like something a psychiatrist would say.

Deepening the kiss, her tongue cautiously exploring Parker's mouth, little electrical shocks rippling through her body. Before she realized it her hands were beginning to unbutton Parker's shirt.

Abruptly he pulled away from her, his hands wrapping firmly around hers and she realized she was breathing as heavily as he was. "You're not ready," he whispered, voice husky, eyes glittering with longing.

Scrutinizing him carefully, "Yes I am," she whispered back, standing on tiptoes to press her lips against the hollow of his neck, her hands running through his hair.

Moaning, he closed his eyes, "Tessa, once you start this, I won't be able to stop," he cautioned softly.

"I don't want you to," her hands started in once again on his buttons, this time a little more fervently, overcome with the desire to have her hands against his bare skin. Shirt coming away, her fingertips ran the length of his smooth, muscled chest, pausing for only a second when they reached his belt, then working quickly at undoing it, and seconds later his pants were dropping to the floor leaving him in only his boxers.

Stooping so his lips were against her ear, "Are you sure?" he asked one last time. Tessa couldn't answer, her heart was beating as fast as if she'd just run a marathon, her pulse was roaring in her ears like the ocean, so she just nodded. Then he was greedily devouring her, his lips on hers as his hands found the zip at the back of her dress, undid it and slipped her arms free, letting the garment join his own on the floor.

Never taking his mouth from hers his hands wrapped around her buttocks lifting her off the floor. Tessa wrapped her legs around his waist and felt his throbbing pressed against her own. Carrying her to the bed where he lay her gently down on top of the covers, his lips dropping a line of kisses from her neck, between her breasts and down her stomach. Little moans escaping from her throat, she had never guessed that it could be like this, so sweet, so beautiful. Then with a hungry growl, Parker was pulling away his own boxers and her panties, tossing them to the floor, and with surprising tenderness climbing on top of her.

After they were done she lay in the crook of his arm, her head against his chest, his breath whooshing across her face, their arms and legs tangled, she felt more at ease than she had thought was possible. Neither of them spoke, they were content just to be together, entwined in one another's embrace.

"Eww that is disgusting," a voice shrieked quietly from the doorway.

They both turned, cheeks flaming red, to see Maisy covering her eyes with both hands.

"Hey, Maisy," Parker cleared his throat and forced a smile. "What are you doing up here?"

Laughing, "Trying to find our hosts for the evening. Are you two going to come back to the party you're throwing or should I hang a 'Do Not Disturb' sign from the door handle?"

"That'll be enough of that, young lady," Parker admonished as both he and Tessa scrambled for their clothes. "Tessa and I are coming back down." Maisy pointedly turned her back as they climbed back into their clothes, Parker pausing to kiss her one last time.

"I just have to go to the restroom, I'll meet you down there," she told them when they were fully clothed.

"Alright, I'll be waiting," Parker threw her another hungry smile, and Tessa felt her body begin to stir again as she thought of what they would do once everyone had gone home. "Come on you," he growled playfully at Maisy as he pretended to strangle her, but she wiggled free from his grip and ran down the stairs calling to everyone that she'd found them.

Giggling as she closed the bathroom door, Tessa felt the smile fall from her lips as she saw the envelope taped to the mirror. Her name was typed on the front, just as it had been in the one the Iceman left for her in the backyard. When she's seen that note she'd known that she was right that Jamie wasn't the killer, but then he'd confessed to leaving the note, and she had allowed Parker to convince her to ignore her instincts and believe that Jamie Presland was the Iceman.

With a trembling hand she reached for the envelope, opened it and slid out a single sheet of white paper and another photograph.

Reading it confirmed her worst fears.

* * * * *

10:41 P.M.

Smiling along with the others as he listened to a story that he had to have heard at least a hundred times already. A story about fifteen year old J.J. and his goal winning shot for the varsity basketball team he was on despite being only a freshman. J.J. was playing it for all it was worth, with dramatic pauses, hand gestures; he had his audience's undivided attention.

"I have heard that story so many times," Maisy moaned beside him.

"Me too," Parker nodded, glancing around his living room, which was crammed to overflowing with police officers, CSU techs, a couple of ADA's, as well as Wyatt and Casey's family, everyone who loved them was here to help celebrate the Wyatt's fifteen year wedding anniversary.

Tessa had spent all day decorating the place with pink and blue streamers and balloon's, which somehow managed to not clash with the Christmas decorations. The tables, upon which every spare inch was crammed with food, were decked out with color co-ordinated tablecloths and matching plastic plates and utensils. Although he had offered to help several times Tessa had told him with a raised eyebrow that he knew absolutely nothing about decorating, and that he had better leave it to the professional.

As many people as there were inside, there were just as many outside, not put off by the snow, some of the guests, respected lawyers and police officers, were busily involved in a snowball fight. Scanning the crowd for the one person he sought and couldn't find. "Shouldn't Tessa be down by now, it's been like ten minutes since you busted us in the bedroom."

Unable to control a giggle, "She probably snuck down because she didn't want to get caught and have to listen to another one of

J.J.'s stories," Maisy rolled her eyes.

"Hey you wanna dance," a nervous looking CSU tech about Maisy's age asked apprehensively, clearly preparing himself for rejection.

"Sure," Maisy grinned and as the relieved young man spirited her away she called over her shoulder, "Tess is probably outside, you know how she loves snow."

Deciding Maisy was probably right, Parker begun to weave his way through the throng in the direction of the back door. As he slipped outside, narrowly avoiding a wave of poorly aimed snowballs, he saw no sign of Tessa. Worried that something had happened to her, she'd seemed fine when they were upstairs, but maybe she'd got sick suddenly, or passed out.

Weaving his way back inside, more forcefully this time, and taking the stairs three at a time, upon reaching the bathroom door he banged on it in the most restrained manner he could muster.

"Tessa?" he called.

When there was no answer he started to turn the handle. "Tessa, I'm coming in," he called again.

Opening the door he found the room empty just as he had anticipated, about to go and check the bedroom when he caught sight of something white on the floor, bending to pick it up he felt his heart stop. It was an envelope; eerily similar to the one Sam and Stacey had found in the backyard the other night, and it was once again addressed to Tessa. No longer caring about forensics he tore the envelop in his haste to get to whatever was inside, and almost passed out when he read it.

Before he realized what he was doing he was flying down the stairs aware of the strange looks he was getting but too frantic to care. Catching sight of Wyatt by the door, he ran over and grabbed his partner's arm. Mumbling a quick and insincere "sorry," to whomever Wyatt was talking to then practically dragging him to the den, ignoring his partner's protests.

"Tessa's gone," he announced as he closed the den door behind them.

Confused, "What do you mean gone?"

"What do you think I mean? I mean gone, disappeared, vanished, no longer here . . ."

"Okay, okay," Wyatt interrupted. "Where did she go?"

Thrusting the note into Wyatt's hand. "I found this in the bathroom. It means he was here, inside the house, it means that we got the wrong guy . . ."

Cutting off his rambling once again, "Who was in the house?" Wyatt asked struggling to follow along. "Parker, you have to calm down because you are not making any sense."

"The Iceman," watching shock fly across his partner's face. "Jamie Presland is not the Iceman, someone else is, and that someone was here in my house, and left Tessa this."

"You think he kidnapped her," Wyatt asked already reaching for his phone.

"No, I think she went after him," Parker answered, déjà vu flashing through him. "Just read the note." Feeling giddy with shock, after what had just happened upstairs he didn't understand how Tessa could go off on her own after a killer, again.

Eyes growing wide as he read, by the time Wyatt was finished his face was as white as the paper he held clutched in his hand. "You think Tessa knows who this is?"

"Of course she knows," he roused at Wyatt. "Tessa always knows who everyone is."

"We have to tell J.J. we have to find . . ."

"Tell J.J. what?" Marty asked from the door, Maisy at his side.

"We saw you running around like a lunatic out there then dragging Wyatt in here, what's up, Parker?" Maisy asked scanning the room. "And where's Tessa?"

Not wanting to waste time explaining Parker yanked the note from Wyatt's hand to thrust it at Marty and Maisy and slammed the door closed behind them.

Maisy was shaking by the time she was finished reading. "That means we were wrong and Jamie isn't the killer," she stammered.

"If Tessa figured out who the real killer is then there is no way she would run off after him on her own . . ." Marty trailed off as he realized who they were talking about.

"Of course she would," Parker snapped. Panic making him more aggressive than he should have been, he could still smell Tessa's sweet fragrance on his skin, still feel her body pressed tightly against his, still hear her voice murmuring inside his head that she wanted him.

"Tessa does seem to have a knack of getting herself into sticky situations," Marty agreed.

"No she doesn't get herself into trouble she runs straight for it," Parker growled. "Tessa is self-destructive, she's impulsive, she's rash, she's reckless, she's irresponsible, she's impetuous, she's . . ."

"Parker, that's enough synonyms," Maisy admonished shakily. "You need to calm down."

"Calm down," he repeated incredulously. "Calm down? Tessa just ran off after a serial killer. On her own. Again. How am I supposed to calm down?"

"Because if you don't then we are not going to get her back alive," Wyatt's soothing voice sliced through the panicked haze that engulfed him. "Tessa knows how to take care of herself, so right now the best thing we can do for her is to figure out who the real killer is."

"Maybe we do have the right guy and this is just a hoax," Maisy suggested lamely.

"It has a photo of Hayley holding today's paper," Parker reminded her.

"At least we know Hayley's still alive," Marty mused wanly.

Yesterday that would have made all the difference, now all Parker could think about was that Tessa was once again putting herself in the hands of a madman.

"If Jamie isn't the killer then we're back at square one," Maisy reminded them, "and before Jamie we had no leads."

"We'll get the files back out, hey we have almost the entire police department here," Wyatt remained relentlessly positive. "We'll get everyone to help, someone will be able to come up with something."

"If Jamie isn't the Iceman then why'd he confess?" Marty asked, baffled.

"Who knows, who cares," Parker muttered, he didn't care about

Jamie Presland right now, all he cared about was getting Tessa home safe and sound so he could strangle her for causing him all this anguish. Fingering the scarf she'd given him just half an hour ago, remembering the look of love in her eyes as she'd kissed him, remembering the feel of her body in his arms. He couldn't lose her, he couldn't, without her he had nothing.

"Hey, we're going to find her, Parker," Wyatt gave his shoulder a reassuring squeeze. "If anyone can confront a serial killer and get away with it, its Tessa," he joked softly.

"For sure," Maisy added with a shaky smile. "No one would dare cross that girl once she works herself up."

"And we have something that we didn't have before," Marty spoke up, as they all looked at him. "We have a connection." Holding up the letter, "Tessa. He sent her this for a reason, and that's how we're gonna find him."

An imaginary light bulb going off above his head Parker grabbed for the phone. "And I know just who's going to help us."

* * * * *

11:56 P.M.

It looked just like she remembered it even though it had been fifteen years since she'd last been here.

Glad she'd decided to change before she left as the snow was still falling thick and fast and it was freezing out. After reading the note she'd let it fall to the floor and hurried back to the bedroom, shedding her satin party dress in favor of more sensible clothes, jeans, a lavender woolen turtleneck with matching beanie, gloves and scarf, and a pale pink leather jacket.

Luckily she'd managed to make it away from the house unseen, thanks to her journey out the window and the fact that her car had been parked on the street because of the party so it hadn't been a problem to get to it and drive off without anybody noticing. She knew that if anyone had seen her sneaking away they would have told Parker, who would have hounded her until she'd told him where she was going. Once he knew that she was heading straight for the Iceman he would have handcuffed her to the door before he let her run straight into the arms of a serial killer.

Parker was going to be mad when he found out that she was gone. Tessa knew that Parker wanted her to trust him completely, and she did, as least as much as she knew how to, but she'd spent the majority of her life dealing with things on her own. It was the most effective way she knew to get things done, it was like the saying, if you want something done right then you do it yourself. But he did have a point, they were supposed to be a team now so she wasn't supposed to go off handling things on her own anymore, especially after what they'd just done. Before tonight Tessa had always thought the term 'making love' was corny, a term for soap operas and movies, but after today she understood exactly what it meant. It meant more than mere sex, it meant joining your body and soul with the person you truly loved.

Bypassing the house, to head out into the woods, making a beeline straight for the place she was looking for. It was almost pitch black out, the thick woods blocking out any moonlight that managed to trickle through the mass of grey clouds that had been hovering overheard for days. Thankfully Tessa didn't need to be able to see to know where she was going.

In the car on the way here she had thought about her dream.

Crunching through the snow Tessa wondered how many deaths could have been avoided, how much pain averted if she had put the pieces together earlier. She was so angry at herself, she'd known that Jamie wasn't the Iceman, she'd known that she had to have had that dream for a reason, she should have insisted that Parker keep looking for the killer.

Still it did no good to play the 'what if' game. What was, was, and there was nothing she could do about it now.

Trudging along, the thick woods may have cut out any moonlight, but at least it also cut out a lot of the falling snow, she may be cold but at least she wasn't getting too wet. The woods were beautiful in the snowy night, the trees were delicately laced with dustings of snow, the ground too was covered in a thick, white carpet, the whole world looked magical, too bad looks could be deceiving.

Up ahead Tessa saw a bright light, a fire was crackling merrily, the flames a mixture of red and yellow and orange, splashing a shimmering glow through the trees. Despite the fact that she had almost been burned alive in a fire twelve months ago, Tessa found watching flames mesmerizing, the way they danced and swirled in an awesome display of majesty almost as though they were alive.

Approaching the fire a figure came slowly into view and Tessa knew that this was her last opportunity to back out, to call Parker and bring in reinforcements. Then she focused herself, the reason she had come was to find out where Hayley Geoffries was bring held. The reason she had come alone was she had known it was the only way to obtain this information.

Standing unnoticed in the shadows of the silent night, the only sound the crackling of the wood as the flames burnt them up, and the sizzling of the odd snowflake that landed in the fire.

"Why did you do it?" she asked at last taking a step inside the circle of light that emanated from the fire and knowing that this was it, there was no backing out now, whatever happened, happened.

Leisurely turning around, "Tessa, so glad you could come," the real Iceman said with a creepy, but unbelievably sane, smile.

Even though she had never seen the face before it was exactly what she had imagined and it looked exactly like it had in her dream and in her mind.

"Why did you do it?" she repeated.

Ignoring her the Iceman said instead, "Won't you sit?" gesturing at a log by the fire.

Deciding that for the moment at least it was best to play along, she sat.

"Do you want a drink?" the Iceman held up a cooler.

"You trying to poison me?" Tessa asked only half joking.

"Amateurish, I would never stoop to that level," the Iceman looked offended at the insinuation.

Hiding a smile as she selected a diet coke from the cooler pulled the tab and took a long drink, realizing that she was hungry as well as thirsty, she hadn't eaten since breakfast this morning.

Also choosing a diet coke, the Iceman sat beside her and for a long minute both of them sat watching the dancing flames, and despite the outrageous circumstances, both were enjoying the beautiful night.

Finally the Iceman broke the silence, "Did you tell him?"

"Parker? No, I didn't tell him," detecting an infinitesimal undertone of worry in the Iceman's voice.

Raising an eyebrow, a spark of relief washing briefly across the Iceman's face. "Why?"

"Because he would have stopped me from coming," Tessa answered honestly. "But that doesn't mean that I'm going to let you go."

"Then why not just tell him where I was and let him come get me?"

"Because I needed to talk to you, I need to know why you did it. Besides," she threw the Iceman a cheeky smile, "You knew that I was coming alone or you wouldn't be here waiting."

Laughing like she'd just said the funniest thing ever. "True, true," the Iceman smiled agreeably. "But you have to know that I'm never going to let you go."

Tessa did indeed know this, but she still wasn't afraid. "I know," she nodded with a calm that surprised even herself. "But what makes you think I didn't leave a note to Parker telling him where I was going?"

Unfazed, "Did you?"

"I didn't need to, I left your note . . ."

"Which doesn't say where I was," the Iceman interjected smugly.

"But you're forgetting something," she replied just as smugly.

"What?"

Noting a glimmer of doubt in the eyes that intently watched her every move. "Daniel."

DECEMBER 21ST

Sighing and shivering, trying to keep warm enough to sleep.

Things weren't so bad when she was asleep.

Then the hunger and thirst and cold and pain receded to a dull background annoyance.

The Iceman hadn't been back in a couple of days and Hayley wondered what had happened.

Maybe she'd made the Iceman so angry that she was never going to get another visit, just be left here to die slowly from starvation and dehydration.

Maybe the police had caught the killer and the Iceman wasn't going to tell them where Hayley was, once again leaving her here to die slowly from starvation and dehydration.

Afraid of what the Iceman might do upon return Hayley had built herself a little fortress. She'd dragged the table over to the side where the bed was and put it over the bed so that when she lay down the table was just above her.

After days and days of being cooped up in a small space she'd been surprised that she had actually enjoyed the closed in feeling of being in bed with the table over the top of her. It made her feel safe, like she was in her own little cocoon.

Her thin, naked body was so bony now she could count her ribs.

Hayley remembered all the times when she was growing up that she had wished she was thinner, now that she was she couldn't stand the sight of her own body.

Hardly caring anymore that she was naked; it wasn't like anyone was going to see her anyway.

Neither did she care that she no longer had a toilet. When she had to go she just crawled across to the other side of the small room, did her business and crawled back.

The leg that the Iceman had shot was stiff and sore, the wound an angry red, and Hayley was pretty sure it was infected.

Maybe she would die of that instead, she thought to herself.

So used to being alone now that she could hardly imagine talking to real people, being in a room with them.

It all seemed so foreign to her now.

Tucking her blanket up under her chin, she tried to clear her head so that she could doze off. It was how she spent most of her time now, sleeping.

Sometimes in her dreams she would see the Iceman coming to her and hurting her.

Sometimes she would see the Iceman's other victims.

Sometimes they helped her and sometimes they joined forces with the Iceman and ganged up against her.

But sometimes her dreams were sweet and wonderful.

Being at home with her mom and dad.

The police coming running in to save her.

Swimming in an ocean full of beautiful, colored fish.

Flying through a sky so blue she could hardly stand it.

Hayley didn't care anymore.

She didn't care about being rescued.

She didn't care about dying.

All she cared about was being somewhere where there was no pain, no hunger, no thirst, no cold.

Hayley Geoffries had given up hope.

Hayley Geoffries was simply waiting to die.

* * * * *

12:11 P.M.

"Daniel, its Parker. Again. Where are you? I've already left you like a hundred messages. I need you to come to my place. Now. Tessa's gone, I'll explain when you get here."

Looking at the phone for a moment then with a roar he threw it across the room, taking a small amount of satisfaction when it ricocheted off the wall and bounced across the floor before coming to rest, now in several pieces.

"Do we have anything?" he demanded, glaring around at Wyatt, J.J., Marty, Maisy and the couple of other detectives who had remained behind to scour through the Iceman files. A tense ball of worry and anger, he couldn't seem to settle down for long enough to make any headway through the mountain of paperwork.

"Nothing yet, but we'll find something," J.J. assured him.

After calling Daniel Micah, the first time, he and Wyatt had returned to the party, explained vaguely that something had come up and sent everyone home. While he and Wyatt were ending things with the guests, Marty and Maisy were bringing J.J. up to speed. Immediately taking charge of the situation, as was his way, J.J. organized a few detectives to remain behind and help them, but decided that to keep things under wraps for the moment so the public didn't panic they didn't tell everyone what was going on.

So here they all were, twelve odd hours later, all of that time spent studying each and every piece of paper relating to the case and they were no closing to finding the identity of the real Iceman than they had ever been.

"Are you sure you want to ask Daniel for his help?" Wyatt asked. "You two don't really get along."

"I don't think I have a choice," Parker snapped, either Daniel Micah was the Iceman or he knew who was.

"Wyatt said that you thought it was suspicious that Daniel showed up now," J.J. commented taking a huge swig of cold coffee.

"Suspicious yes but that doesn't make Tessa's brother a killer . . . does it?" Looking around the room for guidance, he didn't seriously think that Daniel was a psychopath but it was clear that Jamie Presland wasn't the killer and someone had to be.

"I thought Daniel only got here a couple of weeks ago," Maisy rubbed her tired eyes and stifled a yawn.

"But he also said he came because he heard about what happened with Dylan, he said that someone sent him a copy of one of the articles, but if he really did come when he first heard about Dylan

Riley then . . .”

“Then he was here when the first body appeared,” Marty finished.

“But not when Hannah Green was abducted,” Wyatt reminded them.

About to begin another tirade Parker was cut short at the sound of someone pounding on the front door. Reaching the door in two seconds flat, yanking his gun from its holster and pointing it at the door as he swung it open to see a fuming Daniel on the other side.

“You lost my sister!” he yelled, his expression swinging from anger to startled as he saw the gun aimed at his chest, then his eyes growing into two huge aqua saucers as he caught sight of the house’s other occupant’s guns also pointed at him.

Unfortunately the blue eyes that stared back at him only served to remind him of Tessa and Parker felt his resolve waver. “Are you the Iceman? Did you take her?” he demanded, he didn’t have enough patience left to play things smoothly.

“What?” Daniel looked genuinely shocked. “I thought you already had the guy in custody. I thought he confessed.” Looking around at the skeptical faces watching him. “You really think I’m the killer?”

“Are you?”

“You honestly think I’m the Iceman, I knew you didn’t like me but to accuse me of being a serial killer, I think that’s going too far even for you,” Daniel ranted.

“Then where have you been?” Parker snapped back.

“I was out of town. Moving. Just like you told me to. When I got back to Tessa’s place to pick up more of my stuff I got your messages.”

“You didn’t think to call and let me know you were coming?” Parker still didn’t like Daniel but his suspicions were starting to waver.

“I can prove it to you,” Daniel announced suddenly. “You’re sure it was the Iceman that attacked Tessa the other night, at the restaurant right?”

“Right,” Parker agreed slowly wondering where this was going.

“Then there’s no way I could be the Iceman,” Daniel told them triumphantly. "When Tessa was attacked I was with . . ." he trailed off nervously.

Frowning, "You were with a prostitute?" Parker asked.

Horrified, "No of course not." Uttering a deep sigh, "I was with my therapist okay." Pulling out his wallet to rifle through it then producing a card. "Here you can call and check it out."

Taking the card with one hand and passing it to Wyatt. "We'll do that," Parker told him, then while his partner went to dial the number he asked, "You were really with a shrink in the middle of the night?"

"First of all it was nine o'clock," Daniel pouted. "And second of all it's none of your business."

"I already told you if it has anything to do with Tessa then it is my business," Parker kept the gun pointed at Daniel, not quite ready to believe in him.

"You lost my sister," Daniel repeated, his anger snap, crackle and popping.

Daniel was shaping up to be the perfect outlet for his anger. "I didn't lose her, she left."

"You let her go?"

Rolling his eyes dramatically. "Of course I didn't *let* her go, she snuck out of here."

"I thought you were supposed to be taking care of her, I would never have agreed to leave Tessa unless I thought you had her back, which obviously you don't since you let her sneak out . . ."

"What does the phrase 'sneak out' mean to you exactly? Are you suggesting that I should hover over her shoulder every second of the day?" Parker snarled sarcastically.

"What I'm suggesting is . . ."

"Okay, okay, children," J.J. materialized between them. "Break it up."

"He checks out," Wyatt called as he hung up the phone. "He was with his therapist. Apparently he's been seeing him every couple of days since he got back into town."

Finally lowering his gun Parker spun on his heel and marched back down the hall to the living room, J.J. followed but Daniel remained on the doorstep. "Are you coming in or what?" Parker glowered over his shoulder.

"I thought I wasn't welcome here?"

"I called you didn't I?" Parker snapped.

Entering the house and giving the door a more vicious nudge than was needed to close it. "Yes and before I ask why let me make one thing absolutely clear. I am not a killer, I do not have Tessa and I will do whatever you need me to, take a polygraph or anything, in order to fully convince you of that so that we don't waste time looking in the wrong direction. Now onto why I'm here, I thought you told me to stay away from Tessa, now all of a sudden something goes wrong and you expect me to drop everything and come running?"

About to make a witty, albeit nasty, comeback when Wyatt jumped in instead, "We called you because you know Tessa."

Narrowing his eyes suspiciously. "And what exactly makes you think I know what goes on behind my sister's big, empty blue eyes?"

"Because as lame as it sounds," Wyatt replied, "Those big, blue, empty eyes are your eyes, Daniel. She's your sister and you know her better than any of us do."

Scoffing, "I agree with Daniel he doesn't know Tess. She told me that the two of them weren't even close growing up." Parker knew that this childish bickering wasn't helping but he couldn't seem to help himself, Tessa's brother seemed to bring out the worst in him.

Defensive now Daniel decided to change his mind. "Oh yeah? Tessa said that did she? Well did she tell you how we used to hide out together in my room when Emilie and Patrick were having one of their raging arguments?"

"As a matter of fact she did," he shot back.

"Well did she tell you how after Eleanor was killed she used to sneak into my room when she thought I was asleep, and curl up on the floor next to my bed to spend the night because she was too afraid to sleep alone?" Daniel was shooting him the exact same angry glare as Tessa did.

Picturing Tessa as a child, scared and alone, the only witness in her friend's murder, too terrified to be by herself in the dark. "No she never told me that," he answered softly.

A faraway look in Daniel's eyes now, Tessa's eyes. "She didn't know that I knew. I wanted to tell her, to talk to her, but she was so closed off and I didn't know what to say."

Drained, he didn't want to argue with Daniel any longer, it wasn't helping him find Tessa, and right now that was all he cared about. Retrieving the letter from the table, Marty had gone over it on the off chance that a stray fingerprint or fiber or anything useful could be found. Of course he had come up empty.

"Here read this," he passed the note to Daniel. "The Iceman left it in the bathroom . . ."

Daniel's already pale face whitened further. "He was here in the house? When Tessa was here?"

"We don't know exactly when he left the note," Wyatt answered. "But it had to be sometime after lunch," with a glance at the clock on the wall, "yesterday, but before the party."

"Anyway he left it in an envelope," Parker continued. "With a current photo of Hayley Geoffries the missing . . ."

"The missing girl," Daniel interrupted, catching on quickly. "So that other guy can't be the Iceman, unless he's working with a partner, which with serial killers is usually unlikely. I don't get it though why would he leave Tessa a letter?"

"That's what we're hoping you can tell us," Parker told him pointing at the letter.

Turning his attention to the note in his hand Daniel read it quickly, Parker following along over his shoulder.

Tessa,
You know where I am
CUI

Daniel swayed as he read the note, reflexively Parker grabbed hold of his elbow but Daniel shook him off, his gaze wild.

"That's impossible," he stammered throwing the note away as though it were burning him.

"Do you know who wrote it?" Parker asked, a bubble of hope

filling slowly inside him.

"That's not possible. That is not possible," Daniel repeated, looking like he was quickly going into shock.

Parker didn't have time for this. "Come on, Daniel, snap out of it, do you know who it is that wrote that?"

But Daniel wasn't listening, his mind apparently connecting dots together that the rest of them weren't seeing. "Tessa's arm."

"What?" Parker asked confused.

"Tessa's arm, it wasn't saying that you were being watched," Daniel murmured distractedly, the wheels in his head still turning.

Giving in to the urge to shake Daniel he grabbed the man's shoulders and shook him, hard. "Daniel, the man who wrote that note is a serial killer if you know who it is then tell me," practically shouting the last word.

"It's Cordelia. I don't know how but it is, it has to be," clearly Daniel was struggling to believe his own words.

"Cordelia?" almost everyone in the room repeated in shocked unison.

"You're saying the Iceman is a woman?" Maisy enquired, flabbergasted.

"Are you sure that the person that wrote the note is the serial killer?" Daniel asked.

"There was the photo of Hayley Geoffries holding yesterday's newspaper, we know that the Iceman abducted her so I don't see who else could have left the letter," J.J. answered.

"Then Cordelia is the Iceman," Daniel looked convinced now.

"Who is Cordelia?" Parker asked at the same time Wyatt asked; "How can you know that?"

Answering Wyatt's question first, "CUI, Cordelia Ula Isis, that's how she writes her name."

"Again, who is Cordelia?" Parker snapped.

"Cordelia is my sister. Me and Tessa's sister."

Everyone stared at him with gaping mouths.

"Tessa never mentioned that she had a sister," Parker said finally finding his voice.

"Tessa didn't know about Cordelia, at least I thought she didn't,"

Daniel amended with a fleeting glance at the note that lay on the floor at his feet.

"What?" was all Parker could manage.

Daniel sighed and took a seat on the couch, hanging his head in his hands as he gathered his thoughts. "Cordelia had just turned fifteen when Emilie found out she was pregnant with Tessa," he began as everyone else gathered around. "I was six. Cordelia was, is I guess although I haven't seen her in twenty-six years, the most self obsessed person I've ever met. She's smart, but not as smart as Tessa, and she had Emilie and Patrick wrapped around her little finger. They did whatever Cordelia said whenever she said to do it. Cordelia loves attention, craves it, she can't live without it."

"Why did you think that Tessa didn't know about Cordelia?" Wyatt interrupted.

"When Cordelia found out that Emilie was pregnant she went bananas, ranting and raving about how she wouldn't play second fiddle to another baby . . ."

"What about you?" Maisy asked.

"Cordelia wasn't happy about me but she wasn't threatened by me either, to her I was nothing. But she somehow got it in her head that the new baby was going to take over, she was terrified that once it was born then Patrick and Emilie would forget all about her. She needn't have worried," Daniel said sadly with all the vulnerability of a neglected little boy, "they never cared about me or Tessa. Anyway Cordelia insisted that Emilie get an abortion and when she refused Cordelia blew a fuse and left. We never heard from her again and Emilie and Patrick told me that we were never going to tell Tessa about her. I think they were worried that Cordelia would come back and take out her anger on Tess."

"Would Cordelia hurt Tessa?" Parker clenched his hands in his lap to keep them from shaking.

"I don't think so, but then again I didn't even know that Tessa knew about her. Cordelia was weird, strange, scary even. She enjoyed seeing other people suffer, she was cruel and malicious, but still I never would have guessed that she was capable of . . . of this," Daniel waved his hand at the stacks of files spread around the room.

"How did Tessa find out about her?" Marty asked.

"Who knows," Daniel shrugged helplessly. "Who knows how Tessa knows the things she does."

Standing, Daniel wandered to the window where he stood staring out at the pitch-black night, and for the first time Parker found himself beginning to feel sorry for the guy.

"It's not your fault, Daniel, what happened, any of it. Even if you never left it wouldn't have changed anything," Parker consoled him.

Daniel turned to face him with doubtful eyes. "She's my baby sister. It's my job to look after her, keep her safe."

Offering a wry smile. "Tessa does that too. Blames herself for anything and everything, her specialty is things that she has no control over."

"Just like you," Daniel gave a mirthless chuckle. "I did my homework. Tessa's not the only one who researches people, I needed to know what kind of guy had stolen my sister's heart."

Finding some common ground Parker ventured, "Why did you leave her, Daniel?"

"I already told you I left because I had to. It was the only way I thought I could keep her safe."

Parker could see Daniel now thought his efforts had been pointless, Tessa had never been safe. "You were going to take her with you weren't you?" he asked.

Daniel studied him carefully for a long moment before nodding. "When I told Emilie she completely lost it, she was already hanging on by only a thread. After Cordelia left she became depressed, she started to drink, then Patrick left, and she got worse, when I told her I was leaving too and taking Tessa with me. She couldn't deal with it, she told me that if she couldn't have Tessa then no one would. That's the last thing I remember, then she knocked me out and tried to . . . I can't even say it."

Daniel turned back to the window to stare dejectedly out at the night, and Parker felt genuinely bad for the guy. Wherever he'd been and whatever he'd been doing for the last fourteen years it hadn't assuaged one iota of the guilt he felt for his part in his mother's actions. Opening his mouth to offer what felt like another pointless platitude when Daniel continued.

"When I woke up Emilie was gone, I checked Tessa's room but she was gone too, then I head Emilie mumbling some chant from the bathroom." His eyes carefully blank as he recounted the story, the same way Tessa's were when she couldn't deal with her emotions. "When I got there Emilie was holding Tessa's head under the water, Tess wasn't moving. I grabbed this statue thing from the hall and hit Emilie over the head, and then I pulled Tess out. She wasn't breathing and I did CPR for what felt like forever, I was sure she was gone, that there was nothing I could do that would bring her back but I couldn't stop, and then . . ."

Daniel paused and shook his head like he still couldn't believe it had happened. "And then she just started to breathe, it was a miracle. I called an ambulance and then I stayed by her side, holding her until they arrived. When they took Tessa to the hospital and I looked in Emilie's eyes I knew that as long as I was there then she would feel threatened. The only way I knew I could keep Tessa safe was to leave, so I did and it was the hardest thing I've ever had to do. What Emilie did was because of me." Pausing once again, "If I hadn't woken up when I did . . ." he let the thought trail off unspoken.

"But you did," Parker reminded him. "You did wake up and you did save Tessa's life, and you did what you thought at the time was the only thing you could to keep her safe."

Daniel nodded but didn't look convinced.

"I ran the name but didn't get any hits anywhere," Wyatt announced as he hung up the phone, Parker had been so engrossed in Daniel's story that he'd half forgotten that anyone else was even in the room.

"How did you run it?" Daniel asked.

"As you said it, Cordelia Ula Isis Micah," Wyatt told him.

Shaking his head, "She would never use that name, any of them. And if I know her she's probably been married half a dozen times, and she probably changed her whole name after each one, like I said Cordelia craves attention, when she gets bored with something she moves on."

"Would she have gone to see your mother, or maybe contacted your dad?" J.J. asked.

"Cordelia hates Emilie and Patrick almost as much as she hates Tessa," Daniel replied. "She would never go to them."

"Tessa does that, call your parents by their first names," Parker commented. "Does Cordelia do it too?"

"Who do you think I learnt it from? Cordelia may have liked their attention but she hated them, other than DNA it's the one thing all three of us actually have in common . . ." his words slowing down as his brow scrunched in concentration.

"What is it?" Parker asked.

"I think I know where they might be."

"Where?" J.J. demanded, already reaching for his phone.

But Daniel was shaking his head. "I'm going after them alone. Cordelia hates Tessa, she wants her to suffer, if we all go barging in there then who knows what Cordelia might do. If I go alone I might be able to talk some sense into her."

"She's a serial killer," J.J. reminded him shortly. "And she could be keeping Hayley Geoffries wherever it is you think she might be."

"And she's also my sister, and like you pointed out earlier who would know either of them better than me. I'll drive there and once I know that Cordelia isn't going to do anything crazy I'll call you and tell you where I am and then . . . what?" Daniel trailed off and frowned at him.

"You are so much like Tessa," Parker couldn't believe how similar the siblings were, not just in appearance but also in mannerisms, disposition and reasoning. "You want to go off impulsively, half cocked, with a plan you think is good based solely on the fact that you came up with it."

"I don't really see another option," Daniel pouted stubbornly.

"How about you tell us where you think your crazy sister is before she kills your other sister," J.J. was quickly becoming exasperated. "This woman has already kidnapped and killed four women, is holding a girl hostage and attacked Tessa once already."

"Well since I'm the only one who knows where they are I don't see that you have any choice," Daniel was already on his feet and halfway to the door.

"You are just as stubborn as Tessa," Parker snapped as he followed him. "I'm coming with you."

"We could follow you," J.J. countered.

"Good luck with that," Daniel was halfway down the driveway.

"At least help us out and tell us what Cordelia looks like," Wyatt called after them.

"She looks like me and Tessa," Daniel yelled over his shoulder, already climbing into his car.

Jumping in after him as Daniel revved the engine. "What is with you? I'm worried about Tess too, but there's something else, something you're not telling me," Parker eyed Daniel as he pulled madly down the driveway and out into the street.

"I just realized who lured me back to town."

* * * * *

3:16 P.M.

Tessa learnt long ago that monsters didn't live in closets or hide under your bed, they were everywhere, they were all around us. As a child it hadn't been the big hairy creature that lived under your bed, or in the closet, or under the stairs that had scared her but the fact that she knew that any person at any moment could turn out to be the most terrifying monster of all. Monsters didn't come in all shapes and sizes; they came in *every* shape and size.

Sitting now beside her sister, Tessa knew that she was in the presence of a true monster.

She hadn't told Daniel, Emilie and Patrick that she knew about Cordelia. They hadn't wanted to tell her so she had decided it was better for everyone if they never knew. She had been three the first time she'd noticed the figure in black that kept popping up everywhere she went. She'd been five when Cordelia had written to her for the first time, explaining who she was. Tessa had replied and on and off for the last twenty years they had corresponded. Their letters were usually short, lacking detail and Tessa usually received one after another of Cordelia's divorces.

After she'd told Cordelia that Parker had all he needed to find them her sister had gone berserk and Tessa had seen a glimpse of a person who was capable of almost anything. She might not know her sister very well but she had still been shocked to realize that Cordelia was the Iceman. Known it she had, however, the second she'd seen the way the note had been signed, CUI, it was the way Cordelia signed every letter she'd ever sent.

Ranting and raving almost incoherently for at least an hour, then Cordelia had declared that there was something she needed to take care of. She'd moved off a little ways into the woods and talked on her cell phone for hours; in the end Tessa tuned her out and put her mind to planning how she could best deal with her insane sister. After finally returning Cordelia had declared that she needed her rest and had promptly lain down and gone to sleep.

Watching her sleeping sister Tessa had been tempted to kill her there and then and end all of this pain, even going so far as to grab a branch and stand with it in her hand above Cordelia. But even as she had done so she had known that it was something she could never do. She wasn't capable of cold-blooded murder even if it did run in her family. And even if she was capable of killing her own sister, Cordelia was the only person who knew where Hayley Geoffries was, and that was what she was here to find out.

"Daniel doesn't know anything you know," Cordelia announced suddenly materializing in front of Tessa with two sandwiches in her hand. "Here."

Taking one of the sandwiches and deliberately taking her time to unwrap it, waiting until she could practically feel Cordelia squirm. At last she looked up at her sister. "You underestimate Daniel. He's a lot smarter than you think he is."

Scoffing as she unwrapped her own sandwich. "Daniel is nowhere near as smart as we are."

"You mean as smart as *I* am," Tessa corrected with a condescending smile. "We both know that I was always the smart one."

Fuming, "my IQ is 153," Cordelia screeched.

"And mine is 178," Tessa reminded her, stifling a laugh, this may be the first time she'd ever actually met Cordelia but reading her was easier than mastering your ABC's.

"And there it is," Cordelia dropped her sandwich into the dirt.

"There what is?" Tessa asked politely.

"The reason why I had to do it," she snapped.

"The reason why you *had* to kill four innocent girls?" Tessa pushed carefully, hoping to keep Cordelia on edge long enough to get what she needed before Parker turned up.

"What makes you think they were innocent," Cordelia queried as though she had just gained the upper hand.

"What makes you think they weren't," Tessa could play this game all day.

"Because I spent time with them," Cordelia smirked. "Lots of time."

Raising an eyebrow at her, "How does that mean you know them?" Tessa questioned reasonably. "You were holding them captive, they would have done whatever it was you wanted in the hope that you wouldn't kill them. The vain hope."

Apparently that amused Cordelia who sniggered, "Oh they did whatever I wanted alright."

"You're planning something," Tessa veered the conversation in a different direction.

"What do you mean?" Cordelia faked a baffled frown.

"You know exactly what I mean," Tessa told her. "You are the reason that Daniel came back. You're the one who sent him the article about what happened last year with Dylan Riley. It's because of that, that he came running back to town. You wanted him here. Why?"

"So he could be here for all of this," Cordelia waved her hands through the air. "I wanted him to witness everything that I have done. I also wanted us to have a little family reunion."

"There's more to it though," Tessa pushed.

"Ah, my sweet little sister never gives up," Cordelia grinned. "I wanted you both to witness my infamy."

"You mean you want to kill us both," Tessa commented mildly.

Trying to hide her surprise behind melodrama. "I would never kill you and Daniel, you're my own flesh and blood."

"It's okay," Tess smiled. "We can be honest with one another."

"How do you do it?" Cordelia asked with sudden genuine interest.

"Do what?"

"How do you always know what someone is thinking?"

Tessa shrugged. "I guess it's a gift."

"Daniel won't find us you know," Cordelia stated more to convince herself than anyone else. "There's no way he will."

"Why are you so threatened by me?" Tessa asked, something she'd always wondered but had never asked in any of her letters.

"I'm not threatened by you," Cordelia protested.

Tessa said nothing, just looked.

"I'm not," Cordelia repeated, sounding like a defensive child.

"You left because Emilie was pregnant with me. You told her that she should get an abortion. You never spoke to any of us, never came to see us," Tessa pointed out.

"And that adds up to me being threatened? You asked before why I've done all of this, and why I brought Daniel back," Cordelia begun. "But you already know the answer. Because of you."

"Because of what happened last year? Because I got the attention you seem to feel you deserve? But you kidnapped your first victim around Halloween. Dylan didn't turn up until November 20th, so there's no way you could have predicted that unless . . ." trailing off as she saw the smug smile that worked its way across Cordelia's plain face. "You tipped him off didn't you?"

No longer able to contain herself Cordelia begun to giggle like a little girl hopped up on sugar, as she stood to cross to the fire that had burned itself out hours ago. "You were always at the centre of everyone's attention," she moaned.

"So you're angry at me for getting too much attention even though you sent Dylan Riley to get me? Cordelia, that is insane," wondering if she'd underestimated Cordelia's grip on reality as she had with Dylan.

"I thought Dylan would break you before the story got so out of control, I had no idea he was going to go berserk. Then after Dylan beat you down I was going to finish you off with the Iceman thing, but things didn't quite go according to plan so I improvised and brought Daniel back instead."

"How could you do that?" Tessa couldn't believe her own sister could be so cruel.

"Dylan was supposed to destroy you, would have destroyed you, if it weren't for that stupid cop of yours," Cordelia snarled. "He ruined everything."

"He saved my life," Tessa wondered why she never told Parker enough just how much she loved him for everything that he had done for her. Why she always let fear, her arch enemy, win out, and vowed that if she made it out of this alive she would spend the rest of her life telling Parker every day just how important he was to her.

"Exactly," Cordelia shot back matter of factly.

"Do you really hate me that much, Cordelia? That you won't be happy until I'm dead?"

"Yes. I hate you that much," Cordelia's whole being radiated pure venomous abhorrence.

"Why don't you tell me where Hayley is Cordelia, this is really between me and you. You can let her go and still achieve what you wanted," Tessa pleaded, knowing rational pleading would do nothing to convince a lunatic.

"But I'm not quite done yet, you told me you knew I was working towards something big and you were right. I want a whole family reunion. You, me, Daniel, Emilie and Patrick," her smile was quickly growing more and more manic.

"You know Patrick is married again, he has two kids."

Rolling here eyes, "I know. Have you met them?" When Tessa shook her head she continued, "I've seen them, they're idiots, nothing like you and me."

"So you want to get us all together, show us how you've made such an unforgettable name for yourself and how stupid we all were not to believe in you and then you're going to kill us all? Does that sound like a good plan to you?"

"Actually it does," Cordelia nodded seriously. "Do you want to know how I'm going to do it?"

"Not really, but I do think I know where you're hiding Hayley Geoffries," Tessa told her.

"Do you now?"

"At the restaurant. It's yours right?"

Cordelia actually looked impressed, "Good job. And as a reward for your insightfulness, and because you're not going to be going anywhere to tell anyone, I'm going to tell you exactly where. Inside the aquarium is a secret room, one you access from the attic."

Nodding the approval she knew her sister craved. "Very clever." Then sobering, "Why did you do that to my arm, Cordelia? Couldn't you just leave a note on paper like a normal person?"

"Because I was angry at you," Cordelia said as though it was obvious. "And anyway it was a good distraction. Your boyfriend was going to catch me and then everything would have been ruined."

"You knew I was coming there that night," Tessa added.

"When I first met him I knew who he was, and then I saw he'd made a reservation for two. If you saw me you would have seen through the disguise. You would have known it was me. So I tried to hide outside, but he saw me so I ran and when I saw you were following me it just kind of happened," Cordelia shrugged indifferently.

Cordelia was right, she would have recognized her disguised or not. All three of them took after Emilie, each had her bluey-green eyes, her pale skin and freckles, her curly blonde hair, Tessa's the lightest Cordelia's the darkest. But while Tessa was short and pixie like, resembling Emilie, Daniel and Cordelia were tall like Patrick. Cordelia was five foot ten, lean, with big hands and feet; she could be mistaken for a man, especially if that was someone's preconceived notion.

"How did you do it, Cordelia? How did you get the bodies in the ice?" she was sincerely interested to know how her sister had managed that.

Obviously Cordelia was particularly enamored with this part of her plan because she begun animatedly. "Once I smothered them I took their bodies and put them in a block of ice I had prepared earlier," pausing to laugh at her own joke. "Anyway I'd left a circular hole in the middle so I simply posed the bodies inside, put the ice in an old bathtub, added the water and stuck it back in the freezer until the whole thing was solid." Laughing aloud, "I must admit it was my favorite part of the whole thing, it was ingenious if I do say so myself."

"What was with the holly and the gloves and leaving them naked?"

"No reason, I just wanted to make it dramatic," practically beaming with pride. "Do you think I'm evil, Tessie?"

"No," Tessa sniggered mockingly. "You're not evil, Cordelia. Self-centered, maybe, insane, possibly, but inside I think you're just a scared and lonely little girl looking for attention any way you can get . . ."

Catching sight of Cordelia's arm lunging for her too late to do anything about it. Aware of the anger and pure hatred in her sister's face, Tessa knew that Cordelia wouldn't rest until she was dead. The Taser sent pain rocketing through her body and then as blackness took over she was falling.

* * * * *

11:46 P.M.

She was tired, she was hungry, she was thirsty and she was in pain.

That about summed it up Winter thought dismally.

When her stepfather, at least she assumed it was her stepfather, had attacked her and knocked her out back at the restaurant, he had also tied her up and thrown her in here, wherever here was. Rope bound her ankles together and her good wrist was pulled behind her back and joined with another rope to her ankles, her broken arm rested uselessly on the floor. Although the ropes weren't too tight, she'd been cramped up for what had to have been days. Besides tying her up Grant had also gagged and blindfolded her before leaving her in what she thought was a cupboard of some sort. She was pretty sure they weren't still at the restaurant because she was almost positive that she remembered bouncing around in a car.

Winter didn't know why her mom didn't come. Surely she must have noticed that her daughter was missing by now, she wasn't that self-involved. Maybe Grant had done something to her mom too, maybe he had her tied up somewhere, or maybe he had . . . killed her.

Tears begun to well up behind her eyes again and she struggled to hold them back. When Winter had first woken in this cupboard, or wherever she was, and had put together what had happened she had burst into frantic tears as she pulled wildly at the ropes. The more she'd cried the more her nose blocked and the less she'd been able to breathe, Winter had used every ounce of self-control she had to calm herself down. Ever since she had been careful not to think of anything that might make her start crying again.

Hope that she was going to be rescued was quickly evaporating, she was trying to stay positive but with each passing second it was getting harder and harder. Her body ached, her stomach grumbled, and she was so thirsty it was almost all she could think about.

Once or twice her stepfather had been by to give her a drink of water, each time she had felt a gun pressed to her ribs, an unspoken threat, then the tape on her mouth had been removed and water held to her lips. Each time he visited he had remained silent, he just gave her some water and then left, leaving her all alone once again.

Just dozing off to sleep when she thought she heard footsteps outside, they didn't come directly to her as they had when Grant had come on previous occasions. Maybe her mother had noticed that she was missing, maybe she had gone to the police, and right now they were standing just on the other side of the door.

Banging her cast against the wall Winter heard the footsteps stop.

Banging again she heard them move slowly towards her.

Positive that there was a presence on the other side of the door that meant her no harm she banged a third time.

She felt rather than saw the light that splashed down onto her as the person opened the door.

Heard a shocked intake of air as whoever it was saw her lying there, bound, gagged and blindfolded.

Winter felt hands slide underneath her as she was lifted, carried a short distance and then set down again on something soft.

Wondering why the person had not said anything as they carefully undid the strip of cloth that was acting as a blindfold. Her eyes, accustomed to the dark, sprung closed in protest to the sudden light, so Winter squeezed them shut as her savior worked on loosening the ropes that bound her ankles and wrist.

At last she regained control of her sense of sight and tentatively opened her eyes, as they adjusted to the light a face came slowly into focus, and Winter's heart stopped.

"You," she tried to mumble but it came out all scratchy, her throat dry and hoarse from days of inactivity. She was trying to drag her deadened limbs into action to get away from him, but his hands gripped her.

"Try to stay still," he told her with surprising gentleness.

"You did this to me," she spluttered, still trying to shrink away from him.

"What?" Grant asked, clearly confused as he took her wrist and began to rub her hand, gently but firmly, to try and restore normal circulation.

"At the restaurant," she explained, her voice beginning to return to normal. "You found me looking through your things, you hit me over the head."

Still confused, "Are you thinking of the day I found you in my den?"

Shaking her head and then regretting it as it sent a waves of pain and nausea coursing through her. "No, after that. At the restaurant."

"Honey, I think you're a little confused," his look said he thought she was out of her mind. "Who did this to you?"

"It . . . it wasn't you?" Winter asked, for the first time taking a look around her surroundings and seeing that she was in her own home, in her own bedroom. The whole time she'd been tied up and stuffed inside her own closet.

"It wasn't me," Grant told her, letting go of her wrist and starting to rub her feet.

"Then who . . . who was it?" she asked herself as much as Grant.

"I got no idea, sweetheart," Grant answered.

Trying to focus her squishy mind. "I was at the restaurant looking for proof that you were the Iceman . . ."

"That I was the what now?" Grant demanded, looking at her in shock.

Ignoring him, "And I found it. In the closet in the office, there was a secret hiding place in the floor, under the carpet. I found it when I dropped the shoes," her mind putting things together faster than she could process. "I found a bag. In the bag were the photos, of each of the Iceman's victims, and the clothes that they were wearing when they were abducted. I thought it was you, that you'd left them there," she turned to study him, but he seemed completely stunned by this.

"That why you were going through my stuff that other time? Looking for proof that I was a serial killer?"

"Yes," Winter answered immediately, there was no point now in covering it up. "Then I put it all back, in the hiding space in the floor, and I was going to go to the police but someone was there, I saw boots, and then they left and I thought you'd gone. I was standing watching the fish when someone hit me over the head. Again I thought it was you but if it wasn't then . . . maybe Jamie?" she puzzled. "Maybe he is the killer and he kept the stuff in mom's office?"

"I don't think so, girly," Grant studied her back, thoughtful now. "He's been arrested. No chance he coulda done it."

"But if it wasn't you and it wasn't Jamie then . . ." an awful thought was brewing in her addled brain, "Where's my mom?"

She could tell the same thought was brewing in Grant's mind too. "I haven't seen her in a couple of days," he answered slowly.

Feeling the blood drain from her head, from her whole body, like someone had drilled a hole in her. "But that means that the only person who could do all this . . . the person who killed all those women, who attacked people, who knocked me unconscious and left me here. It had to be mom. Mom is the Iceman."

DECEMBER 22ND

1:01 A.M.

She was starting to get sleepy.

It had been dark outside for hours now, she could no longer see the time on her watch, but Tessa estimated that it was close to midnight, maybe even one o'clock. Unlike the night before when she had come here in search of her crazy sister, the moon and the stars offered no light. Neither was there a dancing fire to keep her warm and enable her to see.

Tonight it was pitch-black, the sky a thick mass of clouds, it had been snowing lightly all day, now the snow swirled furiously. She wondered whether Parker had called Daniel for help, because without her brother there was no way he was going to figure out where she was. Even if he did call Daniel and her brother figured out where she and Cordelia were, that didn't mean that finding her was going to be an easy task. Looking for her in these woods would be like looking for a needle in a haystack.

When Cordelia had Tasered her she had stumbled backwards into a carefully constructed trap. Apparently her sister had found an old, abandoned mine or well or something, and then covered the top with enough leaves and branches to mask the opening. When her weight had added to the covering it had broken through and sent her tumbling a good ten or eleven feet into this hole, where she was now stuck.

Tessa had no idea how long she had laid down here, unconscious, after she fell, but when she awoke she was covered in a soft layer of snow, so she'd estimated it to be at least an hour. She was sore, but had seemingly survived the fall without breaking any bones or seriously injuring herself. She'd spent the first few hours making fruitless attempt after fruitless attempt at climbing out, but the dirt

233

walls were too solidly packed to allow her any foothold. One time she'd fallen and twisted her shoulder, the shoulder of her already injured arm, that had pretty much put an end to any thought she might have held onto that she would be able to get herself out of this.

While she had escaped serious injury, her biggest problem now was hypothermia, which was already quickly taking hold. Her muscles aching from shivering as well as from her fall. At the bottom of the pit was a small ledge, which she could just squeeze herself underneath; this gave her a little protection from the snow and freezing wind. Once again, she was glad that she had changed into warmer clothes before coming out after Cordelia; they afforded her a little extra protection from the cold.

Even so, it was starting to get to her.

Earlier she'd been so busy trying to climb out, and then the sun had peeked through the clouds long enough to send a few weak sunbeams through the trees and down into her hole. Now that night was in full swing the temperature had dropped even further, and she couldn't stop shaking. If Parker and Daniel didn't find her soon then it would be too late. Tessa wasn't even sure she could make it to morning. Already she was so sleepy that it was using up most of her energy to just keep herself awake.

Rousing herself with a start when she realized that she had been drifting away, she tried to think of something to keep her mind occupied.

Focusing her mind on what Cordelia had said was her ultimate plan, to get her, Daniel, Emilie, and Patrick all together, to teach them a lesson about underestimating her and then to kill them all. Tessa wondered how Cordelia was planning on getting to Emilie and Patrick.

At first Tessa had kept waiting for Cordelia to return, to get her, to gloat, even to hurt her further, but her sister never came. At last she had started to wonder if perhaps Cordelia had abandoned her plan and was now happy with just seeing Tessa dead. If she hoped to return tomorrow to get her then she was sure Cordelia would be in for an unpleasant surprise, surely her sister must realize that she couldn't survive the night out here in the cold.

Stirring herself again, Tessa made herself stand up and walk brisk circles around the small bottom of the hole, which was covered in at least three inches of snow. Trying some jumps her limbs were too numb, too tired, her body already conserving its own energy by slowing blood flow to the extremities so that it could protect its vital organs.

Dropping back down, and wiggling herself back under the little ledge that at least acted as a buffer between her and the snow that continued to fall relentlessly. Winding her scarf so that it covered her face as well as her neck, and glad of her thick curls that added another layer of protection.

Tucking her hands under her armpits in an attempt to stave off frostbite in the event that she actually made it out of here alive. Knees tucked up to her chest she realized with a sleepy start that she was starting to feel a pleasant warmness wash over her.

Wondering tiredly whether Parker and Daniel would ever find her cold, frozen corpse, Tessa drifted off to a pleasant sleep where she was warm and toasty and wrapped up inside a huge, soft flame.

* * * * *

2:02 A.M.

"You have no idea where you're going do you?" Parker asked Daniel with a look of helpless irritation.

"I told you they'd be here," Daniel snapped. "We found her car didn't we?"

Not bothering to answer the rhetorical question.

It was true that Daniel had led them to what appeared to be the place where Tessa had come searching for Cordelia. When they had arrived out here, at the house where Daniel and Tessa had lived as children, before their father had left and they had gone to live with their paternal grandparents, they had found Tessa's car.

Parked back in the woods, out of sight, Tessa's car was well hidden, presumably so she could sneak up on her sister unseen.

When they found the car and then made their way towards the huge house Parker was rocked by a terrifying sense of déjà vu. This search for Tessa was almost identical to the one last year, only this time it was Daniel by his side instead of Wyatt.

When they'd arrived here twenty odd hours ago, they'd searched the mansion from top to bottom. The place was just as huge and just as magnificent as the estate where Tessa used to live. An enormous Tudor style house, complete with several turrets, five floors full of empty rooms, the house had been completely emptied when Emilie, Daniel and Tessa had moved out. Since then the house hadn't been resold, but remained in Emilie Micah's name, so it had sat here unused but in pristine condition. Obviously someone in the Micah family had arranged for the garden to be tended, and any repairs the house needed attended to.

Finding nothing on any of the floors, or the attic or basement, Daniel had led them to a small cottage down the back, nestled deep in the woods, then to the stables and a couple of other buildings. Each time they had come up empty.

Now they had moved on to the woods, but like Tessa's estate, the forest was vast and seemingly endless. There were any number of places that Tessa and Cordelia could be hiding completely unseen. Snow was falling thickly now, lowering the temperature dramatically, and making it harder and harder to see where they were going, or any tracks Tessa or Cordelia may have left behind.

Frustration was quickly giving way to despair, Parker turned to Daniel, "Are you sure they're even here?"

"Why else would her car be here?"

"Maybe Cordelia took her someplace else," he suggested. "You said she'd be somewhere related to your pasts. What about Tessa's place?"

Daniel shook his head, "Cordelia never lived there. We moved there after Patrick left, Cordelia was long gone by then."

"Well it doesn't look like they're here anymore, where else could Cordelia take her?"

When they had first headed out here to search the house his panic had started to ebb, Parker always felt better when he was doing something constructive, now that things had slowed down however his panic was back with a vengeance. They could wander through these woods for the next several days and still never find Tessa and her crazy sister.

"Could she have known?" he asked Daniel suddenly.

"Known what," Daniel paused in his trek through the snow and wiped away a bead of sweat that was trickling down from under his hat.

"Could Tessa have known all along that Cordelia was the killer?" Parker didn't want to believe it but he knew he might have kept things quiet if it was his sister.

"I thought you knew Tessie," Daniel glared at him. "If Tessa knew that Cordelia was the killer before now then she would have gone straight after her. She would never let Cordelia hurt someone if there was anything she could do about it."

Reassured Parker nodded, feeling bad that he had ever doubted Tessa. "What was Tessa like?" he asked, Tessa never spoke about her childhood and he often wondered what she was like back then. "When she was little?"

A wistful smile crossing his face Daniel leaned back against an enormous tree trunk. "She was a handful. She used to get up to the craziest things, it used to drive Emilie and Patrick crazy. One time she decided to see if it would be possible for Santa Claus to actually go down a chimney," chuckling softly.

"She got stuck?" Parker asked with a titter of his own.

"Oh yeah. The fire department came, they had to tear down half the chimney to get her out, Emilie and Patrick were not amused. Another time she convinced me to help her build her own car, which we did, well she did, I was never the smart one, I was always the one who got in trouble for not keeping an eye on her when one of her schemes went awry. She used to love it. She'd do something melodramatic and I'd be the one who was punished."

"Your sister is the ultimate damsel in distress," Parker smiled lightly, remembering a comment Tessa had made the first time he'd met her, she'd called him and Wyatt the 'soap opera' police. Living with Tessa was most definitely like living in a soap opera, things never ran smoothly, and you never knew what was waiting around the next corner. "She's truly an expert at getting herself into trouble." His cell phone buzzed in his pocket and since already he'd ignored at least a dozen calls so far he decided he better not make Wyatt too mad so he pulled it out and answered. "Hello?" he asked innocently.

"Did you find her?" were the first words out of Wyatt's mouth.

"Not yet."

"I've tried calling you a dozen times," Wyatt told him reproachfully.

"I know I'm sorry, but we've been busy searching for Tess."

"We have a lead," Wyatt begun. "We think we know whom Cordelia Micah had been masquerading as."

"Who?" Parker snapped to attention, Daniel too stopped and turned to listen.

"Cece Hamilton."

"From the restaurant?" remembering the way Mrs. Hamilton had been mesmerized by the sight of Tessa bleeding, he'd thought it was just shock and horror but perhaps it had been something more.

"The very one."

Parker could practically hear Wyatt's grin. "How did you get there? She looks nothing like Tessa and Daniel."

"You remember her daughter?"

"Winter Hamilton," he did indeed remember the quiet, timid girl, who so obviously had troubles in her relationship with her mother.

"Well apparently she was convinced that her stepfather Grant Hamilton was the Iceman. So a couple of days ago she was searching the office at the restaurant for proof when she stumbled upon photos of the victims and the clothes they were wearing when they were abducted . . ."

"Why is she only telling you this now?" Parker interrupted.

"If you had let me finish my sentence then I would have covered that," Wyatt snapped, he'd been up for over twenty-four hours too. "When she was at the restaurant she was attacked, knocked unconscious, tied up and left in her bedroom wardrobe. She still thought that her stepfather was the killer until he was the one to find her. When J.J. and I were at her house talking with Winter and Grant, Winter showed us a photo of her and her mother from several years ago. Parker, Cece Hamilton looks exactly like Tessa. She is Cordelia which mean she is the Iceman."

"And you checked out the house?"

"We did the restaurant too. Nothing. But Jamie Presland has admitted that he is not the Iceman."

"Why'd he confess to four counts of first degree murder if he didn't do it?" Parker was always baffled by the intricate workings of a criminal's mind.

"He said that he wanted to show his dead parents that he was capable of anything," Wyatt sighed. "Anyway we still have him on Phoebe Stein's murder. It doesn't explain why Elizabeth Landry ID'd him, maybe she was just too traumatized that she saw what she wanted to see. Maybe it was just a coincidence, a fluke."

"Hold on," Parker told him then turned to Daniel, "Does Cordelia have any scars on her wrist?"

Daniel thought for a second then nodded, "Yeah she does. When she was ten she decided she wanted a pet elephant, when Emilie and Patrick said no she grabbed a knife and threatened to kill herself unless they gave her what she wanted. When they still said no she cut her wrist a couple of time."

"Did you hear that?" Parker asked returning the phone to his ear.

"Yeah I did. I'll tell J.J. so he can look into it. Parker, J.J. wants me to convince you to tell us where you and Daniel are. Look, before you protest, just hear me out. You've been out there for hours, you haven't found Tessa, you don't know what Cordelia did to her, maybe she's hurt. If she is lying somewhere, injured, then you'll need all the help you can get to find her, and it'll help if . . ."

"Okay, okay, okay," Parker cut him off, Wyatt had convinced him back at the beginning of his spiel. He wasn't going to do anything that endangered Tessa's safety. "We're out at the house where Daniel and Tessa grew up, before they moved to Tess's place." Daniel frowned at him and threw his hands up in the air in frustration, but Parker ignored him.

"You got the address?"

Parker told him.

"Okay, I'm sending some people out there, and an ambulance just in case. Good luck," then Wyatt was gone.

As he hung up the phone he saw Daniel glaring at him. "I wanted to talk to Cordelia before your buddies turned up."

"Well I don't care about that, all I care about is finding Tessa, and besides we don't even know if Cordelia is still here," Parker shot back and then stalked off, he may be softening towards the guy but he was not ready to become best friends.

Daniel muttered under his breath and turned in the other direction.

Parker was getting worried that he'd made a mistake in going along with Daniel and not telling Wyatt and the others where they were. The only reason he had let Daniel persuade him was that he had hoped either Tessa or Daniel might be able to coax Cordelia into revealing where she had stashed Hayley Geoffries. Reinforcements could of wiped off countless hours in their search for Tessa, hours that might end up meaning the difference between life and death. If his choice ended up costing Tessa her life then he'd never forgive himself.

They hadn't gone far when Parker heard Daniel call his name, spinning on his heel he dodged quickly through the trees in the direction of Daniel's voice. Reaching him he found Daniel crouching behind a tree, pointing to a pile of wood several yards away, "it looks like it was a campfire," he murmured.

Pulling out his gun. "Stay behind me in case . . ." Parker trailed off as Daniel bolted towards the burnt out fire.

"Tessa! Cordelia!" Daniel called as he ran.

Exhaling a frustrated burst of air, Parker followed, if Cordelia was nearby Daniel had just given her an opportunity to run.

Stopping short at the edge of a deep hole, Parker dropped to his knees and peered down, his flashlight casting a narrow beam of light. "Daniel."

In seconds Tessa's brother was dropping down beside him, leaning over to try and get a better view down into the pit, then gasped, "I think I see her."

"Where?" Parker tried to follow Daniel's gaze.

"There, under a ledge," Daniel was on his feet.

"I'll find something to help us get down . . . there," he finished as Daniel leapt down into the hole without a second thought.

With a deep sigh Parker followed him down, landing with a jarring thud, but thankfully with no broken bones. Daniel had already pulled Tessa's limp body from underneath the ledge and was cradling her in his arms.

"Is she . . .?" Parker couldn't even say it, his heart squeezed tighter and tighter as though someone had thrown it in a blender. If Tessa was dead . . .

"She's alive," Daniel told him as he shrugged out of his jacket and wrapped it around his sister. "But she's ice cold, her lips are turning blue." Taking hold of Tessa's wrist, brow furrowed in concentration. "Her pulse is slow, respiration rate is too. Hypothermia. We need to get her out of here, now."

Pulling off his own jacket, thinking how providential it was that now was the time he had chosen to start getting over his phobia of jackets. "Wyatt's sending an ambulance, but it's going to be a while." Gently extracting Tessa from her brother's arms, Daniel tightened his hold and looked like he was about to protest but then relented and loosened his grip.

Settling Tessa against his chest, Parker wrapped both the jackets around her shoulders, hoping his body heat and the coats were enough to keep her warm until the medics showed up. "Tessa? It's Parker. Baby, can you hear me?" tapping softly on her cheek hoping to spark a response but there was none. Stroking her hair as he tucked her head underneath his chin. "Come on, honey, stay with me. You have to keep fighting okay? You can't give up. I can't lose you."

Snapping to attention, Daniel jumped to his feet. "You are not going to lose her," he announced with such confidence that Parker almost believed it would be true simply because Daniel said it. "I'll get us out of here."

Looking up to the top of the hole a good four or five feet above their heads, not a huge distance, but to get an unconscious Tessa up there would be quite a feat. "How exactly do you plan to do that?"

"I'll climb up then grab some rope from my car," Daniel answered.

"You have rope in your car? You didn't think to bring it with you in the first place?"

"You're right I should have," Daniel murmured immediately.

Exactly the same answer Tessa would have given. It took all the fun out of an argument or some good old-fashioned self-pitying moping when the other person blamed themselves for things that they were quite obviously not responsible for. "You two are like clones. Why do you do it?"

Daniel's face darkened. "Emilie."

Before Daniel could get distracted by his dysfunctional childhood, Parker refocused him, "Why do you have rope in your car?"

"I love to camp, like boy scouts say always be prepared," his eyes clearing a little as he centered himself.

"How are you going to climb out, those walls are like concrete."

"Rock climbing," Daniel answered as he started up the side, managing to find imperceptible finger holds and, like an agile cat, was at the top in mere seconds. "I'll be back," he called down then was gone.

Reverting his attention to Tessa. "Come on, sweetheart, wake up," shaking her carefully. "Come on, don't give up on me." Adjusting himself to rest against the solid wall of the hole and pulling Tessa into his lap, rocking her like one would a baby. "Everything's gonna be okay, Tess, I'm right here, I'm not going anywhere. And Daniel, he really came through for you, he's gonna be back here soon, we'll get you out, get you someplace warm . . ." Parker didn't know how long he sat there cradling Tessa and probably would have mumbled away reassuringly forever if Daniel's face hadn't peeped down at them.

"Hey, Parker," he announced as he threw down one end of a rope.

"How exactly do you expect me to climb up there with Tessa?" Parker asked as he stood, lifting Tessa into his arms.

"Put her over your shoulder," Daniel called down. "You only

have to come a little way up and I'll be able to reach her."

About to protest and point out the innumerable things that could go wrong with Daniel's newest plan but one glance at Tessa's deathly pale, almost translucent, face spurred him quickly into action. Hoisting her across one shoulder, he took hold of the rope, cleared his mind, and somehow managed to make it halfway up the solidly packed dirt wall.

"That's enough," Daniel told him, leaning down and wrapping an arm around Tessa's waist, wiggling backwards slowly, until they both disappeared back over the edge.

* * * * *

2:46 A.M.

The giant flame that was cradling her in its spongy warmth suddenly began to dance. Bouncing her backwards and forwards, sending a sharp sliver of cold stabbing through her body and making her moan quietly.

Slowly she started to become aware of her surroundings as her cozy, comfortable sleep ebbed away. Tessa realized that it was no longer a flame that was cradling her but a person. Someone was sliding their arms underneath her back and knees, lifting her, holding her. Someone warm and strong and solid. Someone familiar.

Then she was being passed from one set of arms to another, her head drooping to rest on a strong shoulder, above her voices jumbled together and then they were moving.

Tessa tried to lift her head but found that she seemed to have lost control of her body.

Summoning all her strength, she managed a slight twitch of her fingers, which were resting against the shoulder of whoever was holding her.

The person carrying her stopped immediately and she felt eyes staring down at her. "Tessa?"

It was Parker's voice.

Once again, he had come running to her rescue, it was becoming

243

a recurring pattern for them; she got herself into trouble and he came running to save her. Before Parker she had actually been very proficient at looking after herself but lately . . .

"Is she okay?" asked another anxious voice.

Daniel's voice.

Cordelia had been wrong Parker *had* gone to her brother for help, and just as she had predicted Daniel had figured out where they were.

"Sweetheart? Can you hear me?" Parker asked, his voice softly commanding.

Unable to gather enough strength to speak Tessa jerkily nodded her head.

"Just hold on," Parker urged her as he resumed his trek through the snowy woods. "Everything's going to be okay."

She wanted to answer but she was starting to fade again, instead she sank down into the softness of Parker's arms, the bouncing motion of his jogging lulling her back to sleep. Thankfully, she thought absently, the snow had stopped its seemingly endless downpour, but the air was still as cold as ice. She was shivering violently despite the warmth of Parker's body that was pressed against her.

Then the sound of sirens was filling the air and the house where she had been born loomed above them.

Footsteps pounded towards them, voices bumbled above her, she felt Parker lay her gently down on something soft and firm.

"What happened?" a voice asked as someone covered her with a thick, warm blanket.

"She fell, or was pushed, into a hole, about ten feet deep," Parker explained. "We found her unconscious, she doesn't seem to have any injuries but we're worried about hypothermia."

What happened, Tessa thought as sleep pulsed at the edges of her mind like rising floodwaters, was that my sister tried to kill me.

"Honey, can you hear me?" Parker's voice rumbled beside her ear as he bent over her. Something important was tugging at her mind, something she needed to tell him.

Trying to focus on his voice as the medics bustled about covering her in more blankets, checking her vitals, inserting an IV, putting an oxygen mask over her face.

Managing a nod in answer to Parker's question.

"Tessa?" he pushed gently. "Open your eyes for me."

"Miss Micah can you tell me where you're hurt?" one of the medics asked with a light hand on her shoulder.

Forcing open heavy eyes and pulling a shaking hand out from under the blanket to tug away the oxygen mask. "Cordelia?" she asked, voice strained and weak.

"She's gone, honey," Parker told her as the paramedic repeated his question and replaced the mask.

Ignoring the well-meaning EMT as she pulled the oxygen mask away again, her gaze fixed on Parker's. She knew what she needed to tell him and she knew she didn't have much time before she lost her battle with the sleep that tugged relentlessly at her brain. "Restaurant," she said weakly.

"I know sweetheart, we found out Cordelia's alias," he gently pulled the oxygen mask from her hand and once again replaced it over her mouth and nose, then brought her hand to his lips. "Try to rest, you're safe now, everything's going to be okay," he told her soothingly, a big smile on his face as he brushed his knuckles across her forehead.

Shaking her head, that wasn't what she was trying to tell him but her strength was quickly failing, her body starting to tremble. "Hayley, fish, restaurant."

Frowning slightly as realization flashed in his glowing gold eyes. "Did you talk to your sister?"

She nodded, relieved that he seemed to have caught on to what she was trying to say.

"Did she tell you that Hayley is at the restaurant?"

Again, she nodded as her eyes fluttered closed.

"Do you know where?" Parker asked but this time Tessa didn't answer, she had lost her battle with sleep. "Tessa?"

"She's unconscious," the medic announced, "and we need to get her to the hospital now. You coming?"

As much as Parker wanted to stay glued to Tessa's side, he knew she would want him to find Hayley Geoffries before it was too late. Looking over at Daniel, hovering forlornly on his own by the mansion's front door, Parker called him over.

Casting a nervous glance in his sister's direction as he jogged up. "Is she okay?"

"Yeah she'll be okay, but Cordelia told her where she's keeping Hayley, I have to go, I want you to go to the hospital with Tessa. I'm gonna send an officer over with you, I don't think Cordelia's coming back to finish what she started but I don't want to risk it."

Pressing a kiss to Tessa's forehead before the paramedics bundled her into the back of the ambulance, Daniel climbing in behind her. Parker watched it drive away, lights and sirens going, then his gaze turned to the officers as they fanned out to search the grounds for anything that might be helpful to the case. Feeling his excitement begin to bubble up, they knew who the killer was, they knew where the victim was being held, and the Iceman's reign of terror was finally over.

* * * * *

6:13 A.M.

"Nothing," Wyatt announced as Parker pushed open the restaurant's front doors.

After the ambulance had taken Tessa to the hospital, he'd called Wyatt to tell him what Tessa had said and to get him to send a team back to search the restaurant. On the drive over he'd kept his phone by his side, expecting a call at any second to tell him that Hayley Geoffries had been found safe and sound.

None came.

Well that wasn't completely true. Daniel had called from the hospital to update him on Tessa's condition. Apparently her body temperature had dropped to 92.4°F, putting her in stage two hypothermia. Thankfully, the doctors were confident they could re-warm her with hot water bottles and blankets without the need to resort to active core re-warming with warmed IV fluids, or by flushing them through her internal cavities. Daniel had promised to call if anything changed otherwise Parker would meet him at the hospital as soon as he knew that Hayley Geoffries was found safe and sound.

"Tessa said she was at the restaurant, she has to be here somewhere," Parker told him.

"We've searched the whole place, she's not here," Wyatt gave him an odd look.

"What?" Parker asked.

"Are you sure that's what Tessa was trying to tell you?" his partner asked carefully. "You said she was pretty out of it, maybe she was just trying to tell you about Cordelia's alias," he suggested.

Shaking his head, "No I thought that at first, but I told her that we already knew about her sister's alias and she kept saying it to me. Hayley, fish restaurant. Those were her exact words. Hayley is here I know it."

"We've checked the whole place, Parker, she's not here," Wyatt looked tired and frustrated.

Pacing slowly around the room, waiting for something to jump out of the background, hoping this was one of those times where what you were looking for was staring you straight in the face only you couldn't see it. Stopping in front of the aquarium, letting the peaceful gliding of the fish calm his jangled nerves. "You're sure you've checked everywhere?" he asked, not because he doubted his partner's ability to do his job but because he knew that if Tessa said Hayley was here then she was here.

"It's a restaurant, Parker, not a shopping mall, there's only so many rooms, only so many places Hayley could be," Wyatt snapped irritably.

"We're missing something," Parker mumbled, ignoring his partner's edginess.

"I don't know how else to say it," Wyatt growled. "We have checked everywhere and she is not here."

Watching as a particularly bright fish darted up to the glass and seemed to stare with it's googly little eyes straight into his own, then turned just as quickly to dart back towards the centre of the aquarium. A fuzzy thought springing to mind, slowly coming to focus.

Wyatt must have seen something cross his face because he frowned and asked, "What?"

Thinking aloud, "This is going to sound crazy," he cautioned. "Tessa said, Hayley, fish, restaurant, I thought she meant that Hayley was here at the seafood restaurant, but what if she meant, Hayley was in the fish in the restaurant?"

Following his gaze, Wyatt's green eyes grew wide. "You mean Hayley is inside the aquarium?"

"I think that's what Tessa was trying to tell me before she passed out," the excitement that had extinguished when he first heard they hadn't found Hayley reignited.

"How?"

"I don't know." Pacing around the aquarium, it was certainly big enough to have a secret room inside; the problem was how would you get someone inside it. "Does this place have a basement?"

"No," Wyatt's face was thoughtful. "Besides it would be too easy for Hayley to get out when Cordelia brought her food and water. Hayley could just wait and knock her out when she lifted up the door. And you couldn't go straight through," banging a knuckle against the smooth, thick glass. "That leaves."

"The top," Parker nodded, he too had been thinking that. "There's an attic?"

"There is, but we checked it out already, apparently it's a little library," Wyatt told him. "Armchair, bookshelf, lamp. No sign of any trapdoor or anything that might lead to a hidden room."

Fighting disappointment before an idea popped into his head, "Carpet. Is the floor up there covered in carpet?"

Wyatt didn't need to answer, the look on his face said it all, he turned and ran towards the kitchen, Parker on his heels. In the kitchen Wyatt grabbed hold of a small rope that hung from the ceiling and pulled on it to reveal a set of steps that led up to the attic. Hurrying up and without a word between them they began to roll back the thick tartan carpet that covered the floor. When they reached the middle of the room they found exactly what they'd been looking for; a trapdoor, locked shut with a combination lock.

"How are we going to get in?" Wyatt asked.

"I've got Daniel's car," Parker was already halfway to the steps. "If anyone would have bolt cutters in their car, it's him."

Racing through the restaurant, pleased he hadn't bothered to lock the car, swinging open the trunk and rifling through the giant pile of survival equipment, finding what he was looking for he was back in the attic in under a minute.

About to cut open the lock when Wyatt stopped him, "Parker, we have to be prepared for what we might find in there. If Hayley's there she might be dead."

Not wanting to think about that just yet. "But she might be alive," and with that he snapped the combination lock in two and swung open the door.

* * * * *

6:20 A.M.

The lady, the Iceman, had been here earlier.

She was all worked up.

Rambling about some other woman who was trying to ruin her plans.

Hayley was too tired to listen to her ranting and stayed in her little fort ignoring the tidal wave of angry words.

Not bothering with the bucket the Iceman had simply thrown down today's ration of food.

Hayley hadn't bothered to eat it.

She wasn't hungry anymore.

Just tired.

The Iceman had left her in the dark this time, not that it mattered.

In fact, Hayley decided she liked it better this way.

She could feel death tickling at her feet, like when you stood at the beach and the waves lapped at your toes.

Turning on her other side, her injured leg burning at the movement, Hayley snuggled down under her blanket and waited for sleep to take its hold.

Pleasant rest was just coming when she heard a noise.

Surprised that the day could have gone so quickly and it was already time for the lady's next visit.

Wincing when light came pouring down.

Scared when she heard male voices chattering.

This was it; the Iceman had sent someone to kill her.

"Hayley?" a voice called.

Shrinking back against the cold concrete wall.

"Hayley, my name's Parker, I'm a police officer, can you hear me?"

Surely it had to be a trick, her addled mind told her.

"How are we going to get down?" the voice asked.

"There has to be a ladder somewhere," another answered.

"Hayley, just hold on, we're coming," the first voice assured her. It was calm and reassuring, and Hayley wanted to believe it, but she was terrified that she was hallucinating again.

She heard shuffling and clunking, and wiggling to the front of her fortress, she peeped out to see the ladder being lowered down and remembered back to the day she had arrived here.

"We're coming down, Hayley," the voice told her.

Ducking back into her little home like a turtle ducking back into its shell.

"Hayley?"

Footsteps came towards her, stopping in front of the table, a kind face peering in at her.

"Hayley, I'm Parker, you're safe now," he told her with a smile.

Unsure whether to believe it or not she stayed put.

"She's never going to hurt you again, Hayley," he reassured her.

Wanting desperately to believe him but still scared.

"We're going to get you out of here, Hayley," he held out a hand towards her. "Take you home."

His hand was steady, patiently waiting until she was ready. She started to move her hand towards his but hesitated. She'd seen him before, she realized suddenly. He was the police officer who had been here that day so long ago, he had been the one who'd stood watching the fish, the one who seemed to have seen through the glass and concrete to her small cage. And now he was here, inside her cell, and he seemed so real, so lifelike. Could it be true? Could he really be here?

"We called your parents, Hayley, they're going to meet us at the hospital," smiling reassuringly and continuing to hold his hand out.

Mention of her parents made her chest squeeze and her eyes well up and she decided that she had nothing to lose by trusting him. If he was here to kill her then he would, either way she was going to die, and if he really was a police officer then her dreams had come true and she was saved.

Slowly she brought her trembling hand towards his steady one, finding herself surprised when his hand gently closed around hers. His touch was solid and firm and real.

"Come on, lets get you out of here," he said and gently pulled her forward.

Fleetingly embarrassed as her scrawny, naked body came out of her little cave, the police officer didn't comment merely rested her carefully on the ground as he examined her wounded leg.

"Ambulance on its way?" he asked his partner, who nodded.

Completely sapped of all energy Hayley rested her head against the policeman, Parker she thought he'd said his name was, and wondered how she was going to make it out of the room. She didn't have enough strength left to drag herself up the ladder.

The other policeman handed Parker a jacket and he wrapped it around her shaking shoulders and stood, lifting her into his arms. And for the first time Hayley felt safe, really and truly safe, she didn't know how long the feeling would last but she enjoyed it while it was here.

It all felt surreal as he carried her up out of the room that had been her home for the last three weeks, the room where she'd thought she would die. Down out of the attic, through the restaurant, past the aquarium that she had spent hours watching on the small monitor in her cell. Outside he deposited her on a stretcher where two paramedics immediately started fussing over her.

Overwhelmed and unused to being out in the open, Hayley found her breath started to catch in her throat and she grabbed hold of Parker's hand. He squeezed it reassuringly and smiled down at her. "Hey you're not going to get rid of me that easily," he told her.

Giving him a wobbly smile as the EMT's maneuvered her into the ambulance, Parker remained at her side, and called to his partner, "I'll ride with Hayley to the hospital, then I can check on Tessa."

"I'll meet you there," his partner called back as the doors swung closed.

Wondering fleetingly who Tessa was and what had landed her in the hospital, tugging on Parker's hand until he leant over her, licking her lips she spoke the first words she had in days, "Thank you."

"Anytime," he smiled, his eyes glittering with unshed tears. "Anytime."

As they sped towards the hospital Hayley tried to convince herself that this was all real, that it was really happening. She was safe, the police had rescued her, the Iceman wasn't going to kill her, she was going to see her parents.

She had her life back.

* * * * *

12:40 P.M.

It was ruined.

It was all ruined.

And Cordelia knew exactly whose fault it was.

Her ever sweet, ever angelic, ever perfect, ever loved and adored by all, little sister.

Tessa was right when she had said that she was the reason Cordelia was doing all of this. Twenty-six years of living in her baby sister's shadow was enough. Ever since she was born, Tessa had got everything that she ever wanted. She was the pretty one, the cute one, the smart one, the one whom everyone seemed to love, and the one for whom everything simply seemed to fall into her lap.

It was unfair, plain and simple, and so it was only fair that Cordelia take back the place that was rightfully hers as the star of the

Micah family. Her family had been disrespectful by throwing her away in preference of Tessa, they had not treated her as she deserved, they had not seen her for who she really was. They had been brainwashed by that little fake innocent angel, Tessa. Cordelia would right this wrong, hence the plan to bring back Dylan Riley and, after that had failed to do the job, the Iceman scheme.

While Tessa had thought she was on the phone earlier this morning she had in fact ducked away quickly to come back to the restaurant to check up on Hayley Geoffries. The girl had been completely out of it, and Cordelia had decided that once she got Tessa someplace safe she would come back and kill Hayley now. No point in dragging out the girl's pain any longer than was necessary.

As she'd been leaving she had seen an entire battalion of police cars screech to a stop in front of the restaurant and she knew that her identity had been compromised. That hadn't bothered her too much, she knew that the police would never find where Hayley was hidden, and she had an entire portfolio of alias' to use.

The thing that had bothered her was that there were only two people who could have could have turned her into the police.

The first was Tessa. Who might have somehow managed to call her idiotic boyfriend who couldn't seem to solve a case unless she handed it to him on a silver platter. This, however, seemed unlikely, and when she'd returned to check up on Tessa she had known that it was not her baby sister who had ratted her out.

That left only one other person who could have done it.

If someone had found her daughter Winter then the silly girl was bound to have spilled her guts about her stupid suspicions. She knew that Winter had found the clothes and photos in the office at the restaurant, and although she hadn't particularly wanted to, she'd known that locking her daughter away was the only way to keep herself safe. Cordelia also knew that Winter thought her stepfather Grant was the Iceman, the reason she hadn't taken care of her daughter earlier.

Cordelia wasn't sure how she felt about her daughter's betrayal. She had never been close to the girl, had never felt the bond that was supposed to be shared between mother and child. But neither did she hate the girl or wish her any ill, she hadn't felt right about locking her child away but she certainly cared more about herself than the girl.

After her encounter with Tessa, she had driven back out here to check up on Hayley only to find that the irritating police were still there. Luckily Cordelia owned the property across the road, under a different name of course, so she'd been forced to kill the couple renting the house in order to safely watch the police's progress. Estimating that Tessa could probably last through the night before she died from hypothermia, Cordelia had planned to watch for a while then go and retrieve her sister and lock her away someplace safe.

It was around three a.m. when she realized that something had gone drastically wrong. The police presence grew from a couple of stragglers to a couple of dozen, and then Parker Bell turned up, and Cordelia knew that Tessa had been found. No way would her sister's sappy cop boyfriend have left the woods unless he knew Tess was safe. Obviously that pesky Daniel had managed to figure out where Tessa was and make up with Detective Bell long enough to locate her.

She had underestimated her brother.

She would not make that mistake again.

Still she had maintained that there was no way the police would find Hayley. No reason that they should think to check inside an aquarium. Unless of course that idiot Tessa had regained consciousness long enough to tell Parker, which it soon became clear that she had, since not long later Cordelia had watched him walk out of the restaurant carrying the girl in his arms. Apparently, he was one of those cops who always had to play the hero, since he had also travelled with Hayley to the hospital.

That was when she knew it was all over.

There was no way she could continue on the Iceman's plans.

No way that she would be able finish what she'd started.

It was a disappointment, but she could still achieve the main event.

The whole point of the exercise had been to destroy her family and that she could still do. Tessa was at the hospital and since Detective Bell had come here, he must have left Daniel with her. He probably also left an officer on Tessa's door in case she came back. That was smart but it would not slow Cordelia down, in fact leaving Tessa and Daniel together only made her job easier.

Once she had her brother and sister locked safely away she could work on bringing Emilie and Patrick back. Then for the first time ever their whole family would be together.

Grabbing a bag containing her gun and several disguises, Cordelia ignored the bodies of the elderly couple lying dead in the bed behind her, their blood dripping down into a puddle on the carpet. Slipping out the door, borrowing the couple's car since they no longer needed it, she had one stop to make before she headed to the hospital to put the last stage of her plan into action. And then once everything was taken care of she would continue her game so that the Iceman would become the greatest legend of all time.

* * * * *

4:17 P.M.

Sitting in her mother's room, feet dangling down the side of the bed, staring blankly out the window, oblivious to anything but her own thoughts. Winter was still in shock, but she was also still holding on to the vain hope that somehow she and Grant and the police had got it wrong, that somehow her mother was not a psychopathic serial killer.

After her stepfather had found her tied up in her own closet and they had put it all together they had phoned Detective Bell, unable to reach him she had spoken with his partner Detective Wyatt. He had come right over and she had told him everything, from her initial suspicions against Grant to what she had found in the bedroom here at the house, to what she had found and what had happened at the restaurant.

Detective Wyatt had listened patiently, interrupting occasionally to ask a question or to clarify something. When she was finished, he had promised her that he would call her when he knew more.

That was well over twelve hours ago.

Grant had surprised her, behaving nothing like his usual smug, conceited self. He had been kind and thoughtful, checking on her regularly but giving her space like she'd asked for. She could tell he was as shocked and horrified as she herself was. And just like herself he was clinging to the hope that all of this would turn out to be one gigantic misunderstanding.

"Winter?"

She jumped a mile at the voice, and turning she saw Detective Bell and Detective Wyatt standing in the bedroom doorway. She knew from the looks on their faces that the news they were bringing was not good. Turning her back on them she walked to the window and pressed her nose to the cold glass, when she was little she had loved to stand like that watching the goings on of the world.

"Are you sure?" she asked at last, watching the Detective's reflection, hoping to see something in their faces that might suggest she had read them wrong.

"We found Hayley Geoffries at the restaurant," Detective Bell told her gently.

Shocked she turned to face them. "Where? I searched that whole place, the only spot I didn't check was the attic, but there aren't a lot of hiding places up there, just my mom's library."

Exchanging glances for a moment she thought they weren't going to tell her but then Detective Wyatt begun, "She was inside the aquarium," explaining before she could jump in. "There was a trapdoor in the attic, under the carpet, that led down into a secret room inside the middle of the aquarium."

Taking it all in, Winter still couldn't grasp the fact that her mother had done all of this. "Are you positive that it was my mom? Maybe it was someone else who worked at the restaurant. Maybe it really was Jamie Presland."

Detective Bell shook his head. "I'm sorry, Winter, but we have a witness. Someone that your mom confessed to."

Still clinging to blissful denial. "Maybe your witness was wrong. Maybe they made a mistake."

Noticing Detective Bell wince. "The witness' name is Tessa Micah, she's my girlfriend," he paused. "She's also your mom's sister. Your mom's real name is Cordelia Ula Isis Micah and she tried to kill Tessa, almost succeeded. She Tasered Tessa pushed her into a deep hole and left her out there in the snow to die. If I hadn't found her when I did, she would have died from hypothermia. I'm sorry, Winter, but there's no doubt that your mother did this."

Any shred of hope that still existed now extinguished. "My mom tried to kill her own sister?" Turning back to the window feeling like her whole life was nothing but one huge lie. "I didn't even know she had any siblings, she told me that she was an only child." This was all too much too quickly, Winter was having trouble processing it all, to know her mother was a killer was heart-wrenchingly, bone-chillingly, spine-tinglingly, brain-numbingly horrific, to know that she would try to kill her own sister added a whole new dynamic of evil.

Crossing to her Detective Wyatt took her by the shoulders and led her to the bed, sitting beside her. "Winter, have you seen your mom today?"

Shaking her head, "No. Why? You don't know where she is?"

"No we don't, but we think she might be going to tie up some loose ends before she leaves town," Detective Wyatt told her carefully.

Catching his meaning, "And you think I'm a loose end." Twenty-four hours ago she would never have believed that her mom could kill anyone, now it hardly surprised her to know that her own mother wanted her dead. "I haven't seen her since before she attacked me at the restaurant. Do you think that she might try to hurt her sister again?"

"I have an officer outside Tessa's hospital room, she's safe. We want to post an officer here too, just in case your mom comes back here," Detective Bell explained.

Winter nodded, "If you think that will help." Considering asking a question of which she was almost to scared to know the answer, "Does she know I'm the one who ratted her out?"

Once again exchanging glances, Detective Bell came to sit on her other side. "We think she was watching the restaurant from one of the houses across the street," he began slowly.

"What?" she asked looking from one to the other. "What aren't you telling me?"

"We think that your mom killed the occupants of that house so that she could keep tabs on what we were doing at the restaurant," Detective Wyatt told her. "We don't know what she's thinking but we want to make sure we cover all our bases."

They stood to leave, "If you need anything at all, you can call us okay," Detective Bell told her. "You still have my card?"

She nodded and watched them go. "Detective Bell?" she called as they reached the door. "When my . . . my aunt is feeling better, do you think it would be okay if I maybe came to see her?" All alone in the world, betrayed and abandoned by her mom, her stepfather didn't like her and with her mom gone wouldn't want to look after her, so her mom's sister might be all she had left.

"Tessa would love that," Detective Bell smiled at her, a genuine smile as he thought of his girlfriend, he must love her a lot, and Winter wondered if she would ever find a love like that or if she was destined to be alone forever. "You also have an uncle," he told her. "His name is Daniel and it's because of him that we were able to save Tessa."

"So Tessa and Daniel, they're not like my mom?" wondering whether insanity was hereditary.

"No they are nothing like Cordelia," Detective Bell answered fiercely. "And neither are you. Tessa is the strongest, kindest, most loving person I have ever met, she would never hurt another person. You are not your mother, Winter, make sure you remember that. When Tessa's feeling better I'll bring you to see her."

Winter managed a weak smile as she waved goodbye, but once they were gone, she dropped to her knees and cried a flood of tears.

DECEMBER 23RD

1:23 A.M.

For once, she was dreaming pleasant dreams.

She was with Parker and the two of them were dancing in the snow, the stars were sparkling like thousands of diamonds in the sky, the moon shining as brightly as the sun, snow was falling from the clear sky but neither of them were cold.

"Tessa."

Looking at Parker but he too was turning to see where the voice had come from.

"Tessa."

She knew whose voice it was but she couldn't see them anywhere.

"Tessa."

Someone was shaking her.

"Come on, Tessa, wake up."

Her eyes popped open but it took a moment for her to figure out where she was. She was still in the hospital, but for the first time since Parker had found her she was no longer cold. Most of what had happened before she'd woken up here a few hours ago was like a fuzzy mist, she was pretty sure she remembered telling Parker where Cordelia was keeping Hayley Geoffries but she wasn't sure. The first thing she'd asked about when consciousness returned was whether the girl had been found alive. Luckily, Parker had left a message with the nurses to tell her that Hayley was okay; she smiled as she thought about how well he knew her.

"Finally."

Cordelia's face came slowly into focus as she loomed above the bed.

"How did you get in here?" Tessa asked, pushing herself into a sitting position with arms that felt like jelly. "Parker put a guard on my door."

The wicked glint in her sister's eyes gave the answer.

"You killed him didn't you?" she asked and Cordelia nodded gleefully, her face now clearly displaying the insanity that filled her mind. "It's over, Cordelia. They know your alias, they found Hayley, it's done, just turn yourself in and put an end to this, no one else needs to die."

"It's over when I say it's over," Cordelia snapped, pulling out her gun, complete with silencer. "Get out of bed."

Tessa saw that Cordelia was dressed as a nurse, she was also wearing a red wig and green contact lenses, obviously this was how she had entered the hospital and managed to kill the guard without being spotted. Cordelia pulled out the IV from the back of her hand, causing a small stream of blood to flow from the pin-pick wound. Forcing her weak muscles to work Tessa climbed shakily out of bed, swaying and nearly toppling over as she stood. "You still think you can do it don't you? Get me and Daniel, Emilie and Patrick all together."

"Yes I do think that," Cordelia nodded vehemently.

"Parker will never let you get away with it. Even if you kill me he will never let you get away, he'll spend the rest of his life hunting you down," Tessa told her.

Scoffing, "Has your boyfriend ever even solved a case where you didn't hand the answers directly to him?"

Ignoring the snide comment that didn't warrant a response. "Don't you feel even a little bit bad for everything you've done?" Tessa really wished that she saw something in her sister's eyes to show that she had at least a shred of humanity. "Remorse, guilt, regret, anything?"

Cordelia stared back at her with a blank mask; as though she couldn't comprehend what Tessa was saying. "Is that some sort of joke?"

"Why are you so jealous of me, Cordelia, you never really answered me before. You keep acting like it was because of me that Emilie and Patrick never loved you, that Daniel and I had some sort of magical existence that was denied you. You know that's not true,

Cordelia. You know that they ignored us just as much as you. Emilie didn't even notice when I was missing. Patrick never even came to see me after Emilie tried to kill me. You're nothing special, you weren't singled out by the world for bad treatment."

Bubbling with rage, "How dare you speak to me like that," she whispered angrily, their location the only thing keeping her slightly in check. With her back to the door, Cordelia didn't see it slowly start to open and Daniel's face peer around.

Keeping her sister's attention focused away from Daniel. "I'll speak to you however I want, Cordelia. I'm not afraid of you, those girls you kidnapped might have been, they might have been scared of what you would do to them, but I'm not. I've already been to hell, and you are not the most terrifying person I've ever come up against."

Grinning manically. "I know all about your visit to hell, Tessa. I know better than you could ever imagine. You're not the only one who's met the devil and lived to tell about it . . ."

"Freeze, Cordelia," Daniel had maneuvered into the room, gun in hand, which, like brother like sister, also had a silencer attached, and closed the door behind him.

Taking no notice she turned to smile at him, keeping her gun trained on Tessa. "Hello, Daniel."

"Put your gun down," he told her.

Of course she didn't. "What wonderful timing you have, Tessa and I were just discussing how great it would be to have a family reunion."

Scoffing, "We all hate Emilie and Patrick, the one thing we actually have in common, none of us ever want to see them again," Daniel told her.

While Cordelia's attention was focused on Daniel, Tessa carefully edged herself out of the line of fire from Cordelia's gun, her eyes scanning the room in search of a weapon.

"You sent me the article about Tessie and Dylan," Daniel was accusing Cordelia. "You're pathetic, Cordelia, trying to use Dylan to get to Tessa. That's right," he continued when he saw surprise cross Cordelia's face, "You and Tessie aren't the only smart ones in the family you know, you think I can't figure things out? You have a problem with Tessa you don't get someone else to do your dirty work for you."

"Is it really worth it?" Tessa asked. "Is everything you've done, Dylan, the Iceman thing, bringing Daniel back. All those people who are dead because of what you did. Is it really worth it just to get back at me?"

Face bright red, "It was worth it," Cordelia spluttered. "But you are so darn resilient, you just keep bouncing back time after time no matter what I threw at you, you just wouldn't break."

"Oh, Cordelia," Tessa said with a sad smile. "You can't break something that's already broken and I was broken a long time ago."

Scrambling for a response but finding none, Cordelia spun around, flung something at Daniel and then whirled back again.

For Tessa everything that happened next seemed to move in slow motion.

There was a flash as the gun went off and she felt a burning sensation rip through her stomach as she was flung backwards.

Daniel screamed her name.

Sensing the disturbance in the air as two more bullets were fired, sending both Daniel and Cordelia dropping to the floor.

Pain swirled through her body; her vision turned red and then black, and then faded out all together.

* * * * *

1:40 A.M.

It had been a long, long couple of days. All Parker wanted was to hold Tessa in his arms and go to sleep.

After riding with Hayley Geoffries to the hospital, he had stayed with her in the ER until her parents had arrived, then he'd gone to check on Tessa, who had been sleeping peacefully. Wyatt had come by and they had interviewed Hayley, who was proving to be one strong young woman. Halfway through the interview they'd gotten the call about the old couple that lived in the house opposite the restaurant, and after going to check it out had made their way to the Hamilton house to update Winter. Tessa's niece reminded him a lot of Tessa. Her strength, her denial of the facts, the guilt he'd seen in her eyes when she spoke about her mother. Then he'd managed to grab a couple of hours sleep before returning to the station to see if they'd made any progress in tracking down Cordelia.

Rounding the corner on his way to Tess's hospital room, he knew immediately that something was wrong. The guard that he had insisted be placed on Tessa's door until Cordelia had been apprehended was gone.

The corridor was quiet, most of the hospital's staff home for the night, the remaining nurses were down at the nurse's station, chatting and drinking coffee. Hand hovering near his gun as he stopped in front of Tessa's room, the door was closed and all was quiet within. Drawing in a shaky breath he calmed himself before he entered, after everything that had happened it was natural to be on edge, but if everything was fine then he didn't want to worry Tessa unnecessarily.

Opening the door slowly he came to an abrupt stop, the bed was empty, two bodies were lying on the floor, neither of them were moving. All his training fled from his mind, eyes roving the room frantically in search of anything that moved as he dropped to his knees beside Daniel Micah. Hands pressed to the man's neck in search of a pulse, Daniel flinched at the touch, his eyes popping open.

"Where are you hurt?" Parker asked him.

Daniel's hands strayed to his chest. "Cordelia shot me," he answered. "Bullet proof vest," he supplied when he saw the frown creasing Parker's brow. "Where's Tessa?"

Scrambling over to the other body, which was lying in a pool of blood, eyes staring lifelessly at the ceiling, a bullet hole marring the forehead. Thankfully, the body was too big to be Tessa's.

"Cordelia," Daniel supplied as he pushed to his feet, wincing and clutching at his chest, a bulletproof vest might prevent the bullet from penetrating the chest, but it didn't prevent it from leaving one nasty bruise. Staggering around to the other side of the bed Daniel let out a strangled scream.

Following him Parker felt the air rush from his lungs. Tessa laid on the floor, soaked in blood, a gaping hole in her stomach, her eyes were closed, her face as pale as death.

"Get help," Parker heard himself say as he knelt at Tessa's side, grabbing the pillow from the bed on his way and pressing it against the deep wound, leaning down so his cheek was near her mouth he felt a small puff of air. Glancing up to see Daniel still standing, staring in horror at his sister. "Daniel, go, she's still alive but she's lost a lot of blood."

With a last look, Daniel turned and stumbled from the room leaving Parker struggling to ignore the stinging in his eyes and the burning in his chest.

* * * * *

1:50 A.M.

"Parker?" speaking used up almost as much effort as opening her eyes had.

Head snapping back to face her, Tessa saw in his eyes pure panic, but then he locked it tightly away for her sake and smiled. "Hey, baby," with his spare hand he gently stroked her face, his touch feathery soft, as though he thought he might hurt her if he wasn't careful.

A sharp burst of pain made her wiggle, desperately trying to get away from it as though it were some sort of living being that had taken hold inside her body.

"It hurts," Tessa moaned softly.

"I know it does, sweetheart, but Daniel's getting help, the doctors are gonna fix you up good as new." Mustering up a small smile for her. "Hey trust you to get shot in a hospital, could there be a more perfect place?"

"Cordelia?" she asked weakly, still a little hazy on exactly what had happened but sure that her sister had something to do with it.

"She's dead, she's never gonna hurt you again," Parker told her with a glance at something on the floor out of sight. "You know all the serial killers in the city huh?" he joked lamely, but even dazed with pain Tessa could see the worry that wasn't completely hidden in his golden eyes.

Playing the game she offered a tiny smile back. "Just two of them," she managed before she broke off, her breathing labored, eyes closing, the pain overwhelming.

"Stay with me, sweetheart," Parker urged her. "Come on, honey, fight with me, you can do this, you're gonna be fine."

Shaking her head, Tessa could feel her life quickly ebbing away.

"Yes you are," he told her with false confidence as he pressed the pillow he held to her wound more firmly causing her to cringe in pain. "You are a fighter, Tess," he continued. "You're strong, you just have to hold on a little longer, okay. You're gonna be fine, I'm right here with you and I'm not gonna let you die, okay, I love you, I can't imagine my life without you. You just hold on, keep breathing, try to relax, everything's gonna be fine. I promise."

His babbling voice was sounding further and further away, so was the pain that before had been all consuming, now it seemed to be nothing more than a distant tingle.

"Marry me, Tessa," Parker said suddenly.

The words catching her off guard and with the last of her strength she forced her heavy eyes open one last time, locking them onto Parker's, "I love you, Parker," was all she could manage. She wanted to say more but her lungs were now refusing to do their job, her heart had ceased it's pointless pumping of blood around her body, blood that was quickly oozing out from the hole in her stomach, soaking the pillow and staining Parker's hands. Her vision started to fade; her hearing grew fainter and then stopped all together.

And then everything was gone but a glowing, all encompassing, white light.

* * * * *

1:59 A.M.

The room suddenly sprung to life. Doctors rushed in, pulling him away from Tessa, putting a tube down her throat, shocking her heart with a defibrillator, loading her onto a gurney and rushing her from the room.

In his head all Parker could hear were the same words spinning over and over again like a relentless spinning top. Tessa is gone. Tessa is gone. Tessa is gone.

His hearing deserted him, eyesight faded to fuzzy; he lost all sense of time and any connection to his surroundings.

"Parker."

Snapping out of his haze to find that he was no longer in Tessa's hospital room. Someone had moved him to another room, a quieter, cleaner one, but identical in layout to the bloody room that was imprinted in his mind. "Wyatt," surprised to see his partner. "When did you get here?"

"One of the doctors called, I came straight over."

"What time is it?"

"About three thirty," Wyatt told him.

Shocked that so much time had passed, time that was a complete blank. "Tessa?" he asked remembering the way she had looked at him right before she'd stopped breathing. When she had first regained consciousness her eyes had been unfocused and glazed with pain, but when she had opened them that last time they had been clear and lit with love, it had simultaneously warmed and broken his heart.

"She's still in surgery, she's still hanging in there," Wyatt assured him. "She's tough, Parker."

Rubbing tired eyes, he saw that someone had washed away Tessa's blood form his hands, nothing remaining but a few flecks on his fingernails. "Daniel?"

"In worse shape than you are if that's possible. He's a mess, trying to get out of him what happened in there was quite an ordeal. He's got some cracked ribs from the gunshot, but other than that physically he's okay, emotionally is a whole other story, if Tessa . . ." he didn't say the word they were all fearing. "Anyway Casey's with him now."

"Cordelia. Daniel shot her." Parker couldn't deny that part of him felt comforted by the fact that Cordelia Micah was dead. Never again could she inflict her twisted plans of revenge and self-glory on an unsuspecting public.

"I know, they've taken her body to the morgue, Zak'll do the autopsy himself," Wyatt explained.

"It was self-defense," Parker felt the sudden need to defend Tessa's brother.

"I know, Daniel told us what happened, Cordelia shot Tessa then was about to shoot him when she and Daniel shot at each other, no one's going to charge Daniel with anything. The Iceman stuff is over, right now we just need to focus on Tessa . . ." Wyatt broke off as the door behind them swung open to reveal Daniel, Casey and a doctor still dressed in surgical scrubs.

Wyatt had understated just how bad Daniel was looking; he appeared to be holding on by a thread. "This is Dr. Hannigan, he was . . . he was operating on Tessie. He came to tell me how she is but I wanted you to be there when he told us," Daniel explained.

Appreciating Daniel's gesture, since obviously the suspense was killing him, killing all of them. Casey slipped through the doorway to wrap her arms around Wyatt's waist, each of their gazes fixed firmly on the doctor's face, trying to read in it the answer they were seeking.

"Why don't we sit?" the doctor suggested with a calm that had been refined from years of delivering news, both good and bad, to anxious families.

"Is she dead?" Parker asked unable to wait another second, he didn't want to deal with pleasantries.

Taking a deep breath before answering, "No."

Relief flooded through him, Casey, crying quietly, collapsed against Wyatt, who muttered a prayer of thanks, Daniel sank wearily onto the bed, his head in his hand, but Parker remained standing, his focus on the doctor.

"But?" he asked.

The others all looked back up.

"But," the doctor nodded. "She lost a lot of blood, we had to give her several transfusions. The bullet did a lot of damage and we had to remove one of her kidneys. The hypothermia from the other day that her body was still trying to recover from didn't help. She's in the ICU, we have her heavily sedated, it's still touch and go but if she makes it through the next twenty-four hours or so, then barring infection, it's likely she'll make a full recovery."

"Can we see her?" Parker asked, needing to see and touch Tessa to really believe that she was still alive.

Nodding, "But only one of you at a time."

Glancing over at Daniel, as much as Parker wanted to see Tessa he knew that Daniel did too and was about to tell Tessa's brother to go first when Daniel spoke.

"You go," he sighed. "Tessa would want you there. She doesn't want to see me."

"Are you sure?" as thankful as he was to Daniel for saving Tessa's life, twice, he didn't have time to spend reassuring him.

Daniel nodded.

"Tell her we love her," Casey called to him as he followed the doctor from the room.

As he followed the doctor to Tessa's bedside Parker couldn't stop the horrified gasp from escaping his throat when he saw her. She wasn't breathing on her own, a respirator hissed quietly with each rise and fall of her chest, a heart monitor cheeped rhythmically, wires and tubes ran from her body to a host of machines standing guard around her bed.

"There's a chance she can hear you, you can talk to her but I don't want her worked up," the doctor explained somberly before departing.

Alone with Tessa Parker took a seat at her side, almost afraid to take her hand for fear of damaging her further. Gently tucking her hair behind her ear he leant over and brushed a kiss to her forehead. "Hey, Tess, it's me, it's Parker. The doctor said you're going to be okay, you just have to stay strong. I'm going to be right here when you wake up, waiting for an answer to my question," squeezing her hand tightly and praying that he would get a chance to make Tessa his wife. "Come on, honey, wake up. Please, Tessa, wake up, don't you dare die on me." Convincing himself that Tessa had been through worse than this before and survived, she would make it through this too, and together the two of them would be stronger than ever before. "Everything's going to be fine, Tess," he told her determinedly, then less confidently, "Everything's going to be okay."

* * * * *

11:14 P.M.

She hadn't stirred in the nineteen hours, forty-one minutes and twenty-seven seconds since she had been brought to the ICU.

Daniel was sitting at Tessa's bedside, holding her thin, fragile hand, listening to the reassuring beeps of the machines that proved that his unresponsive sister was in fact still alive. Several hours ago the doctors had lowered the dose of sedatives they'd been pumping into Tessa hoping that she would begin to wake up. So far, she hadn't.

He and Parker had been taking turns sitting with her, talking to her, willing her to come back to them. As much as he didn't want to, Daniel had to admit that Parker Bell was starting to grow on him. The love and panic on his face when they'd been searching for Tessa in the woods and found her barely alive in the snow, and again when she'd been lying on the floor in her hospital room drenched in blood. Clearly he loved Tessa very much, and unlike himself, Parker had never betrayed her.

As he sat here, he kept reliving that moment over and over again. Wondering whether he could have done anything different and changed the outcome. He didn't care that he'd shot Cordelia, he'd done it to protect Tessie and himself and he'd do it again in a heartbeat, but he'd been too slow. Cordelia had thrown her keys at him, and the momentary distraction was enough for her to shoot Tessa. She'd tried to kill him too, would have if he hadn't been wearing the Kevlar vest, as it was he had an almighty black and blue bruise. They'd fired their rounds at the same time, the force of the bullet to his chest enough to momentarily knock him unconscious. His aim slightly different than Cordelia's, he'd gone for the head; the result was she was dead and he wasn't.

What he should have done was shoot Cordelia as soon as he'd entered the room and seen her holding a gun on Tessa. He'd wanted to but he hadn't been able to force himself to pull the trigger, it would have made him no better than his sister, and part of him had still believed that they could somehow work things out. But because of his hesitation Tessa might end up losing her life.

It wasn't the first time his hesitation had almost ended in Tessa dying.

He remembered that night with crystal clear clarity. Tessa asleep on her bed, his bags already packed, Emilie alone in her room, painting the moonlit night. He could still hear her voice screeching at him that he was an ungrateful son, that she'd already lost Cordelia and now he wanted to take her baby from her. Even at eighteen, Daniel had known the reason for her ranting had less to do with Tessa and more to do with the fact that she was terrified of being alone. He'd tried to reason with her, saying that he and Tessa weren't happy here, that it would be better for all of them if he and Tess just left.

When Emilie had come at him with her cane, screaming that if she couldn't have Tessa then no one could, he had hesitated, not wanting to hurt his mother, that hesitation had been enough for her to hit him in the head and knock him out. That had given Emilie the opportunity to drug a sleeping Tessa, drag her to the bathroom, fill the tub and half drown her own daughter. Regaining consciousness, he had been frantically searching the house when he'd heard the chant coming from the bathroom. Seeing Emilie holding a limp Tessa under the water he hadn't hesitated that time, knocking his mother out and pulling a dripping Tessa from the bath.

Her small body had seemed even tinier as he'd laid her on the cool tiles, pumping his hands on her thin chest he'd been worried the force would break her ribs and send them piercing straight through her heart. At the time, he'd thought it was pointless, that Tessa was gone, but he hadn't been able to stop, and when she had suddenly taken that first breath his own heart had almost stopped. Cradling his baby sister in his arms, he'd known that as long as he was there she wasn't safe, Emilie would always see him as a threat, and so he'd left.

And because of that, he hadn't been there to protect Tessa when she'd needed him. As Detective Parker Bell had so astutely noted, guilt was a way of life for himself and Tessa. Growing up with Emilie their childhood's had been filled with blame, everything bad that had ever happened to them Emilie had managed to twist so that her children were at fault. Over time, he and Tessa had learnt to believe her and blame themselves for everything. It was because of that guilt that he had stayed away and hadn't known Dylan Riley was hurting his little sister, he hadn't known that Patrick had dared to come back and try to insinuate himself into her life, and he hadn't known that Dylan Riley had come back to haunt her.

Squeezing Tessa's hand as he leant over her. "Come on, Tessie," he pleaded. "Wake up." He couldn't let Tessa die when things were like this between them, while she hated him and wanted nothing to do with him; he had to explain to her, had to make her understand why he did what he did.

Forcing himself to think of a time when he and Tessie had been happy together. Recalling the first time he had taken her camping, he begun to recount the tale to her. "Remember, Tessie, the first time we went on one of our campouts. You were three and I was nine, it was early spring, blossoms and flowers just starting to come out. We waited until Patrick and Emilie were asleep and then we snuck out. You insisted on carrying your own stuff in a little backpack, it was so full you could barely hold it but you refused to let me help." Little Tessie had been every bit as stubborn as grown up Tessa.

"We found a perfect place in the woods, a little clearing, it was always our favorite. You helped me set up the tent, then we made the campfire, cooked marshmallows," chuckling. "You hated them but you knew they were my favorite so you ate them and never said a thing. It was cold so we climbed into my sleeping bag and we just lay there watching the moon and the stars."

That night was the first of many the two of them had spent together out in the woods, their favorite way to escape the house they both hated with every fiber of their beings. "It wasn't until early morning that we eventually fell asleep, and when I woke up I knew that if we didn't get back soon we'd be in big trouble. You were still sleeping; you were so peaceful that I couldn't bring myself to wake you, so I carried you back. I had to leave the tent and everything behind. I got you into bed just as Emilie was getting up so I didn't have time to get the camping gear. One of the gardeners found it, they told Patrick, he was so mad at me, but I never told him you were there. He never knew."

"You can't die, Tessie," a tear splashed down onto her cheek and he brushed it away. "I would do anything to save you, I would trade places with you in a second if I could."

Laying his head down on the bed, his cheek resting against her hand, recalling aloud every pleasant memory he could think of, until he felt her hand twitch slightly beneath him.

"Parker."

DECEMBER 24TH

12:02 A.M.

Hearing the swish of the door as it softly clunked closed Tessa forced open heavy eyes to see Parker hovering beside her bed. Giving him a weak smile. "Hey."

Opening his mouth then snapping it closed again without a word, Parker couldn't wipe the silly smile off his face as he slid into the chair at her bedside. Taking her bandaged hand, the one where Cordelia had ripped out the IV earlier, and bringing it to his lips he kissed it tenderly, continuing to stare at her with wonder.

"Lost your voice?" she asked with a small laugh that ended in her wincing in pain.

Shaking his head, "I can't believe I'm talking to you, I was so terrified that I was going to lose you," cupping her cheek in his hand, his thumb gently stroking her temple. "Everyone was so worried about you, Casey and Wyatt are right outside, J.J. was here earlier, and Maisy's been calling every five minutes."

"Sorry I scared you," Tessa whispered faintly, already fighting to keep her eyes open.

"It's not your fault, baby," Parker soothed.

Panic suddenly knifed through her sharper than the pain and she tried to push herself up. "Daniel?" she asked. "Cordelia shot him. Is he . . .?"A machine screeched its protestations at the sudden spike in her blood pressure.

"Shh, it's okay, just relax, he's okay," placing his hands on her shoulders and gently pushing her back against the bed. "Daniel's fine," Parker reassured her. "He was wearing a Kevlar vest, he has a bruise and some cracked ribs but that's it. He's right outside."

Sinking back into the mattress, relief mixing with exhaustion Tessa let her eyes fall closed.

"Tessa?"

Unable to summon enough energy to answer, sleep was already dribbling into her pounding head, and she was debating whether or not to ask for some painkillers.

"Honey?" fingertips softly brushed against her brow.

"Mmm?" she moaned tiredly but didn't open her eyes.

"Sweetheart, I need to ask you something."

Forcing open her eyes this time, Parker had pulled his chair as close to the bed as was possible and reclaimed his grip on her hand, with his other hand he held a sparkling diamond ring.

"Tessa, I love you and I can't imagine my life without you in it, will you marry me?"

Remembering him saying those words to her just before she'd stopped breathing. Tessa had known for weeks that Parker had been thinking about proposing but she needed to know that he wasn't just doing this now out of fear, because she had almost died. Looking him straight in the eye, "Last time you said that to me I was bleeding to death," she reminded him.

"I know."

"Parker, are you sure?"

"Sweetheart, I have never been more sure of anything in my life," he told her.

"You're not just asking me because of what Cordelia did?" The idea of marriage still scared her because she didn't know if she was capable of giving Parker what he needed, what he deserved. She needed to be positive that he was prepared for anything, that he wasn't just terrified of losing her, that he was going to be by her side from now until forever.

"Baby, I knew I was in love with you from the second we met. I love you and I want to spend the rest of my life with you."

At a loss for words, Tessa studied him, wanting to say yes but hardly daring to. It wasn't that she didn't love him because she did, more than she ever thought she could, but if she married him and then lost him, just like she'd lost every other person she'd ever loved, then she wasn't sure she could survive that.

"Do you want to think about it?" Parker asked at last, trying unsuccessfully to hide the fact that he was crestfallen. "I'm sorry, I shouldn't have asked you that now, it was selfish. You just got shot, you're in pain, you're tired, you need to rest, I'm sorry," he released her hand and went to return the ring to his pocket.

Catching hold of his hand. "Yes."

Parker stared at her, a hopeful glimmer is his golden eyes. "What?"

"Yes," Tessa could feel her own face twisting into a silly smile.

"Are you sure?" Parker stammered, his grin returning.

Tears pricking at her eyes, Tessa nodded, and as Parker slipped the ring onto her finger she couldn't stop teardrops from trickling down her cheeks. The bed dipped as Parker sat, leaning over her with an elbow resting on either side of her chest, his face hovering inches from her own.

"I love you," Parker told her then whispered his lips across hers.

"I love you too," she replied softly as he brushed away her tears. As Parker rested his head on the pillow beside hers and Tessa felt herself fade quickly towards sleep she realized that for the first time in her life she was genuinely happy.

Jane has loved reading and writing since she can remember. She writes dark and disturbing crime/mystery/suspense with some romance thrown in because, well, who doesn't love romance?! She has several series including the complete Detective Parker Bell series, the Count to Ten series, the Christmas Mysteries series, and the Flashes of Fate series of novelettes.

When she's not writing Jane loves to read, bake, go to the beach, ski, horse ride, and watch Disney movies. She has a black belt in Taekwondo, a 200+ collection of teddy bears, and her favorite color is pink. She has the world's two most sweet and pretty Dalmatians, Ivory and Pearl. Oh, and she also enjoys spending time with family and friends!

For more information please visit any of the following –

Amazon – http://www.amazon.com/author/janeblythe
BookBub – https://www.bookbub.com/authors/jane-blythe
Email – mailto:janeblytheauthor@gmail.com
Facebook – http://www.facebook.com/janeblytheauthor
Goodreads – http://www.goodreads.com/author/show/6574160.Jane_Blythe
Reader Group – http://www.facebook.com/groups/janeskillersweethearts
Twitter – http://www.twitter.com/jblytheauthor
Website – http://www.janeblythe.com.au

sic enim dilexit Deus mundum ut Filium suum unigenitum daret ut omnis qui credit in eum habeat vitam aeternam

www.ingramcontent.com/pod-product-compliance
Lightning Source LLC
Chambersburg PA
CBHW070846250626
47159CB00003B/957